◆ THERE'S ◆
SOMETHING
IN A SUNDAY

• THERE'S • SOMETHING IN A SUNDAY

A SHARON McCONE M·Y·S·T·E·R·Y

MARCIA MULLER

THE MYSTERIOUS PRESS
New York • London • Tokyo

A-1

 The Mysterious Press, 129 West 56th Street, New York, N.Y. 10019

Printed in the United States of America

First Printing: February 1989

10 9 8 7 6 5 4 3 2

Library of Congress Cataloging-in-Publication Data

Muller, Marcia.
   There's something in a Sunday / Marcia Muller.
     p. 224 cm.
     I. Title.
PS3563.U397T5 1989
813'.54—dc19   88-22005
ISBN 0-89296-270-4   CIP

For Sara Ann Freed

◆ THERE'S ◆
SOMETHING
IN A SUNDAY

ONE

Sunday morning dawned gray and misty outside the steam-clouded windows of the coffee shop on Lombard Street. Beyond the plate glass lay San Francisco's travelers' row: a fourteen-block stretch of motels and gas stations and restaurants that daily plays host to hundreds of visitors to the city and motorists who are just passing through. Its establishments do not boast the luxurious accommodations found further downtown; Lombard Street is for families, young people on budgets, retirees taking brief respites from their cramped RVs. And for the individual who, for whatever reason, seeks anonymity.

As shadows lifted, the ugly functional buildings took on hazy definition. The asphalt of the wide boulevard was a black and white–striped no-man's-land, devoid of the weekday stream of commuter traffic. At six A.M. the sidewalks were almost empty of pedestrians.

I'd been sitting in the twenty-four-hour restaurant since five, nursing several cups of coffee and fielding occasional curious glances from the red-uniformed waitress. A couple of delivery drivers for the Sunday *Chronicle-Examiner* had come in and departed with styrofoam cups. A cabbie had bought a bag of donuts. But now only I remained, seated in a front-window booth watching the Kingsway Motel across the street.

It was one of the older motels on the strip, which boasted some two dozen between Van Ness Avenue and Lyon Street. L-shaped and two-tiered, with space for cars underneath, it

1

was painted an odd blue with faded yellow trim. Its still-lit
neon sign sported a crown and scepter. The plate-glass windows of the office looked streaky through the fog; the railed
balconies were shadowed, but not so much that I wouldn't be
able to detect motion should the door to room 209 open. So far
it hadn't, and the subject's aged green Ford Ranchero was still
snuggled into a space below.

I sipped my coffee, burned my tongue, and sighed in
irritation. My alarm had gone off at four in the morning, not my
favorite hour to rise on a Sunday. Normally I like to stay in bed
until noon, drinking coffee, reading the paper, doing both the
Chronicle and *Examiner* crossword puzzles, clipping the cents-
off coupons (which I save but never remember to take with me
when I grocery shop). But my job as staff investigator for All
Souls Legal Cooperative often requires that I work odd hours,
so there I sat yawning and drinking too much bad coffee.

As I continued to stare at the motel, Lombard Street slowly
came awake. A trickle of cars passed by, most of them going
toward the Golden Gate Bridge and sunny retreats in Marin
County or the wine country. A woman in a raincoat and
scarf-covered curlers emerged from the office of the motel next
to the Kingsway, with a small curly-haired dog on a lead. The
door of an Italian bakery in the next block opened, and a man
in a white apron stepped out, stood yawning for a moment,
then went back inside. A few people left their rooms at the
Kingsway, but the door to room 209 remained closed.

My client hadn't been sure what time the man he wanted
tailed usually left the motel. I might be in for a long wait.

Three more red-uniformed waitresses arrived, and the other
departed without a backward glance at me, even though we'd
been constant and almost solitary companions for the better
part of two hours. A young couple entered and ordered a
hearty breakfast. When their plates were carried past me, my
stomach growled, so I ordered an English muffin and ate it
slowly, my eyes on the window. Somehow I managed to drop
jelly onto my jeans; I cleaned it off with a napkin dipped in the
water glass.

It was after eight o'clock when the door to room 209 finally
opened. I tensed, reaching for the check and leaning toward
the window to study the man who came out. He was tall and
lanky, dressed in faded Levi's and a rumpled tan suede jacket.
His dusty brown hair hung limply over his forehead, and as he

loped down the stairs, he brushed at it with his left hand. It riffled up, then most of it fell back down again. He didn't go to the Ranchero, but headed for the sidewalk and turned right.

I didn't need to consult the photo tucked in my purse to know this was the man I'd been hired to follow. His name was Frank Wilkonson, and other than that, I knew very little about him. A description, which had been backed up by a photograph, and was now confirmed by his actual appearance. The type of vehicle he drove and its license plate number. The fact that he worked on a ranch. The fact that he checked into the same Lombard Street motel late every Saturday night and left there before noon on Sunday morning.

I knew only those things, and my client's stated reason for wanting him followed—which I had doubted from the start.

My eyes still on him, I grabbed a handful of bills and coins from my jacket pocket and shoved them on top of the check. Then I hurried along the row of booths and out into the chill morning. The fog had lifted somewhat, and although the day promised to be overcast, visibility was now good. Frank Wilkonson was half a block away, walking north on the other side of the street.

The area was fairly well populated now: joggers pounded along; tourists dressed in their best sightseeing togs consulted maps; neighborhood residents fetched papers and fresh sourdough bread and hurried back up the hill to affluent Pacific Heights or toward the Marina district on the shore of the bay. The shabbiness of the subject's clothing and his listless, shambling gait set him apart from the people around him. I was reminded of an old Kristofferson song that told of down-and-out loneliness on a Sunday morning. Well, I could relate to that; I'd felt that way a time or two recently—and not just on Sunday, either.

Wilkonson kept walking for another block, then stopped at a group of newspaper vending machines and bought a *Chronicle-Examiner*. I watched from the opposite corner as he balanced the paper on top of the rack and extracted the pink entertainment section. He leafed through it, paused, and tore out one of the pages. Then he bundled up the rest of the paper, went to a nearby trash can, and dropped the whole thing inside.

As he turned and walked back toward his motel, I debated going across the street and retrieving the paper, to see which page he'd torn out. But his stride was more purposeful now, and I thought he might be heading for his car. I retraced my steps to where my MG was parked in front of the coffee shop, and waited there to see what he'd do next.

There was a hissing noise, and then a haze of fine mist covered the lens of my Nikkormat. The tiny droplets quickly spread and ran together, fracturing the image before my eyes. The knotty bole of the giant fern I was kneeling behind melted to a shapeless blob of brown; its spreading fronds became smears of green; I couldn't make out Frank Wilkonson's figure.

I lowered the Nikkormat. My subject was still there, on the other side of the room by the lily pond. I let the camera dangle from the strap around my neck and swiped moisture off my face, then pulled off my wool hat and stuffed it in the pocket of my new camel-colored pea jacket. It was hot here in the tropical pond room of Golden Gate Park's Conservatory of Flowers, and now that the fog machine had cycled on, it was also muggy. I unbuttoned the coat but resigned myself to keeping it on; carrying it would be too cumbersome, what with my purse and the camera.

Wilkonson stood gazing into the lily pond, one foot propped on its raised concrete wall. He didn't appear either surprised or disconcerted by the swirl of mist, which led me to believe he'd visited the tropical gardens before. While I located a lens-cleaning cloth, the fog machine cycled off again; I dried the camera as best I could. Then I stood up and circled the giant fern, looking for a better vantage point and feeling absurdly like an actor in a Tarzan movie. The fern stood on a small island in the center of the room's other pond; a waterfall gushed down one side of the island, muting the sound of my move-ments with its splashing. Nearly everything in the room was green, from apple to emerald to almost black. Vines twisted and twined on overhead piping, and the air was rich with the smell of damp earth.

I found a good place and squatted down, propping my elbows on the wall of the pond and aiming the 135mm telephoto lens between the fern and the spindly trunk of a palm tree. My Nikkormat—ancient and beloved—was a recent addi-tion to my bag of professional tricks. For years I'd used the camera only for pleasure: a hobby I'd take up, leave off, then take up again. But during a recent picture-taking binge—which had begun the previous March, some six months ago—I'd finally been forced to admit that I'd never be very good at photography. What I wanted to capture just didn't translate to the film; what I had considered good shots when I'd taken them merely looked trite when revealed by the solution in the darkroom's developing tray. And with that realization, the use of the camera for my work no longer seemed a violation of my personal privacy.

Besides, a camera is a perfect tool for an investigator—and it has nothing to do with actually taking pictures.

A former client of mine—one who had achieved worldwide renown as a photographer—had once told me a camera was great "protective coloration." When you were holding one, he'd said, people very seldom looked at you. Instead, they focused on the black box itself, or began to fuss with their hair or makeup, in case you snapped them. In a place like the Conservatory of Flowers, this aid to anonymity worked particularly well, making me seem merely another harmless tourist.

Now I focused the telephoto on Frank Wilkonson's face. He looked tense, his mouth a thin seam in his tanned, leathery skin. His eyes were narrowed and fixed, not on the water as I'd originally thought, but on a sign sticking up from it. I adjusted the lens again and read: "Do not throw coins in pond—they poison fish." Then I scanned the pond itself: its bottom was littered with nickels and dimes, and there wasn't a fish in sight.

The humorous aspect of this wasn't lost on me, but apparently Wilkonson didn't appreciate the irony. Or perhaps, I thought, he wasn't seeing the sign or pond at all. His pose—forearms resting on his raised knee, hands dangling loosely—was casual enough, but underneath it I sensed a leashed nervousness. As I studied him, the sound of women's voices came from the doorway; Wilkonson's head swiveled toward them expectantly. But then his eagerness died and his mouth twitched, almost angrily. I swung the camera toward the door and saw two women of about my age—mid- to late thirties—dressed in the insubstantial sportswear that tourists mistakenly think appropriate for September in San Francisco.

Is Wilkonson meeting someone here? I wondered. In all the time I'd been observing him—nearly forty minutes now—he hadn't once checked his watch. But every time someone had entered the room he'd looked eagerly at the person and then glanced away. If he was meeting someone, I was willing to bet it would not be a pleasurable encounter: his obvious tension suggested to me that he might be gearing up for some sort of confrontation.

He must have projected a similar impression to the tourists who had just entered, because they hesitated and then came my way, rather than moving toward the larger pond. As they squeezed around me murmuring appreciation of the lush tropical foliage, I refocused on Wilkonson and tripped the shutter—not because I wanted a picture of him, but because I wanted to look like an amateur photographer. After the women had circled the island, they went over to the lily pond and stopped as far from Wilkonson as possible; one began rummaging in her bag, presumably for coins to murder whatever aquatic life was still hanging in there. Wilkonson glanced their way and his thin mouth twitched again. He straightened, looked at his watch, and reached into the pocket of his shabby suede jacket.

I lowered the camera and watched him bring out a piece of pink paper—the page he'd torn from the entertainment section. He looked it over briefly, then put his hand back into the pocket and withdrew a yellow sheet. I raised the camera again and focused on it; the lens wasn't powerful enough for me to make out the printing, but the sheet looked as if it had been torn from the Yellow Pages. Wilkonson scanned it, folded both sheets together, and stuffed them back in his pocket. Then he moved briskly toward the door.

I jammed the lens cap back on the camera and followed. By the time I had reached the conservatory's central room and gone down a packed dirt path through the philodendrons and palms and brilliant birdlike flowers that grew under the towering whitewashed glass dome, Wilkonson was already outside. From the top of the wide steps I watched him cut across the formal gardens toward Kennedy Drive. He was heading, I guessed, to where he'd parked his car earlier, near the bocce ball courts. Banking on that, I went a different way—through a pedestrian tunnel under the main arterial—and by the time he reached the Ranchero, I was waiting a few spaces away in my MG.

The rest of the day was both eventful and puzzling. We—Wilkonson and I—attended a plant sale at the Hall of Flowers, adjacent to the park's extensive Strybing Arboretum. The sale was a fund-raiser for the Arboretum Society, and the plants were testimony to the diversity of talents at the park's nurseries. Delicate roses vied for attention with flashy birds of paradise; clumps of bamboo and Japanese maple stood leaf-to-leaf with lime and fig trees. There were dahlia and rhododendron plants, avocado trees and fuchsias, even a fascinating hairy-leaved thing called a baboon flower. Wilkonson wandered for over an hour but bought nothing. I came away—predictably—with the baboon flower. Protective coloration, I told myself as I followed Wilkonson from the hall.

We then began a jaunt around the city that made me glad I'd thought to pack a couple of sandwiches and some fruit the night before. It began at the Sloat Garden Center, near the beach and the zoo. Sloat was a nice nursery; I'd once bought a live Christmas tree there (which I'd managed to kill before the next holiday season rolled around—my neglect, no fault with their merchandise). Wilkonson, however, ignored the rows of fir and fruit trees and fall flowers and vegetables, going directly to the sales counter. While I fingered the leaves of a chrysanthemum plant, he questioned the two clerks, moving his lean, corded hands as if framing descriptive phrases. As near as I could tell, both replied in the negative to whatever he had asked them.

Next we went to the Sunset District, an area of moderately priced single-family homes where the middle-class residents take pride in their gardens and lawns. Wilkonson made more inquiries at the American Seed and Nursery Company, the Sunset Garden Supply, Blooming Dale's, and Mr. Tree. The replies also seemed to be in the negative.

He then looped around Twin Peaks and hit the large garden centers in the industrial Bayshore District. The clerks there were busier; he waylaid those he could and again seemed to receive no encouraging responses. As he left the last place, his shoulders had a distinctly dejected droop.

At a small nursery on Potrero Hill I tried to get close enough to listen to what he was asking; his eyes rested briefly on me, so I bought a bag of potting soil and retreated to my car.

At the Red Desert off Market Street, I shed my pea jacket and donned a paisley scarf before entering. Once inside I lurked among a group of tall, spiny, deformed cacti near the sales desk. Again I couldn't make out what Wilkonson was saying, but I left with a weird-looking succulent called a *Crassula cornuta*.

As I noted my latest purchase in my expense log, I wondered what the client would think when he saw my itemization. If he objected, I decided, I would give him the plants and soil.

After a few more stops the MG had begun to look like a combination rolling nursery and changing cabana. The baboon flower rode on the passenger seat; the bag of soil lay on the floor; on top of it sat the crassula, a six-pack of brussels sprout plants (someone had told me they grew well in San Francisco's cool fall months), a sack of tulip bulbs (to be planted no earlier than November), and two different kinds of fertilizer (fish emulsion and something optimistically labeled GROW!). The space behind the seats was littered with cast-off clothing: my pea jacket; my favorite green sweater; two scarves and a knit cap; and a white acrylic poncho made by the grandmother of a friend who had hated it and donated it to me as an inconspicuous and dowdy disguise. (The damned thing had caught fire once; it didn't even burn, just melted.) I was now down to a bleached cotton blouse, which was just as well because the day had gone warm and sunny—unpredictable, as fall afternoons usually are in the city.

What on earth am I doing with all this stuff? I thought, looking around at my purchases while stopped at a light on Divisadero. I'm not even good with plants. I destroy everything I lay hand to. Everything, an inner voice reminded me, except those wild blackberry vines in the backyard. *They're* out to destroy *you!*

At the next couple of nurseries I stayed in the car. After a stop on Union Street, we zipped along Van Ness toward Lombard, and I breathed a sigh of relief. Wilkonson was going back to his motel; my ill-advised horticultural shopping binge was over.

But he overshot Lombard, staying in the right-hand lane, and turned on Bay, heading toward the godawful Sunday afternoon traffic crush at the city's worst tourist trap—Fisherman's Wharf.

Cost Plus, I thought. Dear God, Cost Plus. . . .

Cost Plus is a San Francisco institution. Every day it draws hordes of customers from every corner of the globe. They buy mass-produced brass elephants and teak salad sets; esoteric kitchen gadgetry and candles and incense; teas and caviar and rum cakes and wine—and plants, at the nursery outlet. The crowds at Cost Plus's various buildings in the Wharf area are always horrendous. Unlike most of the surrounding businesses, it provides its patrons with a parking lot; like most of the parking lots around here, it is perpetually full.

We inched along Bay to Columbus, where cross traffic jammed up in the intersection and blocked the flow for two changes of the light. Then Wilkonson made several turns, none without difficulty and two of them wrong for Cost Plus. I followed, my aggravation level rising. Cars executed strange and illegal maneuvers; strollers wandered outside the crosswalks, oblivious to danger; at Taylor a man blocked the street taking a picture of the cable car. I clutched the wheel harder and reminded myself that my dentist had recently warned me against grinding my teeth.

Wilkonson's Ranchero finally reached the entrance to the Cost Plus parking lot. He would have to make a left turn to enter, and the line of oncoming traffic was bumper-to-bumper. I waited two cars behind him, wondering what he'd decide to do.

He put on the Ranchero's left-turn signal. The oncoming cars crawled by unheeding. He extended his arm from the window and gestured at the lot. A man in a Cadillac kept moving, looking determinedly ahead. Someone—in the car behind Wilkonson, I thought—beeped his horn.

Wilkonson might be from the country, but he understood city driving. He ignored the beep and just sat there. Finally there was a break in traffic. The Ranchero inched forward. A camper with Illinois plates speeded up and tried to cut it off. Both Wilkonson and the camper's driver slammed on their brakes.

Sometimes when you're tailing a person—surreptitiously privy to his or her every movement for a long period of time—you develop a certain empathy. It's as if you begin to read the subject's thoughts: no matter how far you are from him, no matter how obstructed your visibility, at a given crucial moment you have a flash of warning about what he's going to do.

A flash came to me now. And Wilkonson did it.

He had stopped the Ranchero only inches from the camper's front bumper. They were close, but the Ranchero had the edge. Wilkonson extended his left arm out the window in that time-honored middle-fingered salute. Then he wrenched the steering wheel and drew in front of the camper, nearly ramming a car parked at the curb. He slammed into reverse, barely missing the VW that had been behind him. When he completed the U-turn, he raced the vehicle down the other side of the street, fishtailing wildly, tires screaming.

As he roared past me, I caught a glimpse of his face. It was purpled, viciously twisted—one of the most frightening pictures of murderous rage I had ever seen.

TWO

Today's weird jaunt through the city had come about because, late Friday afternoon, Jack Stuart—the newest attorney at All Souls—had asked me to take on the weekend tail job for one of his clients. The job, Jack said, had nothing to do with any legal work he was handling for the man; he was merely arranging it as a favor. But All Souls makes a practice of extending investigative services to steady clients, so I agreed. I had no definite plans for Sunday, seldom had any weekend plans at all these days; the job would fill up otherwise empty hours and, besides, I would be paid overtime.

At four that afternoon I drove to the South of Market District to meet with Jack's client, Rudy Goldring. Goldring was a custom shirtmaker, and the offices of his firm, Goldring Clothiers, were located on Stillman Street, a one-block alley in the shadow of the I-80 freeway and not far from Moscone Center. The narrow street was lined with cars on both sides, most of them in defiance of NO PARKING signs, and many with two wheels pulled up on the pavement. I squeezed the MG in between a new Toyota and a beat-up van and went looking for Goldring's number. The buildings were an odd mixture of old postwar warehouses and factories and Italianate Victorians; Goldring Clothiers occupied the bottom floor of one of the Victorians, a sprucely painted blue one near the corner.

A bearded derelict in threadbare army fatigues sat in the middle of the marble steps drinking a Colt .45. When I started up to the door, he jumped to his feet. I tensed but kept going. He stepped in front of me.

"May I help you, ma'am?" He had a bad body odor and his breath was rank with beer, but he spoke with great formality.

"What?"

"Who are you here to see?"

"Um, Mr. Rudy Goldring."

"Come this way, please." He led me to the door and opened it with all the correctness of an English butler.

"Uh, thank you."

"You're welcome, I'm sure." He pulled the door shut behind me.

I shook my head, thinking, *Only in San Francisco*, then looked around. I was standing at the beginning of a long hall carpeted in pearl gray with darker gray walls. Several doors opened on either side of the hallway, and I could hear the sounds of voices and a telephone ringing. There was no one in sight, so I knocked on the frame of the first door.

A man's voice called for me to come in, and I entered what had once been a Victorian parlor. It was also carpeted and painted in cool shades of gray, and its walls were hung with framed reproductions of mechanical drawings of cable cars. Its fireplace appeared to be in working order and on its mantel sat a trailing philodendron in a shiny brass pot. The rest of the room was in chaos: shirts of various colors and styles hung from long hooks extending out from the walls; boxes and mailing cartons spilled onto the floor from the shelves and chairs; there was an ironing board in the window bay; the big mahogany desk was piled with what looked like invoices and purchase orders, some of which had also fallen to the floor.

The man behind the desk must have been in his sixties. He had a full head of the type of curly white hair whose highlights make it look yellow. His face was deeply lined—by good humor, I thought. His eyes were the palest of blues, his dark suit and white shirt correct enough for a diplomatic reception, and when he stood, I found he did not quite measure up to my own five foot six.

He extended a hand and said, "You must be Miss McCone."

I clasped his long bony fingers. "And you're Mr. Goldring."

"Yes. Please sit down."

I looked where he indicated and saw a chair that was half-buried under shirts and boxes.

"Oh, I'm sorry." He moved around me, almost scampering, and gathered everything up. "We're starting to ship our Christmas orders, and things get out of hand." For a moment he stood, at a loss as to where to put his burden, then dumped it on the ironing board. Most of it promptly fell off. Rudy Goldring threw up his hands in mock despair and went back to his desk. "Please," he said again, motioning at the now empty chair.

I sat, and he ensconced himself in his desk chair. It was a big padded one and it dwarfed him. I said, "Do you do all your shipping from these offices?"

"Most of it goes from the factory down the street. Maybe you saw it—the tan building on the corner?"

I hadn't, but I nodded.

"It's the merchandise for the stores that goes out from there. Not really custom work, just better-than-average ready-to-wear. Every state in the Union we're into now, and the volume grows every year. A man's going to spend the kind of money he has to pay for shirts today, he wants quality. But this"—he motioned around the room—"is my custom trade. Old customers. Good customers. I like to give them personalized service. We inspect each shirt here, iron it, pin it, pack it nice. Some of these men have been coming to me for more than thirty years now. They expect good personal treatment, and they get it."

"Do you have a retail outlet here in town?"

He smiled, his face wrinkling deeply, and spread out his hands. "This is it. A man wants to be fitted or look at samples, he comes here. We got a nice room in the back, we offer coffee or a drink. The fitting is part of the experience of getting a really good shirt."

"How much does a custom shirt cost?"

"Anywhere from sixty to two hundred dollars, depending. But for that you get a lot of shirt. We take sixteen different measurements, take into account the collar height as well as its size. Maybe you got a husband you want to give a custom shirt for Christmas?"

"No, I don't."

"A nice-looking woman like you? A boyfriend, then?"

I hadn't, not at the moment, but it didn't trouble me to admit it—usually. I shook my head, smiling.

"Ah well, by Christmas you might. Then you remember me. We'll fix him up with something nice."

"I'll remember. But now we'd better get down to business. Jack Stuart tells me you want someone followed this Sunday."

At the mention of business the smile slid off Rudy Goldring's lips and his eyes clouded. He picked up a letter opener from the mess on the desk and held it between his hands, turning it over and over with the tips of his bony fingers. After a moment he said, "Yes. Man by the name of Frank Wilkonson. He checks into the Kingsway Motel on Lombard Street late every Saturday night. Leaves on Sunday morning. Usually he goes back to the motel after dinnertime Sunday evening, stays till one or two in the morning. I want to know where he goes and what he does."

"On Sunday, you mean."

"Monday morning, too. Everything until he gets on the 101 freeway going south out of town."

I waited, but Goldring didn't volunteer any more information. His formerly animated face was flaccid and drained; he looked years older than when I'd come in.

Finally I said, "Why?"

"What's that?"

"Why do you want to find out what he does?"

Momentarily he looked dismayed. "Do you have to know that?"

"It would help. The more I know about a subject and the client's reasons for requesting surveillance, the better a job I can do."

"Oh. Well, I got a picture." He rummaged on the desk again and came up with a color snapshot. I took it from his outstretched hand.

It was a poor snap, trimmed to wallet size—taken outdoors, somewhere where there were oak-dotted hills in the background. The man had a narrow tanned face, sharp features, and wispy dull brown hair. He wore an open-necked plaid shirt and seemed to be leaning against the rail of a fence.

I took out my note pad. "I'll need more details about Mr. Wilkonson's physical appearance. What color are his eyes?"

"Can't you tell that from the picture?"

"No."

"Well . . . I guess they're blue."

"His height? Weight?"

"He's tall. Thin."

"That's as much as you can tell me?"

"Yes. I'm sorry."

"How does he typically dress?"

"Well, he works on a ranch. I'd say casually, like in the picture."

"Not a good customer for your kind of shirts, then?" I smiled, hoping to get him to relax.

He remained serious. "No."

His sudden reserve and the lack of detail about Frank Wilkonson were beginning to irritate me. I said, "I assume he drives a car."

"An old Ford Ranchero. Green." He consulted a scrap of paper. "License number SDK 080."

I copied it down and shut my notebook. "Mr. Goldring, what's your relationship to Frank Wilkonson?"

"My . . . he's a relative. A distant relative."

"I see. I take it he's come to San Francisco and followed this same routine on a number of Sundays."

"Three that I know of."

"And all you want is more detail on his activities?"

"That's right." Goldring paused, his pale eyes anxious. I sensed he was afraid I was about to refuse to take the job, because he added, "You see, Frank Wilkonson is my . . . Cousin Meta's boy. He's kind of peculiar. Always has been. Since he's taken to coming up here on Sundays, she's been worried. A man like Frank can get into trouble wandering around this city alone. She just wants to know what he's been doing, that he's all right. It'll be a relief to her, I couldn't refuse. But I don't have time to follow someone, wouldn't know how to go about it, anyway. I asked Jack, he recommended you. . . . "

As he spoke, Goldring's words gathered momentum, as if this were a script he'd memorized and at first had forgotten. Now, with one sentence cueing the next, he seemed to find it difficult to stop.

I said, "I suppose your Cousin Meta felt it would be easier for you to look into it, since you're here in town and she's down in . . . ?"

Goldring watched me for a few seconds, and after I let the silence lengthen, his expression became resigned. "King City," he said.

I continued to study him in silence. After a few seconds of meeting my gaze, he wet his lips and looked down at the desk.

When he picked up the letter opener again, his fingers trembled slightly.

Rudy Goldring was lying to me—of that I was certain. Whether about King City or Cousin Meta or all of it, I couldn't tell. But at that moment I was willing to wager a week's salary that more than fifty percent of what he'd told me was outright lies.

From the way he was avoiding my eyes, I also knew he was aware I'd realized his deception. A flush had crept up from under his immaculate white collar and spread over his face. I sensed he wasn't a man to whom lies came easily—in fact, he probably hated telling them. The fact that he had lied meant his reasons for wanting Frank Wilkonson followed were of great consequence to him—and possibly not very honorable.

After a good half-minute of further silence he spoke, still looking down at the desk. "Will you do this for me, Miss McCone?" There was a pathetic pleading ring to his voice that I wouldn't have expected to hear from the high-spirited man who had greeted me, and it made me feel sorry for him.

I hesitated. As All Souls' employee, it wasn't really my right to turn down an assignment, not unless the client asked me to do something illegal. If I refused to take on this tail job, I would have to do a good bit of explaining—both to Jack Stuart and my boss, Hank Zahn. Besides, I liked him, which is why I said, "Yes, I will, Mr. Goldring."

He dropped the letter opener and looked up, sighing faintly. "Thank you. Thank you very much."

We concluded by going over the scanty details about Frank Wilkonson once more. Goldring barely deviated by a single word from his earlier recital. When he showed me to the door, the derelict was still on the steps. He looked up and saluted Goldring. "Hiya, Captain."

"Hello, Bob. Isn't it almost time for your supper?"

"Dunno. What time *is* it?"

"Close to five. You'd better get over to St. Anthony's, or you'll miss a place in line."

The derelict looked regretfully at the can of Colt .45 in his hand, then shook it. It sounded empty.

Goldring said, "No more beer, Bob. Not until you've eaten."

The man shrugged philosophically, set the can carefully out of sight behind one of the porch pillars, and extracted a worn, fringed, tooled leather pouch from behind the other. When he stood, he adjusted its strap on his shoulder, then ambled down the steps.

I said, "He seems to think he's your doorman."

"He is, in a way. He guards the steps and shows people in, and I provide him with beer and remind him to eat. I suppose I shouldn't be encouraging him to drink, but if I cut him off, he's not going to stop. It's harmless enough."

"He was certainly polite enough when I arrived, but isn't he off-putting to your clientele?"

"Most of them are used to Bob. He's been here five years or more. The others are forewarned."

"He's your personal charity, then?"

"I guess you could call him that." Goldring was watching the derelict walk away, his face a complex mixture of emotions. "There are so many of them, and there's nothing to be done on a grand scale. But I can't help thinking that if every business concern south of Market took an interest— Oh well, you don't want to listen to an old man's maunderings, Miss McCone. And I have a dozen shirts to pack before the late UPS pickup. You'll let me know about Frank Wilkonson on Monday?"

I said I would, and after shaking my hand, Goldring went inside.

An interesting man, Rudy Goldring, I thought as I walked back to my car. Complicated, vulnerable, curiously appealing. And in spite of his obvious lies, an honest man. Conflicted because of that honesty. Was that really why, against my better instincts, I was taking his case?

Maybe, maybe not. Sometimes I never knew exactly why I took on certain things—just as I never knew exactly where they would lead me.

THREE

At two on Monday morning I was still on the job, parked across from the Kingsway Motel in front of the coffee shop where I'd sat close to twenty-four hours before. I'd lost Wilkonson in the Wharf area, but when I'd returned to Lombard Street, his Ranchero had been parked underneath the motel. About an hour later Wilkonson appeared on foot— probably coming back from having dinner at one of the nearby coffee shops or small restaurants. He went to his room and shortly after that the lights in its window went out.

When I felt certain he would stay in his room for a while, I left the MG and went into the coffee shop. I hadn't eaten anything since the sandwiches and fruit I'd downed while following him from nursery to nursery, and the emergency Hershey bars that I always carry in my purse didn't appeal to me. I took the same window booth I'd occupied earlier and ate a burger and fries while keeping an eye on Wilkonson's darkened motel room, then bought a large container of coffee. Back in the car, I whiled away the hours by listening to the radio and bolstering up my flagging energy level with chocolate and caffeine.

The fog had come in again, thick and blustery. It sheeted up Lombard Street like wind-driven snow. I huddled inside my pea jacket, unable to run the heater because it was broken, and thought about the man I'd been tailing: his visits to places having to do with plants; his questions that I hadn't been able to hear; his obvious anger.

He had to be looking for someone. A man or a woman whose vocation or avocation involved horticulture. That could mean anything from retail nursery clerk to garden club president to landscape architect. When he'd questioned the various clerks, he'd probably been describing the person; the way he'd moved his hands while talking indicated that. Because he'd had to go to such lengths in his search, he either didn't know the person's name or had reason to believe he or she was going by an assumed one. Why? Because of trouble with the law? Because of a desire to hide from Wilkonson? And if the latter—again, why?

Wilkonson was an angry man. Leashed anger, but not so tightly leashed that it couldn't be triggered, as it had been at the Wharf. A potentially violent man. Someone a person might naturally want to hide from.

Violent behavior wasn't part of the picture of Wilkonson that Rudy Goldring had painted for me. He'd described him as "peculiar," had said he could "get into trouble wandering around this city alone." I'd assumed "peculiar" meant inept, perhaps retarded. But Wilkonson had proved himself neither of those.

Did Rudy Goldring know of Wilkonson's potential for violence? If he did, he'd omitted a key factor from his description—one I'd had every right to know before undertaking to tail the man. The omission—or perhaps downright deception—made *me* angry. I'd been duped by other clients and in a few cases hadn't learned what was really going on until irreparable harm had been done. In one of those cases two people had died unnecessarily—and then I'd almost lost my own life.

It wouldn't do any good to fume over it now, though. There would be time to confront Goldring about it when I delivered my report that afternoon. To calm myself, I tuned the radio to a station that played oldies, but after a while they broke for a Sunday-night talk show about the problem of San Francisco's homeless. The participants were a welfare worker, a priest, and a sociologist; their dispassionate discussion reduced those who slept in doorways or on park benches to mere statistics. They spoke of over seven thousand homeless people in the city alone, and more than forty-five thousand in the greater Bay Area. They said that for the city's homeless there were only a little over a thousand beds available in shelters; in the entire area only one bed was available for every fifteen people. They talked about how the homeless problem destroyed the quality of life for all of us; about how the tax money allocated to homeless relief wasn't beginning to pay the bills; about establishing regional support centers and funding more studies.

Studies? I thought incredulously. *Spend money that could go to feed people, on more useless research?*

I thought of my own college sociology major and how—had anything more come of it than a vinyl-encased diploma, whose whereabouts I couldn't even guess at now—it could have been me on the radio, analyzing and dissecting. Then I thought of Rudy Goldring and Bob, his derelict "doorman," and of Goldring's comment—naive and practical at the same time—that if every business south of Market showed an interest in a homeless person, it might make a difference. In light of that, the sociobabble on the radio began to depress me, so I switched to KSUN, "Light of the Bay."

My former lover, disc jockey Don Del Boccio, was giving a spiel about a rock concert KSUN would be hosting at the Oakland Coliseum the next week. He and the station's Wonder Bus would be there, Don said, along with Tina, the terrific traffic reporter. There would be a giveaway of KSUN T-shirts and posters to the first hundred couples. There would be a drawing for a door prize—a date with your favorite KSUN deejay. There would be—

I punched the button for a classical station. Listening to Don was almost as depressing as listening to the dehumanizing discussion of the city's indigents. Not because our parting had been a bitter one; there hadn't been enough of a connection between us by then for its severing to foster rancor. Not because I missed him; I didn't. His departure from my life had been more of a liberation. But hearing his bubbly voice and slick, superficial delivery reminded me again of all that had gone wrong between us—of how easily people can mistake sexual attraction and admiration of qualities that they themselves don't possess, for love.

Don is a cheerful, outgoing man who sees more good than bad in the world, a minor celebrity whose fame rests easily on his shoulders. I'd envied his carefree approach to life and thought he would help me loosen up; he'd envied my sense of purpose and thought I would help him chart a more serious career.

But finally, after a couple of years, Don and I had proved to be too different. His upbeat attitude began to seem shallow to me; it grated, just as my cynicism and jealous guarding of my privacy irritated him. He found my cases too grim and didn't want to talk about them. I found even the in-depth talk show he'd persuaded the station to let him do to be superficial; I was reluctant to accompany him to glitzy KSUN promotional functions. Eventually we took refuge in our long, irregular working hours and just let things taper off.

We'd been apart for six months now. I hadn't found anyone new, wasn't really looking. Now I wondered if Don had. Who was this Tina, the terrific traffic reporter, anyway? Hadn't he said her name with more than his usual enthusiasm?

For a moment I considered tuning in to KSUN again, listening to Don to see if I could detect his feelings and circumstances over the airwaves. Then I laughed aloud. Could it be I was a tiny bit jealous? No, I decided, not really. Don was out of my life for good. But I was interested, as I would be in any former lover.

I didn't touch the radio's buttons, though. The station I had on was playing Brahms, a favorite of mine ever since Don—who had once trained to be a concert pianist at the Eastman School of Music—had educated me to the joys of the classics. Hours passed as the selection switched to Mendelssohn, and then Tchaikovsky. The fog blew dense and snowy. Around midnight I almost dozed off, so I got out of the car and walked up and down the block twice, breathing the misty air. It was warmer, the fog like a thermal blanket wrapped around the city. I walked briskly, swinging my arms, and after a while felt more alert.

Now, an hour and forty minutes later, the lights went on in room 209. I watched a tall shadow move across the drawn drapes. Shortly afterward, Wilkonson emerged carrying a small travel bag. As he went to the Ranchero I started my car. He executed a U-turn and went past me, toward downtown. I hung back so he wouldn't notice my headlights; the sparseness of traffic at that hour made him easy to spot.

Eventually he led me into the light industrial district south of Market where I'd met with Rudy Goldring on Friday. The streets were deserted and so dirty that even the fog seemed begrimed. Warehouses and semitrailers hulked darkly. My headlights washed over the latticework of chain-link fences and gleamed off railroad tracks that crisscrossed the pavement. There were no other cars in sight, and I was beginning to fear that Wilkonson would realize he was being tailed when a lighted area blazed up ahead of us. Suddenly the street was congested with cars and trucks and people. I slowed, momentarily puzzled, imagining that we had arrived at the scene of some horrible disaster. Then I saw a green and white neon sign reading CALIFORNIA FLOWER MART.

The Flower Terminal at Fifth and Brannan Streets—not far from the Hall of Justice—is as much of a San Francisco institution as Cost Plus, but not nearly as well known. Five days a week, while the rest of the city sleeps, wholesalers from all over the northern part of the state gather there to offer their wares to the area's florists and retail nurseries and sidewall vendors. I'd never been there before—no one unassociated with the flower industry would have occasion to—but I'd once read a magazine article that had described the terminal as "an incredible hive of activity." The description could not have been more apt.

Trucks clogged the street ahead of me, double and triple parked. Men and women unloaded crates, boxes, and flats of flowers, as well as trees and shrubs, onto handcarts and fork-lifts at the back doors to dozens of stalls. People crossed within inches of my front bumper, heedless of the car's motion. Ahead of me Wilkonson was experiencing similar impediments to progress: he weaved around a van, slammed on his brakes to avoid a hand truck loaded with saplings, crept around a group of men who were drinking coffee in the middle of the street. It was the congestion of the Wharf area all over again, only much worse, and I began to fear another outburst of violence. Wilkonson kept his speed down, however, weaving through the obstacle course. I lost sight of the Ranchero briefly when it slid around the corner onto Brannan Street, then caught up with it as it passed a busy, brightly lighted establishment called the Flower Mart Restaurant. On the other side of Sixth Street he found a quasi-legal parking space. I kept going, spotted a space further down, but was beaten out by an old Chevy. Finally I left the MG by the loading dock of a ball-bearing company and hurried down the crowded street to the entrance to the mart.

A sign by the door declared it off limits to anyone without a badge. Ahead of me I saw Wilkonson; he was showing some ID to the security guard, who waved him inside. I pushed forward to the guard's post, waited for a break in the steadily moving line, and showed him my own identification. The guard was young, and my license impressed him—much as it would have impressed me in the days when I guarded doorways and office building lobbies for a living—and in a few seconds he was on the house phone to his supervisor. After a brief exchange he handed the receiver to me. I identified myself again and said I was working a tail job on one of their badgeholders—for a civil suit, nothing that would cause danger to any of their customers. The supervisor agreed to allow me inside and asked to speak to the guard again; after he hung up, the guard handed me a temporary badge.

The crowded, elongated space in front of me glared with neon light. It was lined on all sides with stalls that overflowed with plants and flowers; piles of crates and flats and boxes extended out into its center. The mart stretched for a full city block, much of it outdoors under the dark, fog-streaked sky. My gaze skipped over roses and gladioli and carnations and chrysanthemums as I searched for Wilkonson. People in work clothes, most of them bundled against the chill early morning air, moved back and forth, examining the color of blossoms and testing the freshness of leaves with their fingertips. After a moment I caught sight of Wilkonson, walking slowly down the right-hand side, stopping at each stall. His gait was no longer stiff with reined-in anger; he moved almost somnambulistically, stopping at each stall and scrutinizing every face—both buyers and vendors—before going on.

I followed him around the mart twice, but he didn't give any indication that he was planning to leave. After a while he seemed to wake up, but there was still no suggestion of the previous day's tension. He seemed almost resigned, as if he were going through the motions of looking for someone with very little hope of finding him or her. When he began his third go-round, I stationed myself beside a small forest of yew trees and kept my eyes on him from there.

Around me the mart hummed with activity. Vendors brought in more and more wares. Buyers moved briskly from stall to stall, inspecting the plants and flowers, criticizing their freshness, exchanging both pleasantries and good-natured barbs, haggling enthusiastically. A tall man came up and peered intently at the yew trees, blocking my view of Wilkonson. A woman joined the man, shook her head, and dragged him away. When they passed, I spotted Wilkonson standing in front of a sea of baby's breath. Seconds later he moved on to a stall where dozens of Boston ferns hung from overhead wires. He canvassed the room in a methodical manner, not bothering to look at the vendors now, but concentrating on the buyers.

His behavior confirmed my suspicion that he was looking for someone connected with the flower industry; only professionals were allowed in here. But what was Wilkonson's connection? He'd shown a badge to the guard. Rudy Goldring had said he worked on a ranch, though. What kind of ranch—?

"Sharon McCone!"

I jumped. A fat woman in a garish green muu-muu stood next to me. There was a pink carnation in her wildly curling gray hair, and she grinned at me, showing gapped teeth. "Sallie Hyde," I said.

Sallie moved in front of me, holding out a pudgy hand. "What are you doing here?"

She was blocking my view of Wilkonson. I took the hand and tugged her to one side. Wilkonson was standing by a pile of cases topped by some exotic red blooms that I didn't recognize. "Working," I said.

Sallie's face took on a sly, knowing look. I'd met her while on a case in the Tenderloin hotel where she lived, a couple of years ago. "Then I better skedaddle."

"No, stand here and talk with me. You—" I stopped, realizing I'd been about to say something untactful about her bulk hiding me.

Sallie, however, is comfortable with her fat. "I make a better door than window, right?"

"Right."

"Glad to help. How'd you get in here?"

"Security supervisor okayed it." Then I realized this was an odd place to find Sallie, too. The last time I'd seen her, she'd been a clerk at one of the flower stands on Union Square. "You must have changed jobs."

"Still work for the same people, but I'm a sort of supervisor myself now. Oversee the stands and do the buying for the Menottis."

"Sallie, that's terrific!" There are only twelve sidewalk flower stands in the city, and the permits for them are held by a few families who have been in the business for generations. If one of them had entrusted its operation to Sallie, she was moving up in the world.

She flushed with pleasure. "Yeah, it is. I love the work, and I'm learning the business top to bottom. One of these days I might just have a shop of my own."

Wilkonson was coming our way, moving past a stall that was crammed with dried and artificial flowers. I squeezed between Sallie and a yew tree, feeling its needles prickle on my cheek. "You still living at the Globe Hotel?"

"Yeah. I could afford to move to a better neighborhood, but I been there so long it's home."

"What about the Vangs?" They were a Vietnamese refugee family who had been my primary liaison when I'd been hired to investigate strange goings-on at the hotel.

"Bought a house in the Richmond."

It had been their dream, as it was for many of the city's refugees. "Nice for them. Do they still have the restaurant?"

"Sure. It's what pays for the house."

Wilkonson had passed behind Sallie without giving her a glance. Possibly that meant that whomever he sought was not a woman—or at least not a large woman. When he was several yards away, I motioned toward him and asked her, "Do you know that man?"

"The guy in the suede jacket?"

"Yes."

She studied him, squinting so her eyes almost disappeared in the fleshy folds of her face. "Don't know him, but I've seen him here before."

"When?"

"Last week? The week before? I can't really say."

"How long have you been doing the buying here?"

"Almost a year now."

"But he's only been coming for a couple of weeks?"

"Maybe, maybe not. I know I've seen him once or twice this month. Before that, I don't recall. I do know he's not a regular, though."

I was about to ask if there was any way of finding out more about the badgeholders when a man with a hand truck loaded with bamboo plants jostled against her and she lurched into me. I collapsed against the yew trees.

Sallie extended her hand to pull me up and glared at the shrubs. "Damned funeral trees," she said.

The words gave me a prickly little chill, disproportionate to their meaning. "*What* trees?" I asked.

"I call them funeral trees. In Europe they plant them in the cemeteries, or so the Menottis tell me. I've seen them around graves here too, so I guess it's true. I *hate* them."

Her tone was so malevolent and she gave the inoffensive trees such an evil look that suddenly I remembered Sallie Hyde was a murderer—tried, convicted, imprisoned, and paroled. When her eyes returned to meet mine, she must have seen the recollection there, because she changed the subject abruptly, chatting about her new job and prospects, then saying she had better get busy with her buying. Before she left me, she gave me her card and said I should keep in touch. I promised to, but somehow I doubted I would. The flower seller was like dozens of other people all over the city whom I knew from cases: an acquaintance with whom I had nothing in common save the violence that had initially brought us together.

It was close to five in the morning and my energy had completely flagged when Wilkonson finally made for the exit. I followed him on leaden legs to Brannan Street and his Ranchero, then fetched the MG. There was an entrance to the I-80 freeway a few blocks away; I caught up with the Ranchero as it took the ramp, and I drove behind it for a ways until I saw it merge onto Route 101 going south out of the city.

At Army Street I took the off ramp. My long, long workday was over.

FOUR

At ten that morning I arrived at All Souls. The fog now hung still and heavy, making the playground equipment in the triangular park across the street seem alien and somewhat menacing. It was kinder to the big brown Bernal Heights Victorian that had housed the co-op for more than a dozen years: the blistered and peeling paint was obscured, seeming once more an unblemished skin; the badly patched shingles and sagging roofline wore a stately wig of gray mist. I often thought of the building as an old lady living out her last days in a constant struggle against the indignities of poverty. Today it was as if she had decked herself out in tattered finery and temporarily won the battle.

When I came through the front door our secretary, Ted Smalley, looked up from his nearly completed *New York Times* crossword puzzle. "Kind of late, aren't you?"

"Kind of." I looked down at the puzzle and frowned. It drives me crazy that he has enough confidence to do it in ink.

Ted covered the paper with his hand. He hates to share and won't even ask for help unless he's hopelessly stumped.

I pushed his hand aside. "What's that?"

"What's what?"

"That. Number seventy-two across. Seven-letter word beginning and ending with *s*. Fourth letter's an *l*." It was one of the few he had yet to fill in.

He glared at me, then sighed. "Feeble."

"Feeble. Should be easy—that's how I feel today. *S* . . .
l . . . *s* . . . sapless."

"Sapless." He ticked off the blocks with the tip of his pen.
As I went toward the stairs to the second floor, he began
filling in the word. "You're welcome," I said.

"You know I hate it when you do that."

"Why else would I?" Halfway up the stairs I stopped. "Hey,
Ted, would you buzz Rae and ask her to come up to my office."

"She's not in yet."

Tardiness was one of my new assistant Rae Kelleher's few
faults, but a particularly vexing one. It bothered me all the more
because I suspected most of her late arrivals could be directly
attributed to the demands of her perpetual-student husband,
Doug.

Ted obviously held the same opinion, because he said,
"Maybe she had to type a paper for Dougie, or prep him for an
exam."

I grimaced and said, "When she comes in, tell her I want to
see her." Then I continued upstairs to my new office.

When I stepped inside its door, I stopped—as I had nearly
every day for the last four months—and admired my surround-
ings. The room—half of the original master bedroom—was at
the front of the house, and its bay window afforded me a view.
Not that it was one of the spectacular panoramas San Francisco
is famous for; I couldn't see the Bay or the Golden Gate Bridge
or even the downtown skyscrapers. What I could see was the
Outer Mission District: the rooftops were as patched and
sagging as All Souls', the buildings as shabby; the streets were
flat and treeless, their gutters clogged with litter; the people
who walked them were generally poorly dressed, their pos-
tures hunched and defensive. But it *was* a view, and the office
was far larger than my former converted closet under the stairs.
Besides, in a way, what I could see from my desk—which sat in
the window bay—was perfectly fitting for the work I did there;
this was my territory, and any one of those people might have
been my client.

The reason I had come to possess such sumptuous digs was
that my boss, Hank Zahn, who had lived in this room since he
founded the co-op shortly after graduating law school, had
gotten married the previous spring to another of the attorneys,
Anne-Marie Altman, and had moved to her flat over in Noe
Valley. I guess I'd acted pretty mournful about him being so far

away and no longer available at any hour of the day or night for counsel or companionship, because he'd bequeathed me the room for my office—disappointing several others who had been casting covetous looks at it. It didn't really make up for the loss of long late-night talking-and-drinking sessions with Hank, nor for the fact that Anne-Marie, my best female friend at All Souls, was now a married lady who hurried home to have intimate dinners with her new husband. But once I'd outfitted it with a new Parsons table desk and an old oriental rug I'd found rolled up in the attic, and had hung some of my favorite photographs on the walls . . . *well,* I'd started thinking of myself as a career woman of substance, rather than an underpaid, unappreciated lackey.

The event that had completed my metamorphosis into staff member of importance had occurred two months ago when Hank and the other partners had decided that I had too much serious investigating on my hands to continue with such important but time-consuming and essentially undemanding tasks as filing documents at City Hall and the routine interviewing of possible witnesses. Hire an assistant, they'd told me.

I'd called around to other investigators and acquaintances at security firms, and one had finally recommended Rae Kelleher. Rae was twenty-five, a psychology graduate from my old alma mater at Berkeley, and the sole support of her Ph.D.-student husband. At that time she had been working as a security guard, as I had been after receiving my own highly useless degree. We'd met, and I'd liked her enthusiasm and easy good humor, had been impressed with her keen intelligence and willingness to do scutwork for low pay in exchange for learning the trade and eventually getting her investigator's license. In the two months she'd worked for me she'd been amenable and uncomplaining and quick to pick up on what she needed to know. The only problem was that husband and his demands on time she should have been devoting to her duties.

I turned my thoughts away from Rae, sat down at the desk, and began going over my notes on Frank Wilkonson. My eyes felt gritty from lack of sleep—I'd only managed two hours— and my head ached slightly. I reached for my purse to see if I had any aspirin; there was only one Tylenol in a dented tin at the bottom of the bag. I swallowed it dry and kept on studying the notes. When I finished, I had the essence of a report, but no conclusions and no clear-cut way to deal with the subject of Goldring's lack of candor about Wilkonson. Finally I opted for typing up only what I had, then called his office.

Mr. Goldring wasn't in, the woman who answered the phone said. Did I care to leave a message?

I identified myself and said I would drop by the office late that afternoon, around the same time I had last Friday. If that was inconvenient, Mr. Goldring should call me.

When I hung up I looked at the case files on the desk. There were only four, and I intended to turn two of them over to Rae—provided she ever came to work. The others I would have to handle myself, since they involved tracking down a couple of hostile witnesses, and Rae had no experience with skip-tracing. Reluctantly I pulled the phone toward me, made a few calls, and came up empty-handed. It was close to noon when I went downstairs.

Ted wasn't at his desk; he'd probably gone to lunch. I poked my head into my former office under the stairs—which Rae had spruced up in a way I'd never thought possible—but found it vacant. Then I went down the hall to Hank's office; he was in but on the phone. When he looked up at me, I saw his complexion was unusually pale, and there were dark circles under his eyes that his thick horn-rimmed glasses failed to hide. Was he coming down with something? I wondered. Or was this a symptom of something more serious than the onset of a cold or the flu? Come to think of it, neither he nor Anne-Marie had looked too good lately.

I mouthed the word "lunch" at Hank. He shook his head and pointed at a stack of folders in front of him. I shrugged and went to a stack of city papers that Hank—who hoards newspapers and other periodicals—keeps in the corner of his office. I checked the date on the top one, found it was yesterday's, and extracted the pink section. When I held it up questioningly, he nodded that it was okay for me to borrow it. Then he said into the phone, "Look, this is a nonnegotiable point—unless you've got something damned good to negotiate with."

I carried the entertainment section down the hall to the big kitchen at the rear of the house. A couple of the other attorneys were eating lunch at the round oak table in the dining area by the windows. I responded to their greetings and went to peer into the refrigerator. It was chock-full of healthy things—spinach, carrots, tofu, cottage cheese, yogurt. I sighed, remembering the good old days when Hank still lived here and there was always a pot of his leftover spaghetti or chili waiting to be warmed up. Finally I settled on only a cup of coffee and took it out to the combination living-and-waiting room.

As I went out the door, one of the attorneys said, "McCone's being antisocial again."

I bristled at the unfairness of the remark. I love the warm, friendly atmosphere at All Souls and genuinely enjoy the others' company, but sometimes the enforced togetherness is more than I can handle. The co-op has its roots in the poverty law movement of the seventies; the word "poverty" seems to apply more to the employees and partners than to the clients, who are charged on a sliding fee scale according to their incomes. As a result, several people live in free rooms on the second floor. Most of the staff take the majority of their meals there, and those who live out seem to spend more time at the co-op than at home. No one minds the lack of privacy. If anything, they thrive on it—kicking around problems with clients and cases, sharing details of their personal lives, arranging endless social functions and outings. For someone like me, such a living situation would be unendurable.

But at the same time, most of the folks at All Souls are my friends as well as co-workers. I can usually be enticed to their parties, and when I need companionship, it's the place I turn. The remark, good-natured as it was, hurt—all the more, I suspected, because it was the same kind of criticism of my need for solitude that Don had leveled at me toward the end of our relationship.

It also made me wonder if people did indeed view me as prickly, independent and needing no one. If so, they were wrong; the empty place I'd carried inside me since my breakup with Don attested to that. I thought of Frank Wilkonson, and the way his dejected, shambling gait as he'd walked through the fog to the newspaper stand had reminded me of Kristofferson's song about lonely Sundays. Then I thought of how I'd wandered dispiritedly along the misty beach on another recent Sunday. No, I wasn't the totally self-sufficient woman my friends and associates believed me to be. I needed someone—but it had to be someone who would let me be myself, give me room to breathe, not try to change me. And a person like that wasn't easy to find.

I shrugged off the gloomy thoughts and settled on the

broken-down couch in the living-and-waiting room. The big front parlor is usually full of clients, but now, during the noon hour, it was deserted. Toys from the chest by the fireplace—provided for the children of clients who must bring their offspring while they consult with their attorneys—were strewn on the worn oriental rug. Chipped pottery mugs and dirty ashtrays stood on the coffee table; I had to clear a space in order to set my own cup down. Then I opened the pink section and paged through it.

I dismissed such categories as "Nightlife" and "Movies," focusing on the one labeled "Exhibits." There it was—the plant sale at the Hall of Flowers. I went out to Ted's desk and found his Yellow Pages. There were four columns and a number of large ads under "Nurseries—Retail." This was probably the other page Wilkonson had had in his jacket pocket.

As I replaced the phone book I tried to decide whether to go upstairs and work on the skip-traces or wander down to Mission Street and grab a burrito at my favorite taquería. Neither prospect intrigued me.

The Goldring investigation had to do with the floral industry. But what? And why? And was it really any of my business anymore? I'd finished my report for Rudy Goldring; this afternoon I'd deliver it. If he merely accepted it and declared the case closed, that would be that. If he wanted more information, I could go around to the various nurseries Wilkonson had visited, try to find out what questions he'd asked the clerks. But before I'd go on working for Goldring, we'd have to clear the air about the things he hadn't told me. I would need more information about Wilkonson himself. Perhaps it would be wise to set the wheels in motion before I went to my appointment with Goldring. I had Wilkonson's license plate number; I could check him out through a friend at the DMV. Better yet, I could ask one of the people I knew on the SFPD to run a check through CJIS or CJIC—

The front door opened, and Rae Kelleher came in.

Rae is a small woman, around five foot two, with short curly auburn hair, a round, freckled face, and a compact athletic body. That afternoon she was wearing jeans, a mangy-looking brown coat of a style that I could have sworn went out in the early sixties, and a blue and gold–striped scarf like the one I used to wear to the Berkeley football games. She began unwinding it from her neck, then saw me, started, and made a guilty apologetic gesture with her free hand. I looked at my watch; it was quarter to one. Silently I waited for her explanations.

She said, "I can't explain."

"Terrific."

"I mean, I can, but it's unacceptable."

"Try me."

The scarf slid to the floor and she began unbuttoning her coat. "I don't think you want to hear this."

"Let me be the judge of that."

"Okay, Doug had—"

"You're right. I *don't* want to hear it."

"Sharon, he needed—"

"Save it, Rae."

This was more or less what I'd expected, and I wasn't mad at her, not really. But I was exasperated at how she was risking her own future by constantly giving in to Doug's demands. Didn't the woman realize that she, as well as her husband, had a way to make in the world? Didn't she know that husbands might stay or go, but a profession that would make use of the talents she seemed to possess would stand her in good stead for a lifetime?

Rae was watching my face. Hers was pinched now, and her freckles stood out against its pallor. I guessed she expected me to fire her.

Finally I said, "Look, we need to talk."

"Well, I know that. Now?"

I hesitated. I was tired and on edge. I didn't want to enter into what would be a delicate conversation in my present condition. "No, not now. I need to turn over a couple of files to you, and then I've got work of my own, and an appointment around four."

A trace of relief touched her features. "After that, then?"

"Yes. Tell you what: There's an All Souls tradition that I haven't introduced you to yet. At least, it's a McCone-Zahn tradition. Why don't you meet me at the Remedy Lounge around five-thirty?"

"That sleazoid bar down the hill on Mission Street?"

"Right."

Most people would have reacted with disgust—or at least reluctance—but once again Rae proved to be my kind of woman. Her face rounded out in a delighted grin, and she said, "Oh boy, I was wondering when one of you would invite me!"

"Five-thirty, then. And no excuses—even if Doug calls and wants something."

"I promise." Damned if she didn't hold up the fingers of her right hand in the Girl Scout salute.

I said, "Okay, pick up that scarf and dump your coat and come upstairs. I've got to brief you on those two cases."

As I went to my office, I chided myself for sounding exactly like my mother. Well, not exactly—my mother would have told her to hang up the coat, and probably to comb her hair and wash her hands as well.

FIVE

The derelict doorman wasn't on the steps at Rudy Goldring's building, so I let myself in. When I found Goldring's office empty too, I continued down the hallway, calling out his name. A gray-haired woman in a striped smock with straight pins stuck through its lapel came out of the back room.

"You must be the one that called this morning," she said. "He's still not in. I'm Mrs. Halvorsen, his office manager. Can I help you?"

"He hasn't come in all day?"

"Just this morning, for an hour or two, but he left before ten. Said he had an appointment." She paused, frowning and fingering the pins. "And that's odd—you'd think he'd have called. He missed a fitting for a new customer at one, and first fittings are important to Mr. Goldring. He likes to make an occasion of them."

"Maybe he wasn't feeling well and went home."

"Home's right upstairs, the second-story flat. He'd have stopped in first. Besides, I tried to call him up there when the new customer came. No answer, and he wasn't down at the factory, either."

"Do you know who the appointment was with—or where?"

She shook her head.

"Well, I'm sure he'll turn up. When he does, would you ask him to call me?" I gave her one of my cards and went back down the hall.

On the porch I hesitated, both annoyed and puzzled, looking at the door to the upstairs flat. Maybe Rudy Goldring had returned home by now; the woman had only mentioned trying to call him once, around three hours ago. I was about to step over there and ring the bell when the door flew open and a tall figure in a raincoat rushed through it and slammed into me.

I stumbled backward and caught at the person to keep from toppling down the steps. It was a woman of about my age, with luxuriant chestnut hair piled high on her head. Her finely formed features—straight delicate nose, high cheekbones, generous mouth, and unusually large blue eyes—would have been beautiful, had they not been contorted with fright. She stared wildly at my face and down at where my hand was gripping her forearm, then tried to wrench away from me. I hung on.

"What's wrong?" I said. "What's happened?"

"Oh God!" Her teeth were chattering; she put a hand to her cheek as if to stop them.

"What is it? Is it Mr. Goldring?"

"Oh God!" Now she was gripping *my* arm, her fingers so tight they hurt. "You know him, you have to help him!"

"Where is he? Show me."

She cast a panicky look at the street, and I braced myself to stop her if she tried to break away again. The she looked back at the open door to the flat. "Up . . . up there . . . in the kitchen."

"Take me to him."

Wordlessly she led me inside and up the steep staircase, her head bowed, shoulders hunched inside the raincoat.

The upstairs flat was painted and carpeted in the same manner as the offices below. Toward the front was a living room that apparently had been created by removing the wall between two smaller rooms; its double-window bay was filled with hanging ferns. The woman turned the other way, past a bedroom and a bathroom, toward the back of the house. A kitchen opened off the end of the hall—one of the old-fashioned kind like All Souls', with black-and-white–checkered linoleum, a sink with a drainboard, and a hulking black iron range.

Rudy Goldring lay sprawled on his back in front of the range, arms flung wide. It looked as if he had fallen and hit his head on one of its curving legs.

Alarm set my skin prickling; I rushed over to him and knelt

down, fumbling for his wrist and trying to push up the sleeve of his shirt so I could take his pulse. The shirt had French cuffs secured by gold cufflinks. As I undid one, I looked at his drained white face, then saw that blood had oozed out from under his head onto the linoleum. It was mostly dry now. I got the cufflink out and grabbed his wrist. His flesh was cool, and his body beginning to stiffen; rigor mortis was setting in. Rudy Goldring had been dead a number of hours.

I let go of his wrist and looked up at the woman. She had backed up against the old Frigidaire and was watching me, hands over her mouth, eyes darkened by horror. When she saw the expression on my face, she made a whimpering sound and her knees started to sag. Quickly I got up and went to her, turning her away from the body and moving her toward the door to the hallway. Her teeth were chattering again and tremors wracked her slender frame; she leaned heavily on me. I guided her down the hall, experiencing tremors of my own.

In the living room I eased the woman into a recliner chair. She started to bring her hands together, then stared down at them. They were shaking violently. She looked up at me, tears welling in her remarkable blue eyes, and then she lowered her head and forced her hands into a trembling grip. She said, "He's . . . dead, isn't he?"

"Yes, some hours ago."

She made a strange noise—half sob, half sigh. I looked down at the top of her head, where her hair was artfully twined into a loose braid. Tendrils had escaped it and trailed down, making her look bedraggled and vulnerable.

I said, "Are you all right?"

"I . . . yes . . . no. Oh God, I was so afraid it would come to this."

"You mean Mr. Goldring's death?"

She was silent.

"*Is* that what you meant?"

No response. I looked around the room—which was obsessively orderly in comparison to the office downstairs—for a telephone. There was one on an end table next to the couch. I started toward it.

The woman raised her head. When she spoke her voice had a sharper edge of alarm. "What are you doing?"

"Calling nine-eleven—"

"No!" She stood, started toward me, then turned and rushed toward the staircase.

"Come back here! You found Mr. Goldring's body; you can't just leave—"

"Please!" She turned, clutching the railing for support. Her face had been very white, but now a flush—almost a rash—was spreading up from her neckline. "You don't understand. There might be publicity, my name in the papers. I can't have that, especially after this. . . ." And then she bolted down the stairs.

I went after her, but she was faster and had too much of a head start. By the time I reached the front porch, she was jumping into a white BMW parked down the block. I ran down the steps and caught its license plate number—1 GDJ 326—just before it pulled out of Stillman into Third Street.

"One GDJ three two six," I said aloud. It sounded like a curse. I turned and walked toward the building, repeating the numbers and letters over and over until I could find my purse and write them down. The purse was on the kitchen counter; funny, I didn't remember leaving it there. I grabbed it without looking at Rudy Goldring's body and started toward the living room to make my call.

But halfway to the door something caught my eye: a worn, fringed, tooled leather pouch of the sort that I'd last seen Bob, the derelict doorman, carrying. It was lying on the floor in front of the sink, not more than two yards from the body.

The senior member of the Homicide team that caught the call was named Gallagher, Ben Gallagher. I'd known him for a long time. When I'd met him he'd been an owlish, somewhat awkward young man who admired me extravagantly—although silently. In the years since then, he'd worked Vice and Burglary, then been reassigned to Homicide; he still looked owlish, mainly because of the round glasses frames he favored, but the awkwardness was gone. He probably still admired me, because his eyes shone when they first saw me, but his silence was now enforced by a wide gold wedding band.

I waited in the living room while Gallagher examined the death scene and dealt with the medical examiner and lab technicians. When he'd finished, I told him what had happened since I'd arrived at the building, including my encounter with the frightened woman and the make and license plate number of her car. Ben took notes, then held up the fringed leather pouch, now encased in a plastic evidence bag.

"This belong to her?"

"No, to the derelict who sits on the steps downstairs, I think. At least he was carrying one like it last Friday."

"Considering its contents, that makes more sense. Eighty-three cents, a switchblade knife, and no credit cards don't really go with a lady who drives a BMW. Now tell me about this derelict."

"Rudy Goldring called him Bob. The man acts as a sort of doorman for him, in exchange for beer. He's medium height, has grayish hair and a beard, was wearing old army fatigues when I saw him."

"Standard derelict description."

"Well, yes. I didn't pay that much attention to him, to tell you the truth; he looked pretty much like all the other derelicts you see in this area." That, I thought, from someone who'd recently been scornful toward a radio talk show reducing the homeless to statistics! I concentrated on Bob, trying to remember something that would distinguish him. Gallagher waited.

After a moment I added, "He seemed fairly well-spoken. Polite. When he opened the door for me, he acted like a butler. Oh—and he eats dinner at St. Anthony's. I know that because Goldring reminded him it was time for him to get in line, and he went off in that direction. Maybe the people there, or the woman downstairs in Goldring's offices, can tell you more about him."

"Maybe." Gallagher finished making his notes and looked up at me. "Now tell me what you're doing here."

Because Rudy Goldring had hired me through his lawyer, my implied contract with him provided for confidentiality. But Goldring was dead, and from Gallagher's questions I gathered the police would treat his death as a homicide, at least initially. That invalidated the presumption of confidentiality, so I told Ben about the job.

When I finished he said, "We'll trace this Frank Wilkonson, see what he has to say about Goldring. Most likely it'll be irrelevant to what happened here."

"You think Goldring was murdered, then?"

"It's highly possible. The M.E. says there are signs he was involved in a struggle—bruises, the condition of his clothing, that sort of thing. The way it looks now, I'd guess it was

manslaughter—a quarrel that got out of hand. Maybe he cut off
the derelict's beer supply, or something like that."

"What about what the woman who was here said to me—
that she was 'afraid it would come to this'?"

"She could have been speaking about the derelict. It's not the
wisest thing, you know, taking one of those people under your
wing. Anyway, we'll locate her, ask her what she meant."
Gallagher closed his notebook and stood. "We'll need a formal
statement; you know the procedure. You still with that same
outfit?"

"All Souls? Yes." I stood, too, and gave him one of my cards.

Gallagher studied it, then looked back at my face. His eyes
were a trifle wistful now, and I wondered if he was remembering the old days, too. What he said confirmed it: "You ever see
the lieutenant?"

He meant Greg Marcus, my lover back then. "We have
dinner occasionally, but that's it."

"Funny, I always thought the two of you would get it
together."

"So did we—once." I looked at my watch. Six-thirty. I'd told
Rae I would meet her at the Remedy Lounge an hour ago. "Is
it okay to use the phone?"

"Sure, Goldring won't mind." Ben raised a hand in farewell
and left the room.

I stared at the empty doorframe. It wasn't a remark he would
have made in earlier days, nor one that I would have
accepted—not without anger and protest. But the years had
tempered our reactions; now we both wore carapaces of
cynicism. It was the only shield either of us had against the
pain, the only armor that made it possible to go on.

I turned away toward the fern-filled front window. Foggy
dusk enveloped the city, early for September, a forewarning of
a long, dark, hard winter. As the shadows lengthened, my
depression deepened. For me, San Francisco had always been
a brightly lit city, and that illumination mainly came from its
good people. But lately it seemed the lights were going out; one
had been snuffed here today. The loss of Rudy Goldring's
kindness and warmth—even though I'd experienced it for less
than an hour—filled me with a painful emptiness.

I forced myself to go over to the phone and call the Remedy
Lounge. Brian, the bartender, told me that Rae had left about
fifteen minutes before, after asking him to tell me I should call

her later. No, he said, she hadn't been upset with me. In fact, she'd spent the time drinking beer and talking with one of the regulars, Joey Corona, who owned an auto body shop further out on Mission.

Brian's words made me smile. I pictured Rae's rusted-out old Rambler American; knowing her, she'd probably sweet-talked Joey into a cut-rate repair job.

The thought was comforting. As long as men were available to be sweet-talked into things, and as long as women were willing and able to do that . . . well, things couldn't be all that bad. . . .

Or could they?

SIX

I didn't want to go home, not yet. There was nothing much there to eat; my cat had taken to wandering and probably wouldn't be there to greet me; the place's continual and usually interrupted state of construction (I'd recently begun enclosing my back porch to turn it into my bedroom but had run out of money) made it decidedly inhospitable. Besides, I still felt depressed—not a deep funk, but a prickly discontent, under-scored by an odd clear sorrow—and I wanted to be with people who would understand. Jack Stuart, Rudy Goldring's attorney, would surely be one of those, and if the police hadn't already contacted him, he deserved to be informed about the death. I drove to Bernal Heights and All Souls.

It was after seven when I parked at the apex of the triangular playground. All along the street, windows glowed faintly through the fog. The buildings in Bernal Heights are mainly single-family homes, with a sprinkling of two- and three-flat dwellings. The people who inhabit them are a mixture of working-class families, neo-Yuppies, and oddballs like the folks at All Souls. I looked into the windows of the nearby houses and saw a family eating from trays in front of a TV, a couple setting a candlelit dinner table, and a string quartet practicing next to a grand piano whose lid was littered with wrappings from McDonald's.

It was quiet inside All Souls. I shed my coat and, out of habit, tossed it on the desk chair in what had once been my office.

Then I continued to the kitchen. No one was there but Hank and Jack Stuart—the man I'd come here to see. They sat at the round table by the windows, wineglasses in hand, deep in conversation. When I came in, they both glanced toward the door, and when they saw the look on my face, their expressions went from glum to concerned.

Hank said, "Shar, what's wrong?"

In spite of my own preoccupation, I realized with a shock that he looked terrible. I couldn't remember having seen Hank so drained and tired in a long, long time. I glanced at Jack; his eyes moved from me to Hank, then back. I thought I caught a warning there: *Don't say anything to upset him.*

I heeded it. "Nothing much. I need to talk to Jack, that's all."

Hank has known me long and well; he can sense when I'm engaging in half-truths. But that night he seemed to want to believe me. He nodded and drained his glass, looking slightly sick after he swallowed, then stood. "Well, I've got to be getting home, anyway." To Jack he added, "Thanks, guy," and walked unsteadily toward the door.

My own concerns had momentarily been pushed aside by anxiety for Hank. I turned to Jack, my mouth open, about to form a question. He shook his head—Hank was still within hearing—and guided me into the other part of the kitchen, where a jug of Gallo's cheapest stood on the drainboard of the sink. He picked up a glass of dubious cleanliness, filled it, and handed it to me.

"What is it?" he asked.

"Rudy Goldring's dead."

He went very still for a few seconds, then his mouth twitched at one corner. "How?"

"He fell and hit his head on the stove in his kitchen. The police suspect homicide—an accident during an argument."

"Argument with whom?"

"You know the derelict who guards his front steps?"

"My God, not Bob. When?"

"This morning, between ten and noon, I'd say. Judging from the degree of rigor—"

"You were there at his place?"

"Yes, I . . . oh hell." Suddenly I felt queasy and light-headed and annoyed with myself. "Look, let's sit down."

Jack motioned at the table, and I took my favorite place,

facing the window beyond which all the marvelous lights of downtown San Francisco blaze. Only they didn't blaze tonight—they were fog-smeared and dim. And they weren't marvelous, either. To me in my present mood, all they represented was the greed of the developers who were overbuilding and ruining my city.

I looked away from them, at Jack.

He was the newest addition to our staff of attorneys, had come to us about a year before. We'd long needed an expert on criminal law—which was Jack's specialty—and with the departure of Gilbert Thayer, an unpleasant young man who had looked like a rabbit with a stomachache and acted like the proverbial serpent in the grass, we'd also had a place for someone who could handle contracts. Unlike the universally despised Gilbert, Jack fit in perfectly. He was a veteran of the same poverty wars—Los Angeles branch—as Hank and Anne-Marie and the other senior partners. He and Hank had carried on a correspondence for a number of years and were in perfect accord as to how a law cooperative should function. When Hank had heard Jack wanted to relocate because his attorney wife had received a good offer from a prestigious Montgomery Street firm, he'd hastened to ask him to join our staff. Jack had accepted just as eagerly and had plunged into the work as if he'd been with the co-op since its founding. He related well to the clients; was as enthusiastic about his contract negotiations as his criminal cases; and seemed as much at ease wearing his three-piece suits to a meeting in a boardroom as he was wearing his jeans and wool shirts to a conference in the back room of a laundry.

After six months, however, the Stuart marriage had crumbled, and Jack had moved into one of the rooms on the second floor of All Souls. No one said much about it, but I gathered the marriage had been shaky for some time and simply hadn't stood up to the stresses of a major move and two job changes. Jack himself seemed kind of lost. In his spare time he wandered about the house looking for people to talk to; he kept starting books and then setting them down half-read, until they gathered dust and someone else put them away. Those in the know told me that such listlessness and inability to concentrate were common afflictions of the newly divorced, and I had no doubt that Jack would snap out of it soon—especially considering the amount of TLC being lavished on him by the rest of the staff.

Now he ran a hand through his thick gray hair. His lean, bony face blanked as he tried to absorb what I'd just told him. He let his hand rest on top of his head for a few seconds, then placed it on mine.

"Did you find his body?" he asked.

"Sort of. I had an appointment to deliver my report to him and—"

"Are you okay?"

"Depressed, but I'll manage. It was a shock—but then it always is."

Jack took his hand away and reached for his wine. "Are they certain Bob was responsible?"

"No, but his pouch was at the scene. You know—that fringed leather thing he carries." I sampled my wine and took odd comfort from its bitterness. "Did you know Rudy well?"

"Not too well, but I liked him a lot. What I handled for him was his business affairs—contracts with suppliers, the sewing union—so the situation didn't really invite closeness."

"Did he tell you much about the job he wanted me for?"

"Hardly anything. What was that all about, anyway?"

I explained, then added, "You'll get a better picture when you read my report. Tell me—had you drawn up a will for him?"

"No, but there is one. I don't know if Gilbert Thayer handled it, or Hank." Hank is our specialist on family law; most of the attorneys refer their clients to him for such work.

"Speaking of Hank," I said, "have you noticed he hasn't been looking too well lately?"

Jack hesitated. "Yes, I have."

"The two of you were talking pretty seriously when I came in. Do you know what's wrong?"

Again he paused. "Oh hell, there's no reason you shouldn't know—you're a better friend to either of them than I am. Hank's got trouble at home. That's why he was talking it out with me—because I've just been through it."

"Trouble at home? But it's so soon! They're not thinking of getting a divorce—"

"No, God no. They're both just at the stage of acknowledging that things have gone wrong."

"But how?"

"They're both very set in their ways. Hank's used to living

casually—too casually, probably—like everybody does here at All Souls."

"Anne-Marie used to live here. She was that way, too."

"Then, yes. But once she bought that two-flat building over in Noe Valley, she developed her own way of doing things, and Hank's having trouble adjusting to it."

"Adjusting to *what?*"

"Well, nightly candlelit dinners. Weekly social evenings with the couple who rent the upstairs flat from them. Chores done on a regular basis. You know. It's nothing against Anne-Marie. Personally, I'd love that kind of life. *Did* love it. But Hank . . ."

"I see." I'd always envied Anne-Marie her beautiful home, and I'd enjoyed many an elegant dinner there, but I could understand why her life-style might be incompatible with Hank's offhanded—face it, sometimes slovenly—existence.

"She has everything systematized," Jack went on, "even down to who does what. She does the laundry, Hank cleans the bathroom. She cooks, all the time, and he misses making his spaghetti and chili. Each is responsible for buying different things: she pays for the paper goods and cleaning stuff and meat; he's supposed to take care of vegetables and staples and liquor."

"Good Lord, how do they do their grocery shopping?"

"Two carts."

"When I used to shop with my boyfriend, we could hardly control one cart between us! What does Hank want to do about this situation?"

"Nothing, so far. Like I said, he's just at the bitching stage. Frankly, I think part of the trouble is that he misses All Souls."

"Well, everybody here misses him, too, but that marriage is important. Both of them took a risk later in life than most of us would have been brave enough to do, and they've invested a lot of themselves in it. They love each other. Besides"—I smiled, trying to cheer Jack, whose expression told me he was reliving his own failure—"he'd better not miss this place too much. I'm not giving my office back to him."

Jack didn't seem to see the humor in the remark—and frankly, I didn't blame him. He tilted his wineglass to get at the last drops, then went to the sink for a refill. "Maybe they'll work it out. People who are set in their ways have been known to change."

"At our age? I wonder." I hadn't been able to change for Don, any more than he'd been able to change for me. I hoped Anne-Marie and Hank wouldn't end up apart, as we had.

Jack offered me more wine, but I declined and went to retrieve my coat from Rae's office. Tonight I'd be better off sulking at home, where I couldn't inflict my mood on anybody else.

But when I got home, things began to look up. I found that my wandering cat, Watney, had returned and was curled in the center of my bed. When I flicked on the light, he looked up and started purring. I went to the kitchen and rooted around in the freezer; damned if there wasn't a package of my favorite macaroni and cheese. While it heated, I cleared some of the mess from the kitchen and shut the door against the construction zone on the back porch. Then I took my dinner to bed and snuggled down with a good book. When I was done eating, I bribed Watney to come home more often by letting him lick the cheese residue from the aluminum-foil container.

As I went about my business for the next few days, I tried to shove Rudy Goldring's death to the back of my mind. Lord knows I had enough to contend with. Rae didn't show up for work on either Tuesday or Wednesday; she called, claiming she had the flu, but she didn't sound sick, and I attributed her absence to her continuing failure to stand up to her husband. As a result, the caseload piled up on my desk; one interview I'd turned over to her required I travel to Sacramento, losing half a day's time in transit. My statement for the police about Goldring's death took up the whole of one morning. It was late Thursday before I had a breather, and I was just thinking of calling Ben Gallagher at the SFPD to ask if they'd made any progress on the case when the phone buzzed, and it was Ben, calling me.

Without preamble, he said, "Did you write down the license number of that woman's BMW?"

"Yes, I've still got it in my notebook. Hold on a second." I grabbed my purse and rummaged through it. "One GDJ three two six."

"Shit. I was hoping you'd just read it to me wrong. But you must have got it garbled."

"Why?"

"We traced the owner of the car. She's not the woman you're

talking about, says she was in a meeting in her own living room
at the time and the car was right outside in the driveway."

"Maybe she's lying."

"No, she doesn't match the description you gave me. And
there are witnesses from the meeting who say the car was
there. Besides, this isn't a woman who avoids publicity—of any
kind."

"Who is she?"

"Vicky Cushman."

"Oh."

Vicky Cushman certainly didn't hide from the limelight. She
was one of the city's most visible citizen-activists, always
championing one cause or another—from saving the buffalo in
the park to tearing down the unsightly Embarcadero Freeway.
In recent years she'd devoted most of her attention to issues in
the Haight-Ashbury district, where she lived.

I'd met Vicky from time to time at All Souls functions. Her
husband Gerry was a hotshot member of a downtown archi-
tecture firm and a close friend of one of our partners, and
liberal activists like Vicky were always high on the co-op's A
list. Gallagher was understating it when he said she didn't look
like the woman I'd encountered at Goldring's: Vicky was petite,
had waist-length blond hair, and the kind of turned-up features
we used to enviously term "cute" in high school.

I said, "Maybe she loaned the car out, and the witnesses are
lying."

"No, you got the number wrong. Did you write it down as
soon as the woman drove away?"

"There was a time lapse, until I could get hold of my
notebook, but I repeated it over and over to myself."

"Uh-huh."

"Okay, maybe I got a letter or number out of place. Why
don't you—" But then I was struck by the statistical magnitude
of checking every combination of those seven letters and
numbers, coupled with the legendary inefficiency of the Department of Motor Vehicles.

"Why don't I what?"

"Nothing. I was about to say something stupid. What about
Frank Wilkonson? Were you able to trace him?"

"Yeah, he works on a big cattle ranch near Hollister. Sheriff
down there checked him out. He says he never heard of Rudy
Goldring."

Hollister was near San Jose, not King City. Another of Goldring's lies. "Did the sheriff ask him why he comes to the city on Sundays?"

"He says he works six days a week on the ranch and comes up here to unwind."

"He unwinds by checking out the conservatory and plant sale, and visiting every nursery in town?"

"That's what he says." I could picture Ben shrugging. After a moment he added, "The guy's got six kids, Sharon. If I had six kids, plants might look good to me, too."

"Maybe," I said dubiously. "I gather you haven't located Bob, the derelict, yet."

"His full name's Robert Choteau, and he's disappeared from all his usual haunts. That in itself indicates guilt."

"Or fear."

"Whatever. We'll locate him, but it'll take time. He's our only lead, since you muffed the license plate number."

It was on the tip of my tongue to tell him to go to hell. But I didn't say it. Gallagher was overworked and tired; I was overworked and tired; he hadn't meant it.

I said, "Let me know how it goes, all right?"

"I'll let you know." He hung up.

I set the receiver in the cradle and pushed back my chair, staring out the window at the flat gray expanse of the Outer Mission. Dammit, I didn't believe I had muffed the license plate number. I have a good head for figures; all I have to do is call a phone number once or twice and I have it memorized. Maybe Vicky Cushman and her witnesses *were* lying; it could even be for some innocuous reason, or out of sheer perversity. Liberal activists are never overly fond of cops. . . .

I felt I knew Vicky well enough to call her and ask about what she'd told the police. Better yet, I'd simply drop in at the somewhat peculiar home she and Gerry owned on the hill above the Haight. If my questions seemed to stem from a casual, spur-of-the-moment impulse, she'd most likely be open with me. I could say I wanted to verify that the car had indeed been hers for my own peace of mind. I could say I was concerned about the woman I'd run into at Goldring's, wanted to make sure she was all right.

Yes, I thought, that would be the best approach. And it *was* for my peace of mind; I hated to think I'd slipped up on something as simple as remembering a series of seven letters and numbers. I'd go over there right away—as soon as I'd called a friend at the DMV and asked her to get me Frank Wilkonson's exact address in Hollister.

SEVEN

The Haight-Ashbury District is best known for the social and psychedelic explosion that took place there in the 1960s, but its history encompasses far more than the brief hippie era. It was originally settled by livestock farmers who staked out five- to ten-acre plots on the quiet eastern reaches of Golden Gate Park; with the expansion of the city's rail service to the area, "suburbanites" followed, building the splendid Victorians that are so prized today. In the 1880s, excitement of a more wholesome sort than LSD trips was embodied by The Chutes, a Haight Street amusement park with a death-defying roller coaster. Long before the hippies discovered the district, bohemians and college students moved there for the cheap rents; after the hippies left, hard-case junkies and drug dealers took over.

Today the Haight is a neighborhood in search of an identity. Spruced-up Victorians sit side-by-side with dilapidated apartment buildings that approach tenement status. Haight Street itself—the commercial center—is a curious melange of mom-and-pop stores that have been there for generations, chic new boutiques, bed-and-breakfast hotels, and the ever-encroaching chain outlets. Fashionable shoppers from the suburbs and more affluent areas of the city brush shoulders with the punks, junkies, and neighborhood mothers pushing baby strollers. Some residents fear the invasion of pizza parlors and twenty-four-hour drugstores will destroy the character of the district;

others—many of them older people on fixed incomes—are grateful for the lower chain-store prices. Everyone is edgy about the way the University of California Medical Center keeps reaching down from Parnassus Heights to gobble up prime real estate. The Haight seems to be caught in a tug-of-war between gentrification and social responsibility. It is rich soil for neighborhood activists like Vicky Cushman.

I crossed Buena Vista Heights on Seventeenth Street and drove downhill on Ashbury. It was one of those September days when you can tell summer is edging into fall: the sky was the hard clear blue of San Francisco's autumn, and enough of the leaves were turning to signify a change. When I turned off Ashbury onto the Cushmans' cul-de-sac just above Frederick Street, I was confronted by a row of tall Lombardy poplars whose brilliant yellow foliage was so achingly beautiful that it made my breath catch. Directly behind them was the ivy-shrouded brick wall of what local people have always referred to as The Castles. The Cushman Castles, now.

The Castles were a grouping of six small, turreted buildings on a two-acre wooded lot. With the high wall surrounding the place, all that was visible from the street were the dark brick turrets, with their steeply canting slate roofs and mullioned upper windows. Each building served a different function: living area, master bedroom suite, children's quarters, artist's studio, servants' quarters, and garage. They were connected only by stone paths through the gardens and lawn. Gerry Cushman's friend at All Souls had told me that The Castles had been built in the 1930s by a minor newspaper publisher (who soon after had gone bankrupt) who considered himself a potential William Randolph Hearst. Presumably these buildings had been his dress rehearsal for creating his own San Simeon. Over the years they'd passed from hand to hand until the heirs of the last owner had let them stand empty in the 1970s, and they'd been taken over by squatters. Gerry Cushman had picked up the property for the value of the land alone in the early 1980s. After a lengthy court battle to evict the squatters, Gerry, Vicky, and their two children moved into The Castles and restored them to their former splendor.

I parked my MG under the poplars and went over to the metal-studded wood gate. There was an intercom beside it; I pressed the button. When a static-distorted female voice answered, I identified myself and asked for Vicky. There was a pause and then the voice said, "This is she. I've met you, haven't I? At All Souls?"

"Yes. I think the last time was at our Christmas party."

"God, yes. You're the investigator, the one who supplied the recipe for that sneaky bourbon punch that got us all so drunk."

"Guilty."

"Wait a second, I'll buzz you in. I'm in the main building—the big one at the end of the path. The door's open, just let yourself in."

The buzzer sounded momentarily, and I pushed the gate. It swung open onto a wide flagstone path that was flanked by eucalypti. The trees' bark was peeling in great ragged, curled strips; their leaves shimmered silver when rustled by the light breeze. I couldn't believe how quiet and otherworldly it was on this side of the wall.

I followed the path around its curve. Ahead of me stood the largest castle: a one-story building with towers on either end. From this vantage point it looked less impressive than it did when its turrets were viewed from the street; they were too tall, and the middle section too squat, a little out of proportion. A wooden door with metal studding similar to the gate's was set in a protruding entry area; I went up to it, knocked, and stepped inside.

The entryway was slate floored, and from there two steps led down into a living room. I hadn't envisioned what this castle might look like inside, but had I, this wouldn't have been it. The room was ultramodern in decor, and an entire wall of glass overlooked the formal garden that separated it from two of the other castles. The furniture was white and tan with accents of bright green, made of metal and glass and leather, with many sharp angles and—to my eyes—outlandish shapes. The carpet was chocolate brown, the kind that shows every speck of dirt. This one was showing it, too: peanut shells littered the floor in front of the couch; ashes formed a blurred semicircle by the fireplace; near one corner was something that looked like sawdust—until I noticed the scratching post. Then I recognized it as catnip and spotted the creature that had been indulging—a fat Siamese curled up in a cat-drunken stupor at the base of the post. The cat was so out of it that it had pushed its muzzle into the deep pile of the carpet; their colors matched perfectly. In the corner behind the post stood a three-foot stack of folded white paper bags. An open one perched atop the others; red lettering on it said, I DID MY SHOPPING AT A NEIGHBORHOOD BUSINESS!

"Sharon, it's good to see you again!"

It was Vicky Cushman's voice, coming from an archway next to the fireplace. I turned and received yet another surprise.

Vicky no longer looked the cute cheerleader. Her waist-length blond hair had been cropped and permed, but it was a bad perm—too limp and long—and it looked like it hadn't been washed recently. She'd lost weight, too, and it made her bony, her face too drawn. She wore a cotton dress in a dusty rose color; its bodice was held together with a safety pin in place of the top button, and it showed various unidentifiable stains. The dress's hem was ripped out in the rear, so it hung almost to her bare heels. Vicky's voice, however, was as buoyant and warm as I remembered it. I supposed I'd just caught her at a bad time.

I said, "It's good to see you, too. But I shouldn't have dropped by without calling."

"Nonsense." She went to the couch, which was buried in a drift of newspapers, pushed them to the floor on top of the peanut shells, and motioned for me to sit. "It's a mess, I know it is, but I've got a heavy schedule, and the goddamned maid didn't show, and the kids are just back from my mom's—listen, do you want a drink? Or a joint? Which is it you do—alcohol or dope? Oh yes, I remember—you made the punch."

I assumed she was babbling because she was embarrassed at being caught in such a state. I said, "Actually, I didn't make it. I gave the recipe to Hank Zahn, and he doubled all the dangerous ingredients. But if you have some white wine, I'd love a glass."

"Me, too. I've been on the phone all day. We're organizing, you probably read it in the *Chron*. UC has got to be stopped, they're eating this neighborhood alive. And then I'm in on the deal about the way they're managing the project where Poly High School used to be, as well as the fight against the chain stores." She waved her hand at the stack of red and white shopping bags. "They're our latest gimmick, just came from the printer today. The local merchants will be giving them out. I'll get our drinks, be right back. Just relax, enjoy."

She disappeared through the archway from which she'd entered. Looking over there, I guessed from the tile floor that it was the kitchen. When I glanced at the fireplace across from me, the assumption proved correct: it was one of those two-sided hearths, opening into both rooms, and behind it I glimpsed part of a dining table and chairs.

I looked around me. In spite of its untidiness, this was a beautiful room. What would it be like, I wondered, to own such a space? How would it feel to be Vicky—a woman who didn't have to go out to a job, with a maid who came in (usually) to vacuum up the peanut shells and catnip? A woman who was supported by a successful husband and was able to indulge in whatever causes interested her?

My speculations were more curious than envious. Vicky's life-style was one I had little experience with and didn't particularly aspire to.

I also wasn't too sure what I thought of Vicky's brand of activism, which had received both good and bad press in recent years. Opponents had labeled it "NIMBYism"—an acronym for the phrase "not in my back yard." They claimed that NIMBYS displayed the ultimate in selfishness by lobbying—with such bodies as the Board of Permit Appeals and the Planning Commission—for rulings that made their neighborhoods financially off limits to those of lower economic brackets. They suspected a prime motivation behind such activism was the preservation of homeowners' property values. Certainly some attempts were blatant elitism—such as a recent referendum to block a low-cost-housing project for senior and handicapped citizens, because it would interfere with the neighbors' exclusive bay views.

On the other hand, neighborhood activists were avowedly on the side of a high quality of life. They were concerned with overcrowding, lack of parking spaces, preserving open space, and the ecological balance. They were against neighborhood merchants being forced out of business by big chains, and affordable housing being gobbled up by monster corporations or developers. And they were articulate, often vociferous, and seemed to turn up everywhere these days.

Now—as Vicky rattled around in the kitchen—I decided if she asked me, I would have to say I found myself sympathizing with the NIMBYS. As a homeowner, my little earthquake cottage was my only substantial asset, and when you're spending close to thirty percent of your gross income on mortgage payments, you don't want anything going on in your neighborhood that will devalue that asset, or make it not such a good place to live.

Still, I was uncomfortable enough with NIMBYism to have wriggled my way out of attending a block organizing meeting the week before. But that was true to form: in the sixties I'd done a lot of talking against the Vietnam War but very little protesting. Now I was merely hoping somebody else would protect my property values for me. I wasn't proud of myself in either instance, but I was self-aware enough to have little real hope of change.

Vicky came back clutching two big balloon wineglasses full of a pale pink liquid. "No white, we're out," she said. "Hope you don't mind a blush. It's something quite good, but I can't tell you what. Gerry could." She set mine down on the glass-topped table in front of the couch. I noticed smears around the lip of the goblet—probably those "unsightly spots" the dish-washer detergent commercials are always lamenting.

"Actually, I like blush," I said, "but it's a new term, and it always embarrasses me to ask for it." The pun was unin-tentional—as most of my best ones are. It didn't matter; it went right over Vicky's head. I suspected that, like many intense social reformers, she didn't have much of a sense of humor.

"I know what you mean," she said seriously, settling at the other end of the couch. I'd noticed before that when she was being earnest a deep set of wrinkles appeared between her eyebrows, and she screwed up her mouth so it resembled a withered rosebud. With her Alice-in-Wonderland hair and rounded, fuller face, it had seemed appropriate and charming; now with this straggly, greasy perm and new gauntness, she looked as if she were trying terribly hard to understand something but not succeeding all that well.

I sipped my wine. As she'd said, it was very good.

Vicky went on, "All these new things. New styles. Blush wine. The music—my kids play it. I don't even know who the singers are. Or why anybody would bother to listen to it. California cuisine. Is pasta salad still in, or has it gone out? Running? Eastern religions? The new sobriety—God, I just got used to cocaine. I don't know, I don't get out much anymore. At least not in what Gerry calls the right circles. And when we do, I don't know how to talk to those people. I mean, I'm trying to keep the corporations and that damned university from eating my neighborhood alive, and they're discussing exotic varieties of *lettuce*, for God's sake. Or is designer lettuce out too, now? Maybe that was last year. . . ."

I knew how she felt. But unlike her, I didn't give a damn what was in or out, nor did I hang around with people who did.

Vicky set her glass down and reached for a carved ivory box on the table. She extracted a joint and said, "Do you smoke?"

"Not anymore. I guess my drug's alcohol."

"But you don't mind if I do?"

"Why should I?"

She nodded, giving me her terribly earnest look again, and lit up. "That's nice," she said, after inhaling and releasing the smoke slowly. "Nowadays everybody seems to mind—regardless of what it is you do. I can't help it, that's what I tell Gerry, with all this stuff going on and all the responsibility, I get so tense. There's this woman who works for me, she says I should take up a hobby, something peaceful that would give me a chance to be alone with my thoughts. But my thoughts—my God, if I think about everything that's going on, I just get so nervous."

She was making *me* nervous. I wondered if she'd always been like this, or if something had gone wrong in her life since I'd last seen her. At the All Souls functions she'd seemed hyper, but no more so than most of the people on our staff. She certainly hadn't seemed this jittery and ready to fly out of control.

I decided to ask my questions and get out of there. "Vicky," I said, "I need your help."

She let out smoke in a long breath. "Yes, sure. What is it?"

I explained in the way I'd planned: about Rudy Goldring's murder, the woman who had fled the scene, the license plate number of the car, and how I wanted to make sure the woman was all right. Vicky listened, nodding and sucking on her joint. When I'd finished, she'd finished it and dropped the roach in an ashtray.

"Sharon," she said, her voice more mellow now, "what can I tell you except what I told the cops? It's my car, and my license plate number, but I had a meeting of my steering committee for this thing against UC going right here in my living room the whole time. And the car was parked in the driveway."

I glanced through the glass wall; there was no driveway or car visible. "I don't understand how you could see it from here."

"I couldn't, but the garage is inside the compound, and cars can only enter or leave by the gate next to it. It's controlled by electronic openers, and only Gerry and I have them."

The woman I'd encountered at Rudy Goldring's hadn't looked like the criminal type, but I asked, "What if someone had come over the wall and used the opener—"

"No way. The wall is wired, the whole place is. Gerry insisted on a very good alarm system, and it's on all the time. He's very security conscious, Gerry. He even made me learn to shoot. We have a .22 in our bedroom; I hate it. But that's all because of the trouble we had with those damned squatters. Do you know they kept trying to sneak back in here for *two years* after we'd moved in—"

"Mom, we're back! Can we—"

"Betsy, honey!" Vicky twisted around toward the entryway, a look of pleasure wiping the earnest creases from her brow.

I turned, too. A girl of about ten stood there. She was tall for her age, but chunky. Her hair was blond and straight as Vicky's had been before she got her awful perm, but lopped off bluntly at her shoulders; her turned-up nose and heavily lashed eyes were Vicky's, too, but her jaw was strong and square—Gerry's? Yes, like Gerry's.

"Mom, listen," she said, "can Rina and Lindy and I make some popcorn?"

Vicky glanced toward the kitchen, as if she were afraid her daughter and her friends might mess it up. That, I thought, was probably impossible; given the state this room was in, Lord knew what chaos lurked behind that archway.

Vicky said, "Not right now, honey. I have company."

"But, Mom . . ."

"I said, not right now, honey."

"Mom, please— "

"No, dammit!" The vehemence of her reply surprised me. "No, you may not! I want you to go to your playroom, or the swings, or Rina's, or wherever, but just let me alone. I have a friend here, and I'm relaxing for once, and I don't want to be disturbed—by any of you. You make sure you tell Rina that. Am I making myself clear?"

Vicky had twisted all the way around and was looking intensely at Betsy. The little girl crossed her arms over her T-shirted chest and clutched her elbows.

"Am I making myself clear?" Vicky repeated.

"Yes ma'am." Betsy turned and ran out, slamming the door emphatically.

Vicky's face was flushed and she was breathing heavily. She twisted back to her former position, drew her legs up, and covered her eyes with her hands, elbows on her knees. "Jesus," she muttered, "what the fuck am I doing to my kids?"

I was framing a reply—one that would involve the concept of this merely being an off day—when the phone rang. Vicky glared at it, then stalked over to answer. Her curt "Yes?" mellowed to an "Oh, hi," and she dug in a carved wooden box on the table next to her, extracted another joint, and lit it. Did she have little stash boxes all over the place? I wondered.

"You what?" she asked. Dragged deeply on the joint. "Oh yes. I forgot. I see. No, it's okay—"

There was a long pause.

"I'm not, Gerry," she finally said. "I'm just relaxing with a friend. What's wrong with that? Can't I have friends, too?" There was a childish whine in her voice, and I decided this encounter was getting too embarrassing—for both of us. I'd come for information, not to pry into what was obviously a difficult domestic situation. I got to my feet.

Vicky motioned for me to stay, but I mouthed the words, "I'll call you," and hurried to the door.

Outside, the day had gone pinky gold and dusky—a further harbinger of autumn. Somewhere in the eucalyptus grove I heard the caw of a crow. For a number of reasons—the obvious and the purely personal—I always associate that type of bird with death. I listened to it as the trees' leaves shivered and flashed silver in the early evening breeze.

Don't be silly, I told myself. This may be a troubled household, but they'll work it out.

Then I looked at my watch. It was close to six-thirty, and tonight Rae had promised—with her Girl Scout salute and an offer of a stack of Bibles—that she would for sure be at the Remedy Lounge by seven. I dismissed Vicky, Gerry, the hapless Betsy, and even the threat my alma mater's medical center was posing to Haight-Ashbury, and retraced my earlier route to the Mission District.

EIGHT

"**S**haron, I understand why you're not pleased with my work, I really do. It's just that Doug is so needy right now." It was the fourth time Rae had said that—or at least some variant on it. She was reasonably drunk; I suspected she'd fortified herself with something from the All Souls refrigerator before making the trek downhill to the Remedy Lounge.

I said, as I also had three times before, "I'm not unhappy with your work—*when* you do it."

She moved her glass around on the gouged formica tabletop, making wet circlets with the beer that had slopped around its base. "But that's what I'm trying to explain. It's a real bad time for Doug. He's got to declare his intention to go for the doctorate or take a terminal M.A. *Terminal* M.A. Wow, it sounds like you die if you do that!"

I had to admit they could have found a better term for it, but it was a tangential issue that I didn't want to get off on. I sipped wine, giving myself time to think. Finally I said, "Rae, what do you want to do with your life?"

"With my . . . what?"

"With your life. Do you have a dream?"

"Me? Oh yeah, of course."

"What is it?"

"Well, I guess I want to be like you."

It took me aback; I'd never been a role model before. When I didn't reply, Rae flashed me a mildly reproachful look and finished her beer. She looked over at the bar, and Brian, the bartender, gave her a thumbs-up sign and began drawing another Bud. It annoyed me vaguely; the Remedy doesn't have a waitress, but Brian had been bringing Rae's beers to our table as if it were a common practice. In all the years I'd been coming here, he'd never taken so much as one step out of his way for me—or any other customer.

I studied Rae: her untended auburn curls, lack of makeup, mangy coat, and moth-eaten sweater. She looked like hell most of the time, and even on her good days she dragged around half dead. Yet she had so much to offer—so much intelligence and good humor and guts—that it had even caught the eye of Brian, who probably hadn't really seen any of the Remedy's clientele since 1952. It seemed a shame that she was willing to throw away her life for the sake of "needy" Doug.

I said, "By being like me, I take it you mean you want your license and a good job that affords you a certain amount of freedom and flexibility."

She nodded, taking the beer from Brian.

"What about Doug? Does he want that for you?"

". . . I guess."

I tried another tack. "Does Doug also have a dream?"

As soon as I spoke, there was a change in her: her face grew animated, and she even sat up straighter. "Yes—he's a wonderful writer. He wants to sell short stories to magazines like *The New Yorker.*"

Inwardly I winced. I knew a couple of short-story writers; what they mainly did was not make much money at it.

Rae went on, "That's one of the reasons Doug is thinking of taking the terminal M.A. He's in the English lit program right now, but he doesn't like it. He really wants to switch to creative writing."

I thought back to a conversation I'd had with Rae a couple of months ago. She'd told me that before Doug had entered the English program at SF State, he'd been studying filmmaking at UCLA. And two years before that, when they'd first been married, he'd been working on a graduate journalism degree at Berkeley.

My silence told Rae what I was thinking. She said, "If he goes ahead with it, this will be absolutely the last change. He's finally found himself. I really believe that."

She did, too. I could see that in her eyes, hear it in her voice.

And maybe she was right; after all, she knew Doug better than anyone. But it bothered me that she was so committed to living his dream rather than her own.

That, however, was a philosophical point we could argue all night, and I had more practical issues to attend to. I said, "Rae, how much do you make a month?"

"A thousand. You know that."

"And out of it you pay what for rent?"

"Six hundred, and then there's the other stuff."

"Which leaves you . . . ?"

"Well, nothing, on account of the car and the cost of food and utilities— Do you know my damn landlord wants to start charging us for garbage and water? I think that's illegal, and I'm going to ask Hank—"

"Rae, do you want to always live hand-to-mouth?"

"Well, of course not!"

"And do you want to work as a gofer at All Souls for the rest of your career?"

Her fingers clenched on the glass, and her freckles stood out against her sudden pallor. "Are you firing me?"

"Lord no! Just answer the question."

"Well, of course I don't. I want to get my investigator's license. I meant it when I said I want to be like you."

"Getting that license is predicated on you doing a good job for me."

"Oh God, Sharon . . ."

"Don't whimper. I can't take whimpering." Her furrowed brow and trembling mouth were both heart-wrenching and annoying. I thought, If she were a man, she wouldn't dare pull that crap on me. And then I thought, But if she were a man, we wouldn't have a situation like this on our hands because very few men would cater to their wives the way she does to Doug. It's a bind that our upbringing puts us women in, and one that's not all that easy to break free of.

"Listen," I said, "I'm going to give you another chance. I think we've been going about this wrong."

She nodded, looking hopeful and releasing her stranglehold on the glass.

"I realize," I said, "that I've been loading you down with scutwork and not taking time to teach you the things you need to know. So what I'm going to do is—in addition to the routine work—let you take on some special projects." When she started to speak, I held up my hand. "I know it sounds good, but you've got to remember this: they'll take extra time—cause you to work long hours, odd hours. You may have to neglect Doug, so you'd better talk it out with him first."

"I'll talk to him as soon as I get home tonight."

"Good. And after you've completed a few projects, we'll talk again, to evaluate your work and decide if you're really suited to this business." Good Lord, I thought, I sound like a genuine supervisor. I could see myself years hence, directing a full staff of operatives, generously dispensing the wisdom gleaned through years of experience.

"What's the first project?" Rae asked.

The vision of my managerial future faded. "Uh, I don't know yet. When something comes up, I'll brief you. In the meantime, do you think you could try to get to work on time tomorrow?"

I sensed she was disappointed by my lack of a definite project, and I hoped my somewhat wheedling tone hadn't undermined my authority. As it worked out, however, I didn't have to worry about her arriving at All Souls on time the next morning. I decided I needed to get some food into her before she drove home, so we went back to the co-op, and I threw together a pot of spaghetti, like Hank used to do in the old days. Jack and a couple of the other inmates of the second floor joined us, we drank more beer and wine, and before I knew it, Rae had passed out on the waiting room couch. I covered her with Jack's spare blanket and went to call Doug—taking an unreasonably sadistic pleasure in telling him Rae wouldn't be home until after work the next day.

The deep blue Friday morning sky promised a day as splendid as the one before. I took my coffee and newspaper out onto my back deck, studiously ignoring the brussels sprout plants, bulbs, soil, and fertilizers I'd bought on Sunday and left on the steps that led to my weedy, overgrown backyard. (The crassula and baboon flower resided in the living room.) Watney, who had not mended his wandering ways for very long, came bounding out of the shrubbery; when he saw I had nothing for him to eat, he darted off again. I settled down with the *Chronicle*, and after a while, on an inside page, found a half-column item headed SEARCH FOR MURDER SUSPECT CENTERS ON PARK.

The story said that Robert Choteau, wanted for questioning

in the murder of clothier Rudolf Goldring, had been seen by several witnesses in Golden Gate Park, and the SFPD was now concentrating its search there. It didn't surprise me. In recent years the park has become a refuge for many of the city's homeless; estimates of how many make it their permanent abode soar as high as a hundred.

Of course, the park has always sheltered its share of hermits; one of the witnesses who had reported seeing Bob was a self-styled "forager" named John, who claimed to have lived there a dozen years and had told reporters he didn't want "criminal elements destroying the ecology of my home." According to park officials, John may have a point. The problem is more serious these days than at any time since the hippies took to camping out there in the late sixties. Many of these new inhabitants have serious alcohol and drug problems, others are simply destructive, and there's not much that can be done about them. If they're run off or arrested, they simply return later.

As a park administrator whom I'd met at an All Souls party had told me, the situation there wasn't going to get better until society itself improved. My reply to him had been an ironic "good luck."

I set the paper to one side, got myself more coffee, and thought about Bob Choteau. My gut-level instincts—which I wouldn't have mentioned to Ben Gallagher to save my life— said that Bob hadn't killed Goldring. There had been too much genuine affection between the men—as shown in the way Bob had addressed Goldring as "Captain," for one example. More important, Bob had not stood to gain anything by the murder. With Rudy alive, he had a supply of beer, probably a small amount of pocket money, a stoop to sit on, and thus what—to him—must have been a certain standing in the derelict community. Without Rudy, Bob was just another bum on the street, a nobody.

But what about a crime of passion? my internal devil's advocate asked. What if Bob had wanted more beer, and Rudy had been out of it? Or more money than Rudy was willing to give him? The killing showed no signs of premeditation. The ultimately fatal blow was probably impulsive, struck in anger.

But the person who had struck it didn't necessarily have to be Bob. Rudy had had an appointment that day; that was what his office manager, Mrs. Halvorsen, had said when I'd stopped by the office asking for him. I'd thought she meant the appointment was set for someplace away from the building, but she could merely have assumed that. What if it had been for his apartment?

I toyed with my coffee cup, constructing a trial scenario.

First, I thought, Rudy has an appointment. Sometime between ten, because he leaves the office a little before that, and one, when he has the fitting scheduled with the new client. Okay, he's to meet the person upstairs in his flat. Maybe he doesn't want his employees to know he's meeting that particular individual—either because he or she is known to them, or just because he doesn't want them to overhear what he plans to discuss. Either way, he leaves, goes upstairs. The person arrives, they quarrel, the person kills him and leaves.

What next? I wondered. What time had Goldring died? A number of hours before I'd gotten there, from the degree of rigor I'd observed. And surely before the woman employee had called up there at a little after one, to see why he hadn't arrived for the fitting. Would Gallagher have a reasonably accurate estimate of the time of death by now? Probably. I'd have to call and ask him.

But I made myself think through the rest of the scenario first.

Next Bob would have arrived, gone upstairs—maybe because he noticed the door was open. He found Goldring's body, dropped his pouch, and took off for the park. I didn't believe his running was as clear an indication of guilt as Gallagher seemed to think. A streetwise man like Bob Choteau would have known he'd be a prime suspect, and the more than thirteen hundred acres of park would have seemed an easy place to lose himself. He might even know others who made it their home, who would shelter him and share their tricks of "wilderness" survival.

And then? The woman in Vicky Cushman's BMW had arrived. Vicky's claim that the car had been inside The Castles compound at the time was another thing my instincts told me to disbelieve. She might be flat out lying, or she might have been tricked, but I was certain she knew the woman who had been driving her car. Why else, in her mellow marijuana haze, had she so lost her temper when her daughter had interrupted us? Given the morning's hard pragmatic perspective, Vicky's outburst at Betsy seemed out of proportion to the child's request to have friends in to make popcorn. I sensed she had been reacting to the pressure of the questions I'd been asking her, and had directed her panic, or hostility, or whatever, toward a convenient and relatively helpless person.

So there it was—a script with everything but the two key ·roles filled in. Who was the person Rudy Goldring had scheduled that appointment with? And what was the name of the handsome dark-haired woman? Were they one and the same? Possibly, if the woman had stayed in the flat after she'd killed him. But I doubted she could have done so, given the panicked state in which I'd found her.

There was one person, I thought, who might be able to help me make sense of all this. Frank Wilkonson. Because there was something else my instincts cried out against: Wilkonson coming to the city to "unwind."

I went into the house and fetched the cordless phone. Ben Gallagher's extension at the Hall of Justice was busy. I called my friend Sheila at the Department of Motor Vehicles; she pulled Wilkonson's address for me: c/o Burning Oak Ranch, P.O.B. 1349, Hollister. Then I went back inside and rummaged through my collection of road maps to see if I had one for that area. I didn't, and on the California map Hollister was a mere dot about forty miles southeast of San Jose. The only thing I knew about Hollister was that in the late 1940s it had been terrorized by an outlaw motorcycle club, and the incident had been the inspiration for the classic Marlon Brando biker movie, *The Wild One*.

I put the map down and tried the Hall of Justice again. This time Gallagher answered. He was obviously busy, and curt with me, but he provided the information I needed: the coroner's preliminary finding was that Rudy Goldring had died of a cerebral hemorrhage caused by his head striking his kitchen stove at approximately eleven Monday morning. The complete autopsy report wouldn't be available for two weeks or more—testimony as to how overworked and understaffed the medical examiner's office was. The search for Bob Choteau, Gallagher said, was proceeding smoothly, but it would take some time to flush him out of the park.

"But we'll get him," he added—more optimistically than I was sure he felt. "The people who've lived in the park a long time don't want a killer loose there any more than you or I would want one loose in our neighborhood."

It was on the tip of my tongue to tell him I didn't think Bob had killed Rudy, and why, but he had another call and ended the conversation abruptly.

It was almost nine, time to go to All Souls and roust Rae from what I was sure would be her bed—or couch, in this case—of pain. Today didn't seem the proper occasion to inaugurate my new plans for her training, so I decided to turn her loose on my one remaining skip-trace and see how resourceful she could be while suffering from a hangover. That would leave me with notes to transcribe on a couple of interviews, my weekly expense report, and three phone calls that had needed returning for at least two days now.

And then? I could retrace my route of the previous Sunday and talk with the nursery employees, attempt to get a line on who Frank Wilkonson had been looking for. But that seemed a great deal of effort for what would probably be very little return. There was no guarantee that the same clerks would be on duty this afternoon, and even if they were, chances they would remember Wilkonson out of all the customers they'd seen in the past week were slim. Better start with Wilkonson himself. With diligent work, by noon I'd have cleared my desk and be free to take off for the Burning Oak Ranch near Hollister.

NINE

Hollister turned out to be an old farm town situated on the eastern side of a flat agricultural plain that stretched from Highway 101 to the foothills of the Diablo Range. The land was covered with walnut orchards and onion fields, and the town itself had a nice feel of yesterday. The outskirts, as they are nearly everyplace these days, were cluttered with franchise restaurants and gas stations. Hopper trucks hauling fruit and vegetables to the local packing sheds clogged the commercial route. But the central district was full of old brick- and stone-fronted buildings, one with a handsome clock tower, and the residential section had quiet tree-canopied streets and well-kept houses on large lots. I drove slowly through town and finally stopped at a corner liquor store to ask directions to the Burning Oak Ranch. The clerk knew it and seemed surprised that I didn't. He drew me a rough map on a paper sack.

"You follow Route Twenty-five through town, out past all the new developments," he said. There was a touch of contempt in his voice that told me what he thought of them. "The route turns where there's a brand new shopping center, and you keep going through Tres Pinos and Paicines, past the county fairgrounds and the Almaden Vineyards. Then you'll start seeing cattle graze, and pretty soon the ranchhouse, at the top of a knoll. Can't miss it."

I thanked him, bought an ice-cold bottle of seltzer, and went back out to the MG. The afternoon here in the inland valley was a hot one, probably in the nineties, and I drank the water and checked the car's temperature gauge—the engine had always run hot—before I started out.

The liquor-store clerk had meant it when he said "all" the new developments. There were miles of tracts, apartment complexes, and shopping centers, of an antiseptic uniformity that the differences in design, building materials, and colors could not hide. I felt vaguely relieved when I was back in the country, climbing on a two-lane highway into the sun-browned foothills. Even there progress intruded; I passed "country estates" and a golf course. But then a sign appeared for the little (POP. 500) village of Tres Pinos, and had it not been for the cars and trucks, I might have been back in the nineteenth century.

The village was a haphazard collection of frame and adobe buildings, a couple of them abandoned, the others sagging with age. The two restaurants and a saloon looked touristy—and probably were, since this was one of the routes to the Pinnacles National Monument—but they were interspersed with ordinary dwellings and outbuildings, a pretty church and graveyard, and a tiny post office. On the right side of the highway was a weathered brown structure with a western-style false front and a sign that said WALT'S TAVERN. A fat man in a bartender's apron—Walt himself?—leaned against one of the support posts on the sagging front porch, contemplating the road. The place was the country equivalent of the Remedy Lounge, and I resolved to stop in for a beer on my way back. The resolve was strengthened when the man raised his hand in a friendly salute.

Further along the road were the county fairgrounds and a still smaller town—Paicines—which consisted of a general store with gas pumps. Then the valley widened. A brush-choked creekbed ran along to my left, and the hills on either side were wheat colored, dotted by scrub oak and grayish brown sagebrush. The higher peaks beyond them were thickly forested, but a stark rocky cliff face stood out like an ugly scar. I sniffed the dry air and thought of fire danger; as I rounded the next curve, I saw a hillside that had been burnt black, its trees a dead rusty orange. But when I came upon Almaden's Paicines Vineyards, the grapevines were lushly green and spilled over the curves of the hills, crowding into their hollows. Now I began looking for cattle, and the ranchhouse on the knoll.

The cattle range appeared fairly soon, on both sides of the road, but I didn't see any ranchhouse. The hills gentled a bit, and golden, humpy pasture dotted with fat steers extended toward the distant peaks. The land was fenced and posted with NO TRESPASSING signs; I checked the odometer, and by the time the fence joined a whitewashed adobe wall, it had been a good three miles. The wall went on for a half mile more, and then a set of pillars connected by a filigreed wrought-iron arch rose from it. I slowed the car and looked up at the rounded knoll.

It was far off, at least a quarter of a mile, and covered with what appeared to be an elaborate terraced garden. Fruit trees grew there; I could see orange and yellow orbs weighing down their branches. There were multicolored flowering shrubs as well. The blacktop driveway itself was lined on both sides by palm trees and ended up top, near an enormous white adobe house with a terra cotta roof. The house was flanked by yew trees—or perhaps, I thought, *shrouded* was a better word than *flanked*, considering Sallie Hyde's name for them, funeral trees.

I hesitated at the foot of the drive and checked the script letters woven into the filigreed design of the gate's arch: BURNING OAK RANCH. Then I eased the MG into first gear and drove slowly along the blacktop. The driveway widened into a large semicircular parking area, but no other cars were in sight. I left the MG on its shady side and got out, breathing in the fragrant air. I couldn't identify any of the mixture of scents— except possibly flowering jasmine and bay laurel.

The door of the house was enclosed in a small bricked courtyard, and the way in was barred by a wrought-iron gate. Through its scrollwork I could see raised flower beds faced with bright mosaic tile. I located a buzzer set into the adobe to the right of the gate, pressed it, and waited. There was no response. I rang again, then pushed at the gate. It was secured. I was about to go back to my car when I heard the whine of a motor starting up the drive; it was louder than my MG's— which is by no means quiet—but sounded considerably healthier. When an old spoon-shaped black Porsche with personalized license plates saying MR VET—veterinarian?—appeared, I stepped forward.

The Porsche rolled to a stop next to the MG.

The man who stepped out of the Porsche was young, a good six-five, with thick sun-bleached hair and a tan to match. His muscular body and long, strong legs were shown off to perfection by a navy tank top and khaki shorts. His eyes were a clear blue, his teeth an even white, and there was—so help me—even a cleft in his chin. The every-woman's-dream type.

For me, he was an instant turnoff.

I watched warily as he crossed the blacktop. At first I detected a faint suspicion in his eyes, but then they scanned me, and he seemed to relax. The once-over was devoid of the usual sexual come-on you get from that type, and I began to feel ashamed of my visceral reaction. When he politely asked if he could help me, I decided it had been more knee-jerk than gut-level.

I identified myself—as I'd decided to do while cooking up a plausible cover story—as Alissa Hernandez, insurance investigator. The name is that of a friend who works for Allstate and gives me a supply of her business cards; with my one-eighth Shoshone heritage, I can pass for a Chicana if no one looks at me too critically. I don't like to use the cards—or Alissa's persona—unless it's a necessity, but in this case I felt it was. The San Benito County sheriff's men had questioned Frank Wilkonson, and probably his employer, too; Ben Gallagher might have told them the name of the private operative who had been hired to tail Wilkonson, and the sheriff's men might have passed it on.

The man studied the card I handed him. Up close he looked older than I'd first thought: late thirties, rather than mid-twenties. He said, "If this is about that truck accident, you should talk with our ranch manager."

"Actually, it's about the manager. Frank Wilkonson is his name?"

The man nodded.

"Could we talk inside?" I motioned at the gate. "I've been ringing, but I guess there's no one else here."

Now his eyes flicked apprehensively toward the house. "How long have you been here?" It wasn't a polite inquiry—he wanted to know.

"Five minutes, maybe a little more."

"And you got no response at all?"

"No."

"I see." He moved swiftly toward the gate, jamming one of his keys into the lock and jiggling it roughly. The lock stuck. He exclaimed, "Shit!" and jiggled it again. This time it turned. The gate flew open and banged into the tile-faced flower bed next to it. He yanked at the key, and when it wouldn't come out of the lock, let go with a disgusted motion and stalked across the courtyard toward the front door. I followed.

We stepped into a large foyer and the man said, "You'll have to excuse me for a few minutes. I'm concerned about my father and need to check on him. He's been . . . ill and— Will you wait here, please?"

There was a wide stairway at the far end of the room; he sprinted up it and disappeared. I could hear his footsteps pounding on the floor overhead.

I shut the outside door and looked around. There was no furniture in the room other than a heavy antique sideboard, covered with what looked to be junk mail and what definitely was dust. The rough plastered walls were hung with Indian rugs; even to my untrained eyes they looked expensive. On a raised shelf running across the sideboard were Indian pottery vases, the shape and colors of each contrasting with and complementing the others. The room had obviously been decorated by a person of considerable means and taste; it was too bad they had let it get so filthy.

There were dust mice—no, dust *rats*—lurking along the baseboards. The terra-cotta floor was so crusted that I could see footprints leading here and there. In one corner was a blob that looked suspiciously like cat barf. The curtains over the windows next to the stairway were torn and pulled—probably by the same creature that was responsible for the mess in the corner. The doors on either side of the foyer were closed, and the house had an unlived-in atmosphere that contrasted sharply with all the loveliness outside.

I heard footsteps upstairs again, and the man loped down the stairway. "Sorry about the delay," he said. "Have you been standing here the whole time? I should have thought to send you into the living room."

"Is your father all right?"

His handsome features clouded and he said curtly, "Yes, thank you." Then he opened a door to the left and motioned me into a large room decorated in the same Indian motif, with woven rugs, a display of kachina dolls and pottery, and lots of simple leather-and-wood furniture.

I said, "Someone in your household must be an expert on Indian art, Mr. . . . ?"

"Johnstone. Hal Johnstone. Please, sit down."

I took a low-slung chair, and Johnstone sat opposite me, across a rough-hewn coffee table. Before I could speak, he said, "I hope there isn't another problem with Frank Wilkonson."

"*Another* problem?"

He made a gesture of dismissal. "There was some trouble earlier in the week, a case of mistaken identity, but that wouldn't concern you. How can I help you?"

I told him the story I'd settled on as I'd driven down there: One of "our" Allstate policyholders had been parked in the vicinity of Cost Plus at Fisherman's Wharf in San Francisco the previous Sunday afternoon. In his absence his car had been hit-and-run; a witness had left a note on his windshield giving the license plate number of the fleeing vehicle: SDK 080. We'd traced it through the DMV and found it registered to Frank Wilkonson, at this address.

"Would you know if Mr. Wilkonson was in San Francisco last Sunday?" I asked.

Hal Johnstone frowned, obviously torn between telling the truth—which he must have known, since he'd mentioned the other "problem" with Wilkonson—and protecting his ranch manager. After a short hesitation, he said, "I'm sorry, I don't. Sunday is his day off, but I can't say what he does with his time."

"Sunday is his only day off?"

"Yes. Cattle ranches can't shut down on the weekends. Frank has a contract with us that provides substantial bonus pay for working a long week."

"I see. So he's off from . . . ?"

"Saturday evening till Monday morning at eight. As I said, I don't know what he does during that time."

"Does Mr. Wilkonson live here on the ranch?"

"Yes, his place is over by the west gate—two miles south, on the other side of the highway."

"Perhaps you could tell me something about Mr. Wilkonson."

"Ms. . . . I'm sorry, I've forgotten your name and I must have left your card upstairs."

"Hernandez, Alissa Hernandez."

"Ms. Hernandez, I don't understand what your question has to do with an inquiry into an accident. Shouldn't you just go to Frank Wilkonson and ask if he hit your policyholder's car?"

"It would make my job much easier if I could. Unfortunately,

there's some uncertainty about the witness's reliability, plus a
bit of conflicting evidence. You see, your manager's vehicle is
registered as a green Ford Ranchero, but the paint scrapings on
the policyholder's car indicate the one that hit it was white. If
I talk to Mr. Wilkonson and he thinks I'm making an accusa-
tion, it could leave my company open for all sorts of trouble. He
might even sue—"

"But aren't you putting your firm in the same kind of
jeopardy by coming to his employer with basically the same
kind of questions?"

I put on my most ingenuous smile and fluttered my hands
helplessly, trying not to overdo it. "I suppose I am, Mr.
Johnstone. And normally I wouldn't have revealed so much,
but you seemed so . . . well, I'm sorry to have over-
stepped. . . ."

Watch it, McCone, I thought. You don't look like a babbler,
and if you go any farther, he's smart enough to see through
you. "Anyway," I added in a businesslike tone, "if you can give
me some background on Mr. Wilkonson, I'll know how to
approach him—or *if* it's necessary to approach him at all."

Johnstone nodded. "I understand. And I'd like to help Frank
out, if I can. The man's had enough trouble this week."

"This trouble—"

"It's got nothing to do with what you're looking into. I'll be
glad to tell you anything about Frank that would appear in his
personnel file, but at that point I'll have to draw the line."

"Fair enough. Suppose we start with how long he's worked
for you."

"For my father, Harlan Johnstone. He owns the ranch; I just
assist him. Wilkonson hired on"—he paused, calculating—
"about three years ago. Before that he held a very responsible
position at a big spread in Texas. Near Fort Worth? Yes. He
came highly recommended, which is why Dad offered him a
long-term contract with lots of perks."

"What kind of employee has he been?"

"Excellent." He said it so fast that it made me wonder if it
were the truth. "Profits are up by twenty-nine percent, much of
that because of pared-down expenses."

"And you say Mr. Wilkonson lives on the ranch? Is housing
one of the perks you mentioned?"

"It always is, for a ranch manager."

"What about the other perks?"

"Sorry, the employment contract is confidential information."

"Is Mr. Wilkonson married?"

"Yes. Wife's name is Jane."

"Children?"

"Six, one since he's been here. I couldn't begin to tell you any of their names."

"I know what you mean. My sister also has six, and I can barely remember theirs. Tell me, do the Wilkonsons seem happy?"

"What does this have to do— "

"I'm trying to get a feel for the situation, in case I have to interview the wife."

"Oh. Well, yes, I'd say so. As happy as you can be when the husband works dawn to dark six days a week, and the wife's worn out chasing after those . . ." His voice trailed off, but I could have sworn he had been about to say "brats."

"Do you know of any reason Mr. Wilkonson would have been in San Francisco last Sunday?"

He shook his head.

"Or any other Sunday?"

"No."

"Did he arrive for work on time Monday morning?"

"As near as I know." He thought for a moment. "I saw him in the ranch office about ten."

Ten—shortly after Rudy Goldring had left his own office to meet with his killer. That let Wilkonson out for the murder, but I hadn't really suspected him of it.

I said, "Will you describe Mr. Wilkonson—in terms of personality type?"

"He's . . . well, on the surface I guess you could compare him with most of the cowboys we hire, only brighter. Slow talking, easygoing. But underneath it, he's extremely intelligent. He relates well to the help because he doesn't talk down to them."

"A calm individual, then?"

". . . Usually."

"And when he's not?"

Johnstone's face clouded, as it had when I'd asked if his father was all right. The fingertips of his right hand whitened against the wooden arm of his chair.

"Mr. Johnstone? Does Frank Wilkonson have a tendency to become violent?"

"Why do you ask that?" But he didn't appear at all surprised.

"Because the witness to the accident at Fisherman's Wharf described a violent outburst of temper on Wilkonson's part that caused the collision."

Johnstone considered that. Finally he said, "It's possible, I suppose. No, it's probable. I don't think Frank's basically a violent man—I *know* he's not—but lately he's been prone to fly off the handle."

"In what circumstances?"

Johnstone was silent.

"Why, do you suppose?"

"Look, Ms. Hernandez, Frank's only an employee here. I work closely with him, since I've more or less stepped in for my father in the past several months, but I don't really know him, not personally."

"So the trouble's personal, you think?"

He shrugged.

I waited and, when he didn't speak, said, "Is there anything else you think I should know before I talk with Mr. Wilkonson?"

Again he looked torn.

"Mr. Johnstone?"

"All right, just this: be careful when you talk with him. As I said before, he's had a bad week. I wouldn't like to see him fly off the handle with you."

TEN

Jane Wilkonson was a tall, heavy, frizzy-haired woman of about thirty who would have made a great drill sergeant. When I arrived at her rambling white frame house, she was in the sun-baked side lot ordering a ragtag army of nine kids out of a Doughboy swimming pool. I could hear her southern-accented voice from where I'd parked behind an old Honda station wagon in the driveway, nearly half a city block away. The gist of what she was shouting had to do with somebody peeing in the pool, and I was just as glad I couldn't make out any more than that.

As I approached them, one of the older boys pointed at me and said, "Shit, Ma, don't be yelling at us when there's company."

"Don't you 'shit' me, you little—" She clapped her hand over her mouth and whirled to face me, her plump cheeks staining red.

At a signal from the boy who had spoken, the troops scattered and ran shrieking for the house.

Mrs. Wilkonson rolled her eyes, still obviously embarrassed. "Dammit," she said, "I try to be tough, but they've all got my number. Clever little bastards."

"They certainly seem to be—clever, I mean."

"I'm just hoping one of them is clever enough to get rich—and loving enough to support me in my old age." She wiped her hands on the ample seat of her red shorts, then stuck out the right one. "I'm Jane Wilkonson. Are you looking for me or Frank?"

"Both of you, actually." I shook her hand and jerked my chin at the house. "Are they all yours?"

"No, thank God. Only five of them—plus the little one that's asleep on the porch. Or was, before they all went tromping up there. The other four are hellion friends from school, and if their parents don't come to claim them soon, there'll be the devil to pay." She smiled as she said it, but I sensed the pent-up frustration of a mother after a long, trying day.

I took out one of Alissa's cards and handed it to her. "I wonder if I might ask you a few questions."

She studied it, her lips pulling down and puckering like one of the children's might. "Allstate? We've got Allstate, I think. Is it more trouble because of Frank's trip to San Francisco last Sunday?"

"I wouldn't call it trouble, at least not yet. It may be something we can clear up quite quickly. Is there someplace where we can talk?"

"You mean where they can't bother us?" She motioned toward the house.

"Well, yes."

"You're looking at a woman who knows how to escape anyone under the age of twenty-one. Follow me."

Her refuge turned out to be a grape arbor on a rise at the back of the lot. The vines were ancient and gnarled, so intertwined with the latticework that they and the structure had become a single entity. Leaves and stunted bunches of raisinlike grapes hung down, practically obscuring the plank seat behind them. Jane Wilkonson ducked under them and plunked herself down, sighing and pulling a pack of Camels from her shirt pocket. I sat next to her and, when she offered me a cigarette, shook my head. She lit one, inhaled deeply, and let out the smoke in a long, luxurious breath.

"I know they're bad for you," she said. "Lord knows I hear that enough from Frank—he hates for me to smoke. But a woman's got to have some pleasure in life."

I glanced down at the hard-packed earth in front of the bench; it was littered with cigarette butts. Jane Wilkonson apparently escaped to this arbor frequently—and alone, since her husband disapproved of her smoking.

She saw where I was looking and added, "Can't drink—I

wouldn't be able to keep up with the kids if I did. Don't gamble or overeat—in spite of my figure. And now, what with Frank . . . What's this about the insurance anyway? You're a claims investigator?"

I wondered what she'd been about to say about her husband. Was sex another of her lost pleasures? "Yes," I replied, "I'm looking into a hit-and-run collision." Then I told her the same story I'd told Hal Johnstone.

As I spoke, the lines bracketing her mouth deepened. She stubbed out her cigarette in the dirt, looked longingly at the pack on the bench between us, then laced her fingers together. "Chickens to roost," she said bitterly.

"I'm sorry?"

"Oh, nothing. Just some nonsense that occurred to me. So your witness thinks this person who hit the car was my husband?"

"His account isn't quite that clear. It's your husband's license plate number, but the witness describes a truck, not a Ranchero. And the paint scrapings on the other car are white, not green."

"I see." She looked at the pack of cigarettes again, then reached for it and lit one almost defiantly.

"*Was* your husband in San Francisco on Sunday, Mrs. Wilkonson?"

She shrugged irritably. "Seems that way, doesn't it? You couldn't prove it by me. I don't know where he goes on his day off. It's his only day, and a man's got a right— Oh, hell."

I waited. When she didn't go on, I asked, "Does your husband always go away on his day off?"

"Lately he does. He finishes up at the ranch office about eight on Saturday night—needs to go over the week's business with Mr. Johnstone. Then he puts the kids to bed and we have dinner. I try to make it special, and he always stays for dinner, I'll give him that. It's our only meal without the kids at the table, you see. Every week I think maybe he'll change his mind and stay. But right afterwards he packs a small bag and just goes."

"And you've never asked him where? Or why?"

She shook her head.

"Or if there's another woman?"

Her lips twitched, and she drew on her cigarette— deliberately, allowing time to formulate her answer. "I wish it were only that. A woman learns how to ride those things out, how to handle them. But this . . . We don't have the kind of marriage where we ask a lot of questions. Or at least I don't ask them."

Obviously not, I thought. I didn't know a great many women who would have put up with a spouse's repeated unexplained absences without asking—no, demanding—to know where he'd been. I myself believe in a certain amount of room for privacy in even the closest of relationships, but had I been in Jane Wilkonson's place, I would have hounded Frank mercilessly until he told all. I asked, "What time does he usually come back?"

"In time for work on Monday. He's never late, and he never acts like he's been drinking or . . . anything."

"How long has he been going away like this?"

"Not long. Last Sunday was only the fifth time. I know because we went to Monterey to the aquarium—just the two of us, for my birthday—on Sunday six weeks ago. That was really the last good time we had together." She looked me full in the face, her brown eyes terribly earnest. "Five weeks isn't long at all. That's why I've decided just to wait it out, see what happens."

"Do you think perhaps something's bothering him that he needs to get away and think about?"

She shook her head, not in denial, but in discouragement. "Must be, but he's not talking to me about it. Like I said, we don't talk easily about the things that matter. But he got that way last year, about the same time. . . ." And then she became very still, as if she'd realized something she should have known before.

"About the time of your birthday?"

"No," she said, more to herself than me. "Can't be." She continued to sit, turned in upon herself, then shook her head, as if to wake up.

"What were you about to say, Mrs. Wilkonson?"

"Nothing that makes any sense." But sense or no sense, whatever she had thought of badly disturbed her. She threw her cigarette to the ground and crushed it angrily with the toe of her sneaker.

I tried another tack. "Has your husband been in a bad temper lately? Does he get unusually angry with you or the kids?"

"He's never hurt any of us."

Which meant yes. But now she must have reminded herself I was there in a quasi-official capacity, because she hardened her voice and said, "What does all this have to do with the accident he's supposed to have had, anyway?"

I explained about the violent outburst the "witness" had observed near Cost Plus. It made me feel a little better because it was the truth, and something she ought to be aware of.

Jane Wilkonson studied the ground for a moment, then sighed. "It doesn't surprise me."

"Have there been other incidents like that?"

"Not with the car, no."

"With what, then?"

She hesitated. Obviously she needed to talk with someone—and preferably another woman—or she wouldn't have told me as much as she had. In the silence, I envisioned her life here: isolated from even small towns by miles and miles of cattle graze; a cut above the wives of the men who worked for her husband; a step below the Johnstone women—if there were any. And she had a husband who couldn't talk about the "things that matter," was surrounded by children too young to understand why Mom was upset.

She said, "With who is more like it. Frank quarreled with Mr. Johnstone—Hal Johnstone—a couple of times recently. Pretty violently, to hear tell."

That explained Johnstone cautioning me to be careful when I talked with Wilkonson—and perhaps his reluctance to discuss the ranch manager's violent temper. "Over what?"

"Do you think I'd know? The ranch hands and their wives, they made sure I heard about it, but they were mighty careful what they said." Her mouth twisted and she glared angrily at the pack of cigarettes, as if they and not the conversation had left a bad taste in her mouth.

"Nobody here ever tells me anything," she said. "Plain Jane—that's what they think of me. The brood mare who only cares about her kids. I'm Frank's wife, and Randy's mother, and so on and so on. But take Frank and Randy and the rest of them away, and I'm nobody at all. So nobody ever tells me anything."

After that bitter recital, I didn't have the stomach to go on questioning her. I said—fully meaning it—"Mrs. Wilkonson, I'm sorry if I've upset you or made you sad."

She shook her head and briskly rubbed her hands on her big

bare thighs. "Not your fault. If it's anyone's, it's mine. Actually, the talk did me good." Then she picked up the pack of
Camels, stood, and stepped out of the arbor.

I ducked under the low-hanging vines. Jane Wilkonson was
standing still, gazing out over the valley. From the rise that the
arbor stood on you could see across acres of sunburned cattle
graze, the road a grayish ribbon curling through them. The tile
roof of the Johnstone house was visible, and the funeral trees
surrounding it.

Jane turned to me, her face concerned, as if she'd upset me,
rather than the other way round. "You didn't make me sad,"
she said. "Not really." Then her eyes moved back to the distant
ranchhouse, and an emotion that I couldn't quite interpret
crept across her features.

"It's a sad place here, that's all," she added.

Before I left her, Jane gave me directions to the offices where
I could find her husband. They were several miles back the way
I'd come, toward Paicines and Tres Pinos, just inside the
ranch's north gate. A pair of blue and white mobile homes
stood in the middle of a graveled lot, surrounded by cars and
pickups. Wilkonson's Ranchero was parked close to the first
trailer, and I left the MG beside it and climbed the steps to the
trailer door.

I knocked on the door's closed louvers, and a female voice
called for me to come in. Inside the temperature was chill; an
air-conditioning unit hummed noisily. A young woman sat
behind an L-shaped desk that held stacks of files and a word
processor. The trailer was one large room, with three other
desks, file cabinets, and a Xerox machine. A map of the ranch
with varicolored pins stuck in it took up one whole wall. Two
of the desks were unoccupied, but Frank Wilkonson sat at the
third, directly under the map. He was talking on the phone, his
booted feet propped on the desk's edge, his swivel chair tilted
back. He glanced at me, but there was no recognition in his
eyes.

The young woman—a sandy-haired, snub-nosed teenager—
looked expectantly at me. I gave her Alissa's card and asked to
speak with her boss. She compressed her lips nervously—
probably because of Wilkonson's earlier visit from the sheriff's
men—and took the card back to him.

I looked around the trailer. I'd been envisioning something

along the lines of a shed with tack hanging on the wall, and it surprised me to find myself in an office that looked like the business end of a small manufacturing company. Of course, I thought, that was what a cattle ranch was: small manu-facturing—in this case, of steaks and roasts and hamburger.

The teenager consulted with Wilkonson. He looked at the card, shook his head, and gestured at the phone receiver. She came back and said Mr. Wilkonson would be quite a while. Did I want to make an appointment? No, I replied, I'd driven all the way from San Francisco, and it would be inconvenient to come back. Would she tell him I only needed a few minutes of his time? She relayed that to him, and he talked for half a minute longer and then hung up.

Wilkonson stood, tucking his red patchwork cowboy shirt into his faded jeans. He moved in an easy, loose-jointed manner, his posture more relaxed than it had been when he was prowling around San Francisco. I felt that strange smug-ness that always comes when I meet face-to-face a person I've tailed. I knew a good deal about Wilkonson, and the covert knowledge gave me a feeling of power.

Before he spoke to me, he said to the secretary, "Nearly five, isn't it, Ginny? Why don't you pack it in for the night?"

Ginny glanced at me, as if she were afraid to leave her boss in my clutches. Then she looked at her watch—it was only around four-thirty—and pleasure at the early dismissal won out over her protective instincts. "Thanks, Frank," she said, and went to straighten her desk.

Wilkonson looked down at the card in his hand. "Miss Hernandez, is it? Allstate?"

"Yes. Mr. Wilkonson?" I held out my hand.

He took it limply, as if he weren't accustomed to shaking hands—or at least to shaking hands with women. "What can I do for you?" he asked. His accent held more of a Texas twang than his wife's.

"I'm investigating a hit-and-run accident," I began, and went on with my well-practiced spiel. Wilkonson listened, glancing nervously at the secretary. When I finished, he waited until she'd left the trailer before speaking.

"Your witness copied down my license plate number?" he asked.

"Yes."

"What time on Sunday did this happen?"

"Around five."

"I see." He looked down and began straightening a stack of printouts in the IN basket of the desk next to him. When his eyes met mine again, they were genuinely puzzled. "I *was* there at the Wharf, Miss Hernandez. I can't deny that. And I do admit making a U-turn. But I could swear I never hit another car—I'd have felt the impact."

"The witness said you appeared to be angry. Perhaps you just didn't notice . . . ?"

"No," he said firmly, "I'm sure I'd have noticed." Now I sensed tension rising in him, reined in, as it had been on Sunday.

"Well," I said, "there's a possibility the witness could be wrong. He might have just thought you hit the other car, since there were no green paint scrapings on it. My theory is that it was hit earlier, by a white vehicle, and your . . . performance was what attracted his attention. I'll have to look deeper into this than I expected, I guess."

What I'd said didn't seem to ease his mind. He asked, "Look, how much would it cost to repair your policyholder's car?"

I chose a figure I thought would seem high to him. "At least eight hundred dollars."

His lips twitched but he said, "I'll be glad to pay for it. In fact, I'll give you a check right now."

"Don't you want to contact your own insurance carrier? They'd pay—"

"No. I don't want my rates raised. . . . Besides, it's a group policy for employees here at the ranch, and something like this—hitting a car in a fit of temper and then driving off—would make me look bad."

"I understand. And believe me, Mr. Wilkonson, I can understand how the accident could have happened; it's a zoo at the Wharf on Sundays. I suppose you and the family were up there for an outing?"

"Uh, yes."

"Well, I know how those family outings can be: the kids are whining because you won't let them go to the Wax Museum; the wife's stopped and used the MasterCard in every store in Ghirardelli Square; you want a beer, but everyplace is too expensive and crowded; the panhandlers and street merchants. . . . Oh yes, I know what you were going through."

"That's exactly right. I hate San Francisco, anyway. Never go there if I can help it."

"Is that right?"

"It sure is. You want a check now to cover the damages?"

"Are you absolutely certain you don't want me to look into this any further? After all, you may not have been at fault."

"No, I'd just as soon have the matter dropped. You know how it is."

I certainly did. "Well, then, I'll file my report, and someone from the claims department will be in touch with you. I don't need any money now."

"Thanks, Miss Hernandez. You've been real understanding." His words were gracious, but I could feel anger just below the surface. It wasn't necessarily directed at me, but as I'd watched this man, I'd forged enough of an empathy with him that I knew he handled his anger in an inappropriate and scatter-gun fashion. I thanked him for his cooperation and got out of there quickly.

As I reached my car, the wisdom of that decision was confirmed. From the trailer came a crash and a shattering, as if Wilkonson had heaved something against one of the louvered windows.

ELEVEN

I drove slowly up the valley, considering what I'd found out at Burning Oak Ranch. Frank Wilkonson was seriously upset about something—or perhaps obsessed would be a better word. He'd been willing to part with eight hundred dollars in order not to call further attention to his Sunday in San Francisco; he'd twice quarreled with his employer's son; he'd become distanced from his wife. And according to her, he'd been in the same state at some time during the previous year.

Exactly how had Jane Wilkonson put it? "He got that way last year, around the same time . . ." Now I wished I'd pressed her about it.

I wasn't worried about Jane relating our conversation to her husband. Given what she'd told me of the marriage, she'd wait to see if Frank would mention my visit to the ranch offices. And he certainly wouldn't—not after he'd been so eager to have the purported insurance investigation dropped. When Jane realized he wasn't going to bring the subject up, she would merely store the knowledge of our talk with all the other important things that went unsaid in their household.

It was now a little after five, and I supposed I should be heading back to San Francisco, so I bypassed Walt's Tavern in Tres Pinos, where I'd planned to stop for a beer. But by the time I got to Hollister I knew I wasn't returning to the city that night; I had no real reason to, no plans for the weekend, no obligations. Where Route 25 turned northwest toward Highway 101, I saw a Best Western motel called the San Benito Inn. I executed a sudden right turn—enraging the driver of the pickup behind me—drove to the office, and took a room.

Time to think about what you're doing, I told myself.

Fortunately I always keep a bag packed with toilet articles, cosmetics, and a couple of changes of clothes in the car—in case a job unexpectedly takes me out of town and keeps me there for a while. I carried it up to the second-floor room and dumped it on the luggage rack. Then I lay down on the bed and stared at the rough-plastered ceiling.

I'd come to Hollister because I'd sensed Rudy Goldring's reasons for having me tail Frank Wilkonson had more of a connection with his death than Ben Gallagher and the SFPD wanted to believe. I'd thought if I found out more about Wilkonson, I might uncover those reasons. But what I'd uncovered were more free-floating facts and innuendoes. Taken apart, none of them meant anything. Taken together, they merely increased my confusion. I needed to find out even more.

Leave that for a minute, I told myself. You're avoiding the real issue—why you're bothering with this at all.

I had no client, not anymore. My obligation to Rudy Goldring had ended with his death. All Souls still had a responsibility to him because his attorney would probably have been named executor of his estate. But that had nothing to do with me or my job. So why was I acting as if this were an ongoing investigation?

Boredom, because lately I'd had too much time on my hands? Curiosity, because I don't like loose ends? Commitment to seeing the truth come out, because I'm just made that way?

When you become involved in a murder case, I reminded myself, the best course of action is to turn it over to the police and let them handle it. In fact, that's not just the best course of action—it's the only *legal* one.

But I'd never been good at observing the technicalities, or avoiding unnecessary risks. And I *was* bored. I *did* have too much time on my hands. I *was* curious, and those loose ends were bugging the hell out of me. Besides, I've always had this somewhat naive—and probably abnormal—preoccupation with the truth.

I sat up, reached for the phone, and direct-dialed Alissa Hernandez's office in San Francisco. The person who answered her extension said she'd gone for the day. I tried her home; her machine said to leave my name and number and she'd get back to me. I didn't want her to have to pay for a long-distance call, so I simply left my name and told the machine I'd try again later. Then I called All Souls.

Jack Stuart wasn't there, but surprisingly, Rae still was. Her voice sounded weary when she answered, but she brightened when she heard who it was. "Hey," she said, "I located the guy on that skip-trace."

"Great, congratulations!"

"The report's on your desk, and I've notified the client. Where are you?"

"Hollister."

"Near San Jose? What're you doing there?"

"Following up on something. Look, I have a special project for you. It's not much of one, but it'll be a big help to me."

There was a pause—she was probably thinking of getting home to Doug. Then she said gamely, "Okay, sure."

"I'm trying to reach Alissa Hernandez at Allstate." I gave her both of Alissa's numbers, since she was in and out of her office at as many strange times as I was. "Keep trying her for me. Ask her to check the computer for auto policies on Frank Wilkonson"—I spelled it and gave her the Hollister P.O. box—"or Burning Oak Ranch, same address. I want to know if Wilkonson has his own coverage or if it's under a group policy for the ranch. Ask her to pull all the particulars within the last, say, two years. Got that?"

"Just a second." I pictured Rae, hunched over the beat-up desk in my old office, writing down the details. "Anything else?"

"Try to track down Jack Stuart. I want to know about a will for one of his clients, Rudolf Goldring. Ask him if it's been entered into probate, and if so, what's in it."

"Okay. I think he may be down at the Remedy with Hank."

That surprised me; since his marriage, Hank's visits to the Remedy had been infrequent. More trouble at home? More drunken commiserating with Jack? "There's another thing," I said, "but it's a personal favor."

"No problem."

"Thanks. Would you call this number"—I recited it —"and ask whoever answers to stick some food for my cat on the back deck."

"Your neighbors, huh? What if there's nobody home?"

"There will be." The Curleys next door were a large, boisterous family, with big hearts—especially when it came to neighbors and cats.

"When are you coming back?" Rae's voice was a shade wistful, as if she could do with some commiserating at the Remedy, too.

"Soon. Tomorrow, probably." Suddenly I wished she were here, so we could kick around the things I'd found out over a few drinks. I read off the phone number of the motel, told her I'd be there until noon the next day, in case she got hold of Alissa or Jack, and hung up.

Then I said aloud, "McCone, what the hell are you doing?"

"Shut up," I replied.

Reflecting on how talking to oneself is a sign of creeping middle age, I got up and went to freshen my hair and makeup. I wanted to look presentable when I arrived at Walt's Tavern in Tres Pinos, for a couple of drinks and perhaps some gossip about the area residents.

Walt's was a typical country tavern, with none of the frills that would have made it attractive to tourists en route to or from the Pinnacles. A number of work-soiled pickups were parked out front. When I stepped inside I found a barroom with a wood floor, a mixed and mostly unmatched collection of tables and chairs, and moldy-looking stuffed animal heads on the dingy beige walls. The smoke was thick, the music on the jukebox country, and the decibel level of the voices high.

Most of the tables were taken, and some of the people at them were eating food from varicolored plastic baskets; what was in the baskets had been fried beyond recognition, but I guessed it was mainly chicken, since a sign behind the bar proclaimed it the specialty of the house. As I stood scanning the room, I became aware that people—mostly men—were giving me appraising glances. Any stranger, particularly a woman alone, was liable to attract attention in such a place.

As I started for the bar, a fellow in a Stetson had said, "Buy you a drink, honey?"

"No, thanks," I replied and kept going.

"What'sa matter, honey? Too good for a cowhand?"

I stopped, turned, and said, "No. And no, thanks," more

firmly. The look I gave him quieted him—and warned his companions to leave me alone.

I sandwiched myself on a stool at the bar between a trio of middle-aged men with weather-toughened faces who were rolling dice and a young fellow with jug ears who was telling two women who looked like cowgirls about his marital problems. Although the back-bar was laden with liquor bottles, only the more common varieties looked to have been poured from within recent memory; the exotic types, such as a two-foot cone of Galliano, seemed to have been purchased for their decorative value, and were layered with grime. I thought fondly of a cool glass of white wine until I spotted a jug of a particularly vile supermarket brand. When the bartender—the same man I'd seen leaning against the porch pillar earlier—finally got around to me, I asked for a Bud. I suspected it was the kind of place where you didn't get a glass unless you requested it—and I was right.

When he set the bottle in front of me, the bartender's eyes flickered in recognition. I smiled, about to speak, but a great roar of laughter went up from the dice players, and one of them hollered for another round. The man picked up my money and went to serve them, and I sipped my beer and relaxed, waiting to hear something interesting.

". . . and so she says to me, 'Get outta the apartment.' And I say, 'Where the hell do you think I'm gonna sleep?' And she goes, 'I don't give a rat's ass. Bunk in with the other cowboys out to the ranch.' And I go . . ."

The jug-eared fellow had his problems, all right, but I tuned them out and concentrated on the men on my other side.

They were rolling dice again, the leather cup smashing down on the well worn surface of the bar. I glanced over there and saw they were drinking shots of whiskey and beer chasers. Although their red faces and loud camaraderie said they'd been at it for some time, I sensed they were practiced drinkers, the kind who take themselves home with just so many drinks and no more under their belts. Their conversation was mainly about the Forty-niners' performance the previous Sunday, and after a while I tuned them out, too.

At the end of the bar, around the corner from the dice players, was a sort of takeout counter. From time to time people would come in and the bartender would deliver sacks to them, which I assumed contained the house special. The chicken couldn't be all that bad if it was so popular, and I was trying to decide whether to order some and move to a table where I could better mingle with the clientele, when a sheriff's deputy came in. As he went up to the takeout counter and signaled to the bartender, I realized a silence had fallen among the dice players.

After a moment one of them said to the deputy, "How you doing, Larry?"

"Can't complain."

"Buy you a beer?"

"Thanks, but I'm on duty."

"Heard you were on duty down to the Burning O the other day."

"You heard right."

"Something about Wilkonson, wasn't it? And a murder up in San Francisco?"

"Now, you know I can't be talking about department business."

"Come on, Larry, fill us in."

The bartender approached with an extra large sack. The deputy took it, nodding thanks. To the dice players, he said, "Nothing *to* fill you in on. Just routine, that's all. And if I don't get back to the substation with this"—he motioned with the sack—"they'll have my tail."

In silence the dice players watched him leave. I was aware of a hush at the nearby tables. Even the bartender stood still for a few seconds. Then it was as if someone had flicked a switch, and everything started up again.

The first words from the dice players that caught my attention were "Just what they need—more trouble down at the Burning O." I leaned forward, my elbow on the bar, slipping my hand under my hair and cupping my ear in a way that looked like I was merely resting my head.

". . . Shit, man, he'll make himself crazy. The booze isn't going to ease it, not the way he's going at it."

Was it Wilkonson they were talking about? Jane had said nothing about him drinking.

"You've got to admit, though—young Harlan's picking up the slack."

Young Harlan? Hal Johnstone?

"Yeah. Fancy education, fancy car and all, the boy knows ranching."

Yes, Hal Johnstone.

"You wouldn't have thought it, the way he went off to that college back east, rather than a good California ag school like Davis. But the boy's holding his own, in spite of his father being so dog-shit drunk that he can't tend to business."

Then Harlan Johnstone, Sr., was the one who was "easing" his troubles with alcohol.

One of the men laughed, ruefully. "Something, isn't it— what a woman can do to you?"

"Sure is. But this is a peculiar thing. You got to remember, Irene's been gone for over two years. The divorce is final, for Christ's sake. Irene was one hell of a woman: got out fair and clean. Waived any settlement or claims to his property. So why start with the drinking now?"

"*You* got to remember that Irene wasn't Harlan's first wife. When a man loses a young piece like that—"

"She wasn't all that young."

"Late thirties, I'd say, to his sixty-some."

"Sixty-odd's old enough to know better."

Silence. A sigh. A sheepish, "When did any of us ever know better?"

More silence.

"None of us got the kind of ranch Harlan's got there, though. Man's got a lot to lose if the Burning O goes to hell."

"But like you said, the boy's doing okay. And they got a damned good manager in that Wilkonson—"

"Don't mention that son of a bitch to me!"

I leaned further to my right, straining to shut out "The Ballad of Pancho and Lefty."

"You got some beef with Wilkonson?"

Silence again.

"Well?"

"Let's just say that I don't like what he's done at the Burning O. Leave it at that. And now I better haul my ass home. The missus promised me a couple of steaks to grill."

The trio finished up their beers, paid their tabs, and left to a chorus of good-byes from their fellow patrons. As they went toward the door, I watched them, wishing I could place each man with each voice I'd heard. And wishing that the last speaker could have been persuaded to explain his dislike of Frank Wilkonson.

The men's stools were quickly taken by a couple in jeans and western shirts. They began talking about the woman's younger sister who was "running wild." Apparently they'd already had a few drinks, because the man kept saying monotonously, "We got to do something about your sister, Patty. We got to do *something*."

To my left, the fellow I'd started thinking of as "Ears" had had three beers in quick succession and now switched to bourbon. The cowgirls' interested expressions looked as if they were molded in plaster of Paris. After a few more minutes they exchanged exasperated looks, signaled the bartender, and ordered baskets of chicken to be brought to a nearby table that had just been vacated. A man and woman promptly claimed their stools and leaned close together, exchanging the little pats and smiles that come with new love. Ears gave them a venomous, envying look that neither of them noticed.

The bartender stopped in front of me and looked questioningly at my empty beer bottle. I nodded yes, pondering the situation at the Burning Oak. It explained, perhaps, why Jane Wilkonson had called it "a sad place."

Ears sighed deeply.

I ignored him, taking the bottle of Bud and pushing money across the aged patina of the bar.

Ears said, "Oh God, what am I gonna do without her?"

I thought, Oh God, leave me alone.

Ears said, "Excuse me, miss. Never seen you here before. You new in the area?"

Now *I* sighed deeply and turned to look at him. Face on, he was even more jug eared; the damned things stuck out like Dumbo's. But he had a sweet downcast mouth, slightly crossed eyes that gleamed wetly, and he looked as if he'd only begun shaving yesterday. I am a sucker for helpless young things that need me. And this one so obviously required attention.

I said, "Yes, I am. My name's Alissa Hernandez." For a moment I held a forlorn hope that he might have some prejudice against Hispanics.

No such luck. His eyes brightened and he said, "Join me in a basket of chicken?"

It took the young man—who was rather ignominiously named Jim Smith—nearly three hours to pass out. After the bartender delivered our chicken and fries (surprisingly good, or I wouldn't have eaten most of Jim's, too), we moved to a table. There I listened with half an ear to the saga of how Sherri ("She spells it with an *i* at the end, and she always dots the *i* with a little heart") had made him move out of their apartment in Hollister and was now seeing some "jerk" who worked at a gas station. The story was complicated by various rambling asides, and it took me a while to work the conversation around to the Burning Oak Ranch. When I did, Jim allowed as how it was a "hell of an impressive spread," but said he didn't know anything about it or anyone who worked there. He and Sherri, he explained, had only come down from Wyoming a few months ago.

"And now that we're here, our marriage has gone bust," he added. "Folks warned us about California." Then he continued with his story. It didn't matter that I was only half listening; by the end of the evening I knew his tale of woe well, because he told it three times—each at greater length, but with the consistency that comes from a great many rehearsals. I murmured and nodded at appropriate intervals, didn't protest when he ordered us more drinks, and listened to the conversations eddying around us. About the only thing I heard concerning the Burning Oak Ranch was that Frank Wilkonson had had a "visit from the sheriff" earlier in the week, but that the problem had been "cleared up." The group discussing him appeared to be ranch hands, and something about the way they spoke told me Wilkonson was the type of manager who didn't mingle socially with the help. When the place began to clear out at around ten, Jim Smith leaned forward, put his head on his arms—as a schoolchild does during quiet time—and went to sleep.

I finished my beer, nodded at the bartender for another, and then patted Jim's limp brown hair. The sad young man was curiously appealing; he reminded me of my neighbors'—the Curleys'—mongrel puppy. I hoped Sherri would come to her senses and break it off with the jerk at the gas station.

The bartender was about to bring the beer over, but I motioned for him to stay put and went back to the almost deserted bar. "Let me pay the tab for Jim and me," I said.

He shook his bald head. He was portly, with lively brown eyes and healthy pink skin that pulled smooth over his layers of extra padding. "You don't have to do that, miss. Jim's in bad shape—but I guess you know that. I run a tab for him every night, and I'll collect later."

"Nice of you." I looked around at the few remaining patrons.
"They go home early around here."

"They're mostly ranch hands; get up early, too."

"This seems to be a popular place with them. Who's Walt?"

"Me." He jerked a thumb at his chest. "Didn't I see you drive
by this afternoon in a red MG?"

"Right. I saw you, too. I stopped in because the place
reminds me of a bar I go to at home."

"Where's that?"

"San Francisco."

"You pick up strays there, too?" He motioned at the slum-
bering Jim Smith.

"Sometimes."

"And eavesdrop on other people's conversations?"

"I—*what?*"

"I've been watching you ever since you came in, lady. Made
you the minute you sat down at the bar. You're not a cop—
you're too subtle—but I'd wager you might be a PI."

It bothered me that he'd pegged me so easily, but I had to
smile. I said, "What are you—a former cop, or a former PI?"

"Cop. San Jose." He grinned and extended a big hand across
the bar. "Full name's Walt Griscom." When he released my
hand, his smile faded. "I don't like things going on in my bar
that I don't understand, so you'd better tell me why you're
here, what's on your mind."

I hesitated. A former cop in a little town would probably
know a great deal about his friends and neighbors. He also
might be intrigued enough with the matter that had brought
me down here to want to help. But he would have a vested
interest in this community and not want a member of it to be
annoyed or suspected.

Walt Griscom watched my face, then went and got himself a
beer. He came around the bar and sat down on the stool next
to mine. "Look," he said, "maybe I phrased that wrong. Let me
tell you something about myself. This was my dad's bar—
bought it back in the Depression when nobody in his right
mind was opening small-town taverns. Made a go of it by
giving credit to down-and-out ranchers and their hands. When
things got better, they repaid him in patronage. I thought that
kind of life wasn't good enough for me, so I moved to San Jose
and became a cop. When the yuppies took over the department, I retired and came back home."

Griscom paused to swig beer and accept money from a couple who were leaving. He pocketed the bills and continued. "What I'm telling you is that I've got a lot of respect for the people in this valley. I like living here, and I don't want to see folks hassled. On the other hand, I've got a lot of respect for the law. I wouldn't want to see anything illegal going on—or anything that would make me wish I hadn't come back here. So if what you're looking into is something I should know, I'd appreciate your telling me about it."

He was a wily old devil, but I liked him. So I told him—everything, including my real name. It was a risk, but again my instincts proved right. Because when I finished, *he* had quite a story to tell *me*.

TWELVE

As I sat in wait for Frank Wilkonson's Ranchero to emerge from the west gate of the Burning Oak Ranch the next evening, I had plenty of time to think over what Walt Griscom had told me—as well as the information Rae had phoned in at eight-thirty that morning.

The phone had awakened me, and I'd spoken into it with a furred tongue—a consequence of brandies on top of more beers with the bar owner. Rae sounded peppy and cheerful, and for a moment I regretted having bolstered her confidence with the additional job responsibilities; in my present condition, I would have liked her a lot better if she'd sounded downtrodden.

She said, "What's wrong? You sound mean as a snake."

I ignored the question. "What have you got for me?"

"Well, don't bite my head off!"

"Sorry—I'm hung over."

"Having a hot time in Hollister, huh? Well, I got hold of Alissa Hernandez, and she pulled the info on Frank Wilkonson." Now Rae's tone became crisp. "Policy's his own, there's no record of employee coverage for Burning Oak Ranch."

Yet another strike against Wilkonson's veracity.

"The guy's a bad driver," Rae went on. "Or maybe he just gets rattled in unfamiliar territory. Nothing too major, but some fender benders in the past two years, and they're all in different locations."

I sat up and grabbed the pen and memo pad from the nightstand, then propped up the pillow behind me. "Give them to me—location and date."

She did. In August of the year before, there was one in Southern California—Orange County, specifically—and another in September. Later in September he'd had a minor accident in L.A. proper. In August of this year, he'd rear-ended another car on the Bayshore Freeway, some twenty miles south of San Francisco, and there was a more recent incident in the city itself.

I told Rae to hold on and went to get my checkbook from my purse. It had one of those calendars that cover a three-year period; I checked the dates against it. All the incidents had occurred on a Saturday or a Sunday.

I stared at the list, wondering if I should risk paying another call on Jane Wilkonson. I would like to ask her if she'd been with her husband on any of those dates. But I was willing to bet she hadn't.

"Sharon?" Rae said.

"I'm here. Thanks for the information. Were you able to get hold of Jack?"

"Yes. He was taking off for Yosemite—more rock climbing—but he gave me a copy of the will."

I smiled faintly. Rock climbing was what we at All Souls referred to as Jack's "sublimation activity." He wasn't very good at it, but his near obsessive enthusiasm more than made up for his lack of skill. Fortunately, he never got up very high. We were all sure he'd abandon the pursuit once he'd put a certain amount of distance between himself and his divorce. "Give me a summary, would you."

"It's kind of complicated. Most of the bequests are to organizations benefiting the homeless. There are provisions for the sale of his business, and all sorts of trusts set up, along with the details of who's to administrate them and how. And then there's a small bequest to the guy who's supposed to have killed Goldring—Bob Choteau."

"How much?"

"Five thousand."

Wait until Ben Gallagher gets hold of that information, I thought. It wasn't much in terms of Rudy's entire estate, but to someone who was homeless . . .

"Anything more on Choteau?" I asked.

"There wasn't anything in the paper this morning."

"Good . . . go on."

"Why good?"

"I'll explain some other time."

There was a pause that told me Rae felt shut out, but she merely said, "Okay. The rest of the will is just two bequests, each in the amount of twenty-five thousand. One to an Irene Lasser, described as 'friend,' and the other to her daughter, Susan Lasser, to be placed in trust until she's eighteen."

Well, I thought, there's the connection.

I hadn't known her birth name, which was what the Lasser must be, but the first name Irene was not all that common. It had figured prominently, however, in the story that Walt Griscom had told me the night before.

Funny, though: he hadn't known about the daughter, Susan.

What Walt had told me explained Jane Wilkonson's statement that the Burning Oak Ranch was a sad place.

Seven years before, Harlan Johnstone's wife of thirty-one years had died after a long illness. Within months Johnstone had remarried, to a woman named Irene, who was a professor of horticulture at San Jose State. Just how Johnstone had met his much younger bride—she was thirty, he fifty-nine—wasn't clear to Walt, but he said that many of the local people were suspicious of her motives and hostile because Harlan had married again so soon. The bad feelings went away, however, when the new Mrs. Johnstone set about beautifying the ranch-house's grounds with the elaborate terraced gardens I'd seen, as well as organizing classes for members of Hollister-area horticulture clubs. Her workshops for children were particularly effective, and Irene displayed a genuine affection for her young gardeners.

"She really seemed to love kids," Walt told me. "Which was a shame in a way, because none of us could see Harlan starting a second family at that stage in his life."

The first hint of trouble between the Johnstones came about two years later when Irene abruptly withdrew from her community activities. The excuse she gave was that she was needed at the ranch—and she had been known to help out in the office from time to time—but those who knew Harlan well felt that he had become jealous of her outside interests and had forced her to give them up. That viewpoint was reinforced by a marked deterioration in Irene herself: when she was seen around Tres

Pinos or Hollister, she looked withdrawn and depressed, and she seemed to have lost more weight than was healthy. This went on for over two years, and then she snapped out of it, becoming the same attractive, vibrant woman whom Harlan had first brought to the Burning Oak.

"It was a real turnaround," Walt said. "People kept commenting on it. I remember talking with Hal Johnstone, who had just come back here after working someplace on the East Coast for several years. He hadn't seen her since his father's wedding and couldn't believe she'd ever been in such bad shape; he was impressed by his stepmother."

"And what happened then?"

"About six months later, she took off. Just up and left with no explanation, not even a note. Harlan was frantic; at first he thought maybe she'd been kidnapped—there's a lot of money in that ranch, you know. Then he thought she'd run away with another man and he put detectives on her trail. They had no luck tracing her. Finally, a little more than a year ago, the divorce papers, along with a waiver of her rights to her share in the community property, came from an L.A.-area lawyer."

After that, Harlan had given up. What he did was begin drinking—and he'd been drinking heavily ever since. In the past month or two, he'd refused to leave the ranchhouse, and his imbibing had reached monumental proportions. Hal, as the men I'd overheard at the bar had said, was holding things together at the ranch, but just barely. He'd been trained in veterinary science, not in the business end of cattle ranching, and even though Frank Wilkonson was a good manager, there were many things that required the attention of someone with Harlan's skills—and weren't getting it.

It explained a great deal, I thought, about Hal Johnstone's behavior when I'd visited the ranch: his sudden concern when I said I'd been ringing the bell and getting no answer; his quick trip upstairs to check on his "ill" father. It also explained the dirty, rundown condition of the house.

"They'd better take that place in hand pretty soon," I said. "The house is a disaster area, and it'll only be a matter of time before the gardens start showing neglect."

"Jane Wilkonson tries, bless her soul, but it's too much of a job for just one woman."

"You mean she cleans that big house?"

"Tries to. She's the only one Harlan will let inside. It isn't easy for Jane to find the time, what with all her kids. But she cared for Irene, and she knows how she would feel about the place going to hell."

I wanted to say that if Irene had been so concerned with the ranchhouse and its gardens, she should have stayed there and looked after them. But that wasn't fair; I had no idea what pressures had been operating on the woman.

I said, "Why do you suppose she left that way?"

Griscom shrugged. "Who's to say? I asked young Hal about it, but he didn't know. He'd been gone for three months before it happened—some job helping out a colleague with his practice, I think—and had only come back to the ranch a day or two before she took off. Was as surprised as the rest of us. I kind of thought the Johnstones had got things settled between them. Every marriage goes through a rocky period when the partners are trying to accommodate each other's conception of how it should be. The good ones survive, the Johnstone marriage didn't."

It made me think of Hank and Anne-Marie. Would their marriage also be one of those that didn't make it?

I said, "What about Frank Wilkonson?"

Walt's mouth tightened slightly. "What about him?"

"I heard some talk at the bar. One man seemed to dislike Wilkonson pretty strongly. All he would say was that he doesn't like what he's doing at the Burning O. But you, on the other hand, seem to think he's helping Hal Johnstone keep the ranch running."

Walt hesitated, and finally said, "Oh hell. You've been straight with me; I might as well return the favor. There was talk about Irene Johnstone and Wilkonson, back about the time she did her turnaround and came alive again."

"Ah."

"Wilkonson had just come to work on the ranch. Irene helped out in the office. Jane Wilkonson was pregnant and having a rough time of it. The kids were running wild."

"In short, the perfect set of circumstances to drive him into another woman's arms."

"Yes, but I for one don't believe it. Irene was terrific to Jane. She did her shopping, drove her to the doctor, and took those kids—all five of the little hellions—for days at a time." He grinned. "Must have driven Harlan crazy, having them in the house. Harlan loves his son, but the kid gave him a fair amount of trouble while he was growing up, and Harlan always used to say he was just as glad they couldn't have more than the one."

"His first wife couldn't conceive again?"

"There was some medical problem. She was always a sickly woman, I've heard. But like I was saying, if Irene had been having an affair with Frank, I doubt she would have cozied up to Jane that way."

For an ex-cop, Walt Griscom was remarkably innocent in certain respects, I thought. Irene's actions were perfectly compatible with having an affair, to my cynical way of thinking. She might have realized that the best coverup for carrying on with the husband is a friendship with the wife. And she also loved kids and probably knew that the quickest way to a father's heart is through his children. Or she might have genuinely cared for Jane and done the things she had out of guilt. The possibilities were numerous.

But that was beside the point. What mattered was that it all fit: the woman whose vocation was horticulture; her probable romance with Wilkonson; her disappearance; his reconnoitering places where a person in her profession might work, shop, or frequent.

I said, "What does Irene Johnstone look like?"

A former cop was a good person to ask. Without hesitation, Walt replied, "Tall, about five-nine or -ten. Brown hair—not drab, I'd call it chestnut. Used to wear it up a lot, in a fancy braid. Good facial bone structure, fine but strong. Wide mouth. Great big eyes, they're her best feature—like blue lamps."

It was the woman I'd encountered at Rudy Goldring's.

"Did Irene ever mention Rudy Goldring—the man I told you about who was murdered?"

"Irene never mentioned anyone or anything about her life before she came here."

"Why, do you think?"

"I've always assumed it was because she didn't have much of a life up to that point."

"And you never once had an urge to have a check run on her? Just to see what kind of woman Harlan had married?"

He smiled, in a way that said he'd thought of it often. "I stopped doing things like that when I quit the force and became a tavern operator." Then he paused and added, "Now, in a way, I wish I had."

* * *

Now, as I waited in the driver's seat of the MG, watching the ranch's west gate, I thought about Irene Lasser Johnstone—or Irene Lasser, as she'd been called by Rudy Goldring's will, having apparently gone back to her birth name. She was a bit of a vague figure: no one down here seemed to know much about her, including the existence of her daughter, Susan. And my day's researches had failed to provide more than the most basic details of her past before she'd come to the Burning Oak Ranch.

I'd driven up to San Jose shortly after breakfast, but had found most of the resources—the university personnel office, the newspaper morgue—closed because it was Saturday. Eventually I'd settled for the public library's microfilm room and files of back telephone books and university course catalogues.

Irene Lasser had taught at the university for a period of five years before she'd married and left San Jose. Her course load had been primarily freshman and sophomore horticulture lectures and labs, although as her status had risen from assistant to associate professor, she'd been assigned more specialized courses for upperclassmen. In the faculty roster, she was listed as having gotten her Ph.D. in 1976 from UC Davis—the "good ag school" the men at Walt's bar had mentioned.

Lasser had made the newspaper once, for a fellowship she'd been awarded the year before her marriage. From the phone book, I learned she had lived at the same address on Pine Drive for the entire time she'd been with the university. When I drove over there I found that Pine was a one-block street near the campus, in an area that was now predominantly Vietnamese; the address was a small white frame house, and its occupants spoke no English. Some of the neighbors—who were also Vietnamese—did, but none of them remembered the woman who had lived there over seven years before. Neither did the operator of a nearby corner grocery, which stocked rice and Oriental foodstuffs. As he told me, "Here everything is different and everyone is new. We are making another Saigon."

The sum total of my information on Irene Lasser was frustratingly slight. And I'd have to wait until Jack Stuart got back from Yosemite—providing he hadn't fallen off Half Dome and cracked his skull, Lord forbid—to ask him what he knew about her. I wouldn't be able to talk with the personnel department at San Jose State or the registrar's office at Davis until Monday, and by then—

Headlights appeared on the drive that ran from the Wilkonson house to the highway. I glanced at the luminous dial of my watch: ten forty-five. He had had time to finish up his work at the ranch office and have his weekly solitary dinner with his wife.

The headlights moved down the drive and then stopped. In their glare I saw the mechanically activated gate open; the vehicle drove through, and then the gate swung closed. The moon's light was bright enough that I could pick out the distinctive shape of the Ranchero. It turned left and picked up speed, moving toward Hollister.

I waited until its taillights were out of sight, then started the MG and switched on its headlights. Although I was reasonably certain that Wilkonson would go straight to the Kingsway Motel on Lombard Street in San Francisco, I didn't want to lag too far behind him.

THIRTEEN

Wilkonson drove through Hollister and maintained a steady pace north to San Jose. There he merged onto Freeway 280, which runs along the ridge of hills on the western side of the San Francisco Peninsula. South of the city he exited at Skyline Drive; that surprised me, because it was a pretty roundabout way to get to Lombard Street.

Skyline climbs even higher on the ridge, above miles and miles of lookalike tracts. The day had been blisteringly hot inland, and the high temperatures had brought the fog billowing in over the hills. It wafted in wet tendrils across the MG's windshield and hazed the lights of the houses below. Then the road dipped down into a dark, sparsely populated area. Just beyond Fort Funston on the cliffs above the Pacific, it branched; the Ranchero took the arm that became the Great Highway.

Now he had me thoroughly puzzled. This was a very indirect route to his motel, and the weather was too inclement for a drive along the beach. The fog sheeted across the road, carrying with it gritty particles of sand. Visibility was nil, except for the reflected glare of headlights on the white concrete traffic barriers that had been erected to prevent encroachment from both the dunes and the loose dirt created by a seemingly endless waste-control project. Beyond the barriers hulked the primeval shapes of earth movers and scoop-loaders parked in the construction area, backlit by smears of light from the houses and apartment buildings on 48th Avenue.

Ahead of us a traffic light went from green to amber to red.
It had cycled to green again by the time Wilkonson reached it.
I slowed as he turned right onto Lincoln Way, the long street
that borders Golden Gate Park on its southern side. Immediately he pulled into the left lane and made the turn into the
park. The signal changed and I stopped, watching his taillights.
The Ranchero's brake lights flared as it pulled to the curb.

There were no cars behind me, so I waited even after the
signal had turned green. The Ranchero's lights went out. Then
I saw a glint of metal, as if its door had opened, and a faint
series of motions as an indistinct figure crossed the road. When
the signal went amber, I pulled through it, into the first
available parking space on Lincoln.

I unlocked the MG's glovebox, took out my .38 Special, and
stuffed it in my shoulder bag. Then I grabbed my pea jacket
from the backseat, put it on as I hurried across the street and
into the park.

The darkness there was thick and enveloping. An icy wind
rattled the dry vegetation and brought the damp taste of salt to
my lips, the smell of the sea to my nostrils. The hollow bray of
a foghorn came from the Golden Gate to the north; after it bled
away into silence, all I heard was the soughing of the trees and
the faint whine of a motorcycle on the highway. In spite of the
proximity of buildings on the side streets, I felt miles
removed—almost as if I'd stepped back into the time when this
part of the city had been a remote outpost covered with sand
and dune grass.

The foghorn sounded again as I spotted the Ranchero some
fifty feet ahead, pulled onto the verge in the shelter of a
wind-twisted cypress. I moved toward it and squatted by its
rear bumper, peering into the blackness on the other side of the
road, where the figure I'd seen had gone. The trees were
thicker there; a massive conical shape rose from them, stark
against the white mist.

One of the old windmills.

What on earth was Wilkonson doing there?

Quickly I calculated my bearings. This would be the Murphy
Windmill, built around the turn of the century to pump water
to the park's Strawberry Hill Reservoir and now unused and
sinking into decay. Its counterpart, the Dutch Windmill, had
recently been restored and was fully operational, but funding
had run out before work on this one could commence. It stood

moldering away in an overgrown thicket next to a sewage plant.

It wasn't too inviting a place during the day—much less so on a dank, foggy night.

I fumbled in my bag for my flashlight. When I stood and shone it through the Ranchero's windows, I found, as I expected, that the vehicle was empty. Hastily I switched off the flash and once more studied the shadows surrounding the windmill. Nothing moved over there. The only sounds were the regular laments of the foghorn and a distant hum, which I now identified as coming from the adjacent sewage plant.

After a few minutes I came out of the shelter of the Ranchero and moved to the other side of the road. The soil was sandy there; my tennis shoes made little noise as I edged down a slight incline toward the windmill. I stopped next to the heavily overgrown thicket, listening.

Nothing moved here. No one breathed.

After a bit I took out my light and trained it on the windmill. It was octagonal; rough concrete for half its height, then shingled. Most of the shingles had peeled away, creating an irregular checkerboard pattern; the lower windows had been bricked up, but the upper ones gaped blackly. When I moved my flashlight beam over one with a precariously dangling frame, a bird flew out, wings flapping. I followed its flight path with the flash, highlighting the huge T-shaped nut that had once held the vanes and the jaggedly broken support beams that projected like mammoth splinters from the walls. Then I switched off the light, waited to see if anyone would come to investigate my presence.

No one appeared, but I stayed watchful for several minutes. Then I thought I heard a creaking and moaning, as if the vanes of the windmill were straining in the wind. Not actual vanes, of course, but the ghosts of those that had once laboriously turned. . . .

No, just the cypress tree over there, bending in the wind.

After a couple more minutes I moved down into the declivity where the windmill stood. A sandy path led around the building, bordered on the up side by an extension of the thicket. The ground was littered with fast-food wrappers and beer cans and wine bottles; in one place there was a tailing of toilet paper extending from the windmill's wall. I moved slowly around the structure, stumbling twice on some exposed piping, fretting because the ever-louder sounds from the sewage plant would obscure any others that might be made.

About three-quarters of the way around I came upon a double metal door set into the rise opposite the mill. More mechanical noises came from beyond it. I was so busy shining my flash on the padlock and chain that secured the doors that I didn't notice the ground ahead of me had dropped off. My foot found only air—and I pitched forward, jerked back, and landed on my rear.

An arrow of pain shot upward through my tailbone. I said, "Uff," brought my hands down, and felt rough cement. I'd dropped the flash when I'd lost my balance; I groped around and finally located it under the bend of my right knee. In its beam I saw I was roughly a foot below the surrounding terrain, in a concrete area that led to the door of the windmill. The door was of wood, with a massive iron bolt.

I sat still for a minute, waiting for the waves of pain to recede from my spine. McCone, I thought, you're not the agile cheerleader you once were.

In the years since I'd entered my profession—which at the moment seemed a dubious one, even to me—I'd inflicted countless bumps and bruises upon myself. In addition, I'd been stabbed, chloroformed, and kidnapped, almost fallen to my death, almost drowned, and once—humiliatingly—shot in the ass.

Now I asked myself, *How much more of this can you take?*

It was a good question, but right now my attention was focused on the big iron bolt on the windmill's door. The bolt should have been in a horizontal locked position. Instead, it was slightly canted, and the door stood open a crack.

I took the .38 from my bag and stood. Then I moved to the door, placed my other hand on the bolt. As I pulled the door toward me, its rusted hinges squealed. I flicked the gun's safety off and crouched down, waiting.

There was no sound of movement within.

A nervous prickling merged with the pain waves that still lapped at my spine. He was waiting for me to make the first move.

With my free hand I felt around behind me, came up with a chunk of loose concrete. I tossed it around the door. It fell with a clatter.

No response.

No one there—or someone more clever than I?

I waited. Minutes passed. Dead silence.

I stood, straightening slowly against the persistent pain. Took the flash in my left hand and moved around the edge of the door. Blackness inside, cold and musty.

I raised both my gun hand and the flash—steady, very steady.

And saw no one.

The space inside the door was concrete walled and floored. It was full of junk of various sorts, too numerous for me to take in. There was a smell of onions and grease, old and cloying.

The room was empty.

FOURTEEN

When I was certain no one was hiding in the shadows, I stepped inside the windmill. A brief scan with the flashlight told me someone had been camping out there. A pile of tattered blankets next to the far wall formed a makeshift bed; a candle in a red glass globe—the kind they put on your table in cheap Italian restaurants—stood on the ground next to it. There were paper bags and cardboard boxes arranged along the walls on either side of the bed, and scattered refuse bore the names of fast-food outlets and cheap vintners. When I examined the far corners, I found two more nests of rags and blankets—making it a dormitory of sorts.

What I'd stumbled onto was one of the hideaways that homeless people crept into within the confines of the park. This one must have been quite a find for the people who lived here: enclosed, dry, and—so long as none of the mounted police or park personnel noticed their comings and goings—relatively undetectable. The patrols would routinely check the door to make sure it was secure, of course, but the residents would know their schedule and wedge it shut to give the appearance that all was as it should be. If they were careful, they could go on living here indefinitely.

I had appropriated several books of matches from my motel room that morning. I located them in the pocket of my jeans, pulled one out, and lit the candle. The flaring reddish light showed the room in greater—and more wretched—detail.

There were plywood-covered areas on the cement floor where pumping equipment had obviously been removed; the stone walls were cracked and covered with mold; a stairway had once ascended to the upper stories, but that too had been ripped out, its splintered handrails still reaching down, like arms whose hands had been cruelly severed. The room seemed several degrees colder than outside. And beneath the greasy food smell was the stench of rotting garbage.

I turned my attention to the refuse on the floor: discarded wrappings, bottles, styrofoam cups, used hypodermic syringes, cans, chicken bones, food that was decayed beyond recognition. Much of it had probably been spoiled before it was brought here: the park administrator I'd met at the All Souls party had told me the homeless scavenged the trash cans for remains of picnic lunches; they also visited the dumpsters at McDonald's and other neighborhood restaurants. Apparently some of their gleanings had been so unpalatable as not to tempt even their ravenous appetites. When I found an empty cat-food can I shuddered, thinking, Even Watney won't eat this brand.

I straightened and looked around the room once more. It seemed an unlikely place for Wilkonson to have come. Perhaps I'd fixated on the windmill as his destination merely because it was the closest building to where he'd parked his car. What else was in this corner of the park?

The sewage plant. It probably would be staffed twenty-four hours; perhaps he'd had business with one of the crew. There was a caretaker's house a short distance from the windmill, but if he'd been going there, he'd have done better to conceal his car at the end of its long driveway. Otherwise, there was nothing here but wooded area to one side and, at the far end of the sewage plant, soccer fields.

All the places around here seemed unlikely destinations for Frank Wilkonson.

Had he realized he was being followed and left his car here as a ploy to elude his pursuer? No, that didn't make sense. If he were to do that, he would have abandoned the Ranchero in a populous area, one with public transportation, from which he could easily disappear and just as easily return to retrieve his vehicle. Why stage a vanishing act in the dark outer reaches of the park, far from taxicab stands or frequently running bus lines?

I began to prowl the room once more, moving each blanket,

rag, and piece of debris, emptying each paper sack and cardboard carton—trying to make some connection between Wilkonson and its inhabitants. None of the discards or possessions told me anything more about the people who lived here than that they were poor, ate badly, drank alcohol in quantity, and in one case at least, had a drug habit. Then, beneath the last nest of filthy blankets, I found a plywood plank that had been pried up and improperly replaced, which covered a two-foot-deep pit where machinery had once been installed. Inside it was a six-pack of Colt .45—Bob Choteau's brand of preference—and a white sack with red lettering: I DID MY SHOPPING AT A NEIGHBORHOOD BUSINESS!

The sack was identical to the ones Vicky Cushman had had stacked in her living room when I'd visited her the other day.

Inside the sack were foodstuffs: canned hash, tuna fish, sardines, Spam, crackers, instant coffee, peanut butter, rice cakes. There was a box of plastic knives and forks and spoons, as well as a brand-new can opener—both bearing price tickets from one of the chain stores Vicky had vowed she wouldn't let into her neighborhood.

I rocked back on my heels and stared at the red lettering on the sack. Just because Vicky had had the bags—fresh from the printer, she'd said—at her home on Thursday, I couldn't assume this one had come direct from there. Bags could also have been delivered to any number of her fellow organizing committee members; they could have been passed out to hundreds of Haight-Ashbury shoppers between then and now.

But it was too large a coincidence to suit me.

There was a noise outside, a snuffling that might have been animal or human. I blew out the candle, turned off my flashlight, and waited tensely. No one entered.

I took it as a warning that I should get out of there. The squatters wouldn't have left their food and possessions unattended for long. They were probably out foraging; they might return at any time.

I groped across the room to the door and stood listening for more sounds. When I was sure whatever had been snuffling around out there had gone away, I stepped out, made sure I was alone, then positioned the door and bolt as close to how I'd found them as I could. Then I retraced my path around the windmill and up the rise until I could see the road. Wilkonson's Ranchero still sat under the wind-bent cypress.

He'd walked toward the windmill; I'd seen him do that. In the time I'd spent parking my car he could have reached the mill, entered, and left again. But that still didn't explain where he'd gone next. And since his car was still here, he had to be around someplace. *Where?*

Well, I couldn't scour the thickets for him. And I doubted he would respond if I called out to him, tried to persuade him to talk with me. I'd just have to watch the Ranchero and wait him out.

To the right of the windmill, a fair distance away and close to the road, was some kind of debris pile. I moved toward it, saw jumbled wooden beams and sheets of corrugated iron that looked to be the remnants of a shed that had been torn down. It would provide a good view both of the mill and the Ranchero—plus a shelter from the fog and wind.

I climbed the slope and probed the heap with my flashlight. There was a triangular space about two feet high into which I could curl, between a pair of crisscrossed beams. It looked singularly uninviting but dark and secure.

With a flicker of regret because after this night my camel-colored pea jacket would never again be truly new (and with a stab of pain over the dry-cleaning bill I was likely to incur), I dropped to my knees and crawled under the angled beams.

For a time I felt warm and cozy in my hideaway; it made me think of long-ago rainy days when my brothers and sisters and I would pull the covers off our parents' double bed, leaving them anchored at the foot, and pretend the space between them and the floor was an Indian cave. But nifty childhood memories only go so far: soon my tailbone was throbbing again. No matter how I shifted, stones cut painfully into my ass, and it was getting even colder.

I turned up the collar of my jacket, hugged my arms over my breasts, warmed my hands in my armpits. After a few minutes I felt so toasty that I almost went to sleep. I brought my hands out into the damp, icy air. Soon I was miserable and shivering again. I began to think fondly of home, and the thick quilts on my big soft bed.

It really was the height of stupidity staying there in the park. For all I knew Wilkonson could be miles away by now. In any event, he probably wouldn't appear tonight. At best I'd be stiff and sore and exhausted all the next day. At worst, I'd catch a horrendous cold or end up with pneumonia.

But all the arguments I marshaled for giving up and going home failed to move me. I am extremely stubborn, and while many times that stubbornness has proved to be too much for my own good, there have been times when it's paid off. So I waited, thinking about Frank Wilkonson and Bob Choteau to take my mind off my discomfort.

The only connection between the two men was Rudy Goldring. Rudy, who had hired me to tail Frank. Rudy, who had left bequests in his will to both Bob Choteau and Irene Lasser, Frank's probable former lover. All four of them were connected—in ways I didn't understand totally, but connected nonetheless.

But then there was Vicky Cushman. Vicky, whose car—whether she was willing to admit it or not—Irene had been driving the day of Rudy's murder. Vicky, who had had the I DID MY SHOPPING AT A NEIGHBORHOOD BUSINESS! sacks in her living room on Thursday.

Maybe I was placing too much emphasis on that sack. But it looked too fresh to be someone's discard, and the foodstuffs inside were expensive.

Maybe Bob Choteau was also connected to Vicky Cushman.

Vicky bothered me. Her lie about the car . . . her frenetic behavior . . . her efforts to sedate herself with wine and grass. . . . Something wrong between her and Gerry . . . and something else there . . . maybe. . . . What? . . .

A noise brought me back to full wakefulness. I'd been dozing, not really asleep. Hastily I looked at my watch. When I'd checked it after crawling in here, it had been close to two; now it was twenty after four.

What had awakened me was the police patrol. I could hear the motor of the cruiser and the mutter of its radio. I raised up and peered around the crisscrossed beams at the road. Two uniformed officers were inspecting the Ranchero, one shining his flashlight through its windows while the other stood back, hand ready on his gun butt. After a bit more inspection, the one with the flashlight wrote out a ticket—it was illegal to park there at this hour—and stuck it under the windshield wiper; then they both returned to the cruiser and drove off.

I started to settle back into shelter, but my body was still cramped and cold, and my stubbornness had diluted some. The noise of the cruiser's engine faded, and I realized that the foghorn no longer cried. That meant the insulating mist had retreated to the sea; the land had been cooled, and now real autumn-morning iciness would set in.

I crawled out of my hiding place and started for the road. As my eyes rested on the Ranchero, I remembered having seen a blanket on the seat when I'd shined my flash through the window hours ago. There was no reason I shouldn't curl up in Wilkonson's car and await his return there. After the last few miserable hours, I was in no mood to play any more games. I'd simply confront him and demand explanations.

Only he didn't come back.

When traffic on the surrounding streets increased, I knew the city was waking up, and I began to get worried. I sat up, refolded the blanket, stared through the gray morning haze at the windmill. It looked even more deteriorated now: shingles were flaking away as if it were molting; where the support beams for the vanes weren't sagging and splintered, they were rotted away. The surrounding terrain was clogged with dead vegetation, and the wind-tortured cypress trees bent low, scoured silver branches clawing at the dull sky.

The crackle of another police radio drew my attention away; it must be time for the next patrol. Quickly I ducked down, opened the car door, and slipped out. As the cruiser pulled to a stop behind the Ranchero, I moved through the undergrowth and found a path that would take me to where the MG was parked on Lincoln Way.

FIFTEEN

Eight o'clock on a Sunday morning was probably an impolitic time to go calling on a potentially hostile witness, but at this point I just didn't care to observe the proprieties. The presence of the shopping bag in Bob Choteau's hideaway, coupled with her lie about Irene Lasser using her BMW, placed Vicky Cushman squarely in the middle of what I was coming to think of as my case. It was time I established the precise nature of her connection to the other principals.

Vicky had better not cross me, I thought as I stopped my car next to the wall of The Castles. She may think she's tough because she takes on the chain stores and Cal's medical center, but she's never had to contend with a determined McCone before!

Surprisingly, when I pushed the button on the intercom, I received an immediate answering buzz, rather than the sleep-choked inquiry I expected. I went through the gate and followed the path under the eucalyptus trees. The air was still, and their leaves hung heavy with dew; moisture blanketed the lawn with a silvery sheen. Ahead of me I heard a door close, and when I looked in the direction of the noise, I saw Gerry Cushman coming out of the castle to the left of the main one—the master bedroom suite, I supposed.

Gerry was a tall, slender man who walked in a bouncy gait that reflected his high energy level. His black hair was curly and stood up from a widow's peak in a funny little corkscrew.

When I'd seen him at All Souls parties, he'd been quiet at first; after he'd gotten a couple of drinks in him, he'd become animated and had dominated conversations with his quick wit and expansive gestures. In spite of his somewhat odd appearance, his obvious keen enjoyment of life made him very attractive to women; I'd heard that he wasn't above a romantic fling from time to time. Presumably Vicky was too busy with her civic causes to notice—or perhaps she just didn't care.

This morning, however, Gerry didn't look as if he was enjoying anything very much. He carried a set of rolled-up blueprints under one arm and was scowling ferociously. His hands were thrust in the pockets of his trendy baggy houndstooth jacket. When he saw me, he stopped and stared, not saying anything.

"Gerry," I said. "Sharon McCone, from All Souls Legal Cooperative."

"Oh, right. I was trying to place you. Vicky mentioned you'd dropped in the other day."

As if on cue, one of the upper windows of the turret behind him opened, and Vicky stuck her head out. Her frizzy perm was wildly disheveled; even at this distance I could see that her eyes were red and swollen. She ignored me, focusing on Gerry, her mouth twisting in anger.

"Fuck you, Gerry!" she yelled. "Fuck you!" Then she withdrew from the window and slammed it shut.

Gerry seemed to shrink inside the loose jacket. He didn't even look back, just started walking toward the gate, his head bent, eyes on the ground.

"I really needed that," he said. "It's just the way I wanted to start my day."

I fell in step beside him, deciding to talk with him first and get a feel for the situation before I went inside to see Vicky.

"I've got to go down to Carmel Highlands, look over a building site with a client," Gerry added. "He's picking me up, that's who I thought you were when I buzzed you in. Would have been great if it *had* been him. Nice scene for a client to witness, right?"

"People have their off days—everybody understands that."

He laughed bitterly. "Vicky seems to have cornered more than her fair market share." Outside the wall, what sounded like a van with a diesel engine drove up. Gerry glanced apprehensively at the gate. "Look, that's my client. I'm just going to take off. Will you do me a favor?"

"Sure."

"Go in there and try to talk some sense into her. Calm her down. Try to keep her from getting into the grass or wine this early. Will you do that for me?"

"I'll try."

"Try's all anyone can do with Vicky."

He went through the gate, slamming it as hard as Vicky had the window, and I retraced my steps toward the smaller castle. When I tried the door handle it turned, so I stepped inside and called out to Vicky. She didn't reply. I shut the door and looked around.

The ground floor was a sitting room, with a fireplace fitted into the curve of the wall. In the center of the room, a spiral staircase rose to the second story. The place was in total disorder: bedding materials were heaped in one chair and on a hassock drawn up in front of it, as if someone had slept there; on a table between it and a second chair stood an empty jug of red wine and a half-full brandy snifter. My eyes moved from it to a trail of red stains that led across the pale blue carpet toward the hearth. A smashed wineglass lay there, and there was a great splash of red on the wall above the mantel. I shook my head, then went toward the staircase, calling out again.

"I'm up here," Vicky's voice said. "Has the fucker gone?"

I climbed the stairs to the bedroom. It too was round, decorated all in blue; a door opened to a combination bath- and dressing room set in the square area over the entryway. Vicky huddled on one of the most enormous beds I'd ever seen—obviously custom-made because of the way its padded head-board conformed to the turret's curving wall. The sheets and blankets were twisted and rumpled, and most of the pillows—there had to have been at least ten—had fallen to the floor. Vicky wore a long ruffly white nightgown that would have looked virginal had it not been for the red spatter marks that matched the stains downstairs. She was smoking a joint.

Sorry about that, Gerry, I thought. I *would* have tried.

"Has the fucker gone?" she repeated.

"If you mean Gerry, yes. His client came, and they took off. I thought I'd check to see if you're okay."

"Now that he's gone, I am." She extended the joint to me. I shook my head and sat down at the foot of the bed.

"Oh, that's right. Your drug's alcohol. I'd give you some wine, but I drank it all. What I didn't throw at the wall, I mean." She giggled.

"I take it you two had a fight," I said. "Do you want to talk about it?"

"What's to talk about? It was just one more episode in the big serial fight. The other day I was thinking that we might as well make a soap opera out of it. What do you think? We could call it *As the Worm Turns.*"

"Vicky—"

"I like it, don't you? Of course all the characters except Gerry would be women. He'd like that. Gerry and his women."

Ah, I thought, she does know—and cares.

Vicky stubbed out the joint in an ashtray and scuttled over to the edge of the bed. She picked up a pillow and retreated to the headboard, where she sat Indian-style, the pillow cradled against her breasts as if for protection.

"You know when I found out what he was like?" she said. "It was years and years ago. My oldest daughter, Lindy, had just been born. She was just a little baby and we were living out in the Sunset and I drove up and saw Gerry necking with this woman in her car in broad daylight in front of our own house."

"What did you do?"

"Waited till he got out of her car and tried to run him down with mine. It went out of control and I hit a fireplug instead. Water went spurting all over the place. I jumped out of the car and ran into the house and locked myself in this walk-in closet we had. I stayed in there for twenty-four hours, screaming off and on."

She was silent for a moment, her gaze darkly inward as she relived those hours in the closet. "When I came out the fucker told me he wanted an open marriage. That was the first episode in our soap opera. It's been number one in the ratings ever since. I can't have an open marriage, I won't have one, and Gerry—he just *does.*"

I didn't know what to say, so I just sat there, wondering why she persisted in making me a sort of unwilling voyeur. If Vicky had been a close friend—Anne-Marie, for instance—I would have been glad to listen. But she was a mere acquaintance, and the primary emotion her revelations aroused in me was embarrassment. I suspected she would also be embarrassed when she recalled our conversation in a calmer, more sober light.

After a bit Vicky sighed and crawled over to one of the nightstands. She fumbled through its drawer, came up with another joint.

"Maybe," I said, "you should leave the grass alone for a while. You look like you could use some food. Why don't we go over to the kitchen and I'll cook you breakfast—"

A look of alarm passed over her features. I guessed she was afraid I'd confiscate her dope. Then the alarm faded and was replaced by irritation. "Maybe," she said, in a good imitation of me, "you should mind your own business."

I shrugged, trying to control a flash of anger. "You're right. So, since we're speaking of business, I'll get to the reason I'm here."

"Somehow I didn't think this was a social call. What do you want this time?"

"The truth—for once."

"About what?"

"Irene Lasser."

Vicky set the unlighted joint down and scurried back to the headboard, where she once again cradled the pillow defensively. "Who?" she said.

"Come on, Vicky. You know Irene. You loaned her your car last Monday, and you gave her one of those neighborhood-business shopping bags so she could load it with goodies and take it to Bob Choteau at the place he's hiding in the park."

"I didn't— Who's Bob Choteau?"

"No more lies, Vicky."

"I don't know what you're talking about. *Who* you're talking about. You copied some license-plate number down wrong, and now you're trying to blame me for things I didn't do, for knowing people I've never heard of. I didn't loan my car to anybody, I didn't take a bag of food to some bum—"

She realized her mistake; that showed in her eyes. Quickly she got off the bed, ran into the dressing room area, and slammed the door. The lock clicked into place.

"What are you going to do, Vicky?" I called. "Sit in there and scream off and on for twenty-four hours?"

Her reply was *close* to a scream. "There's a phone in here. If you don't get off my property right away, I'm calling the cops!"

That I didn't need. I got off her property.

SIXTEEN

The elderly desk clerk at the Kingsway Motel knew Frank Wilkonson but said he hadn't checked in as usual the night before.

"Funny about that," he added. "He's got a standing reservation."

I looked disappointed and said, "I was so hoping to see Frank. Are you sure he didn't just come in later than usual? Maybe somebody else checked him in."

"I'm the only one on duty Saturday nights, miss. There's no way he could have escaped my notice."

"Well, I'm sorry to have missed him. A couple of my other friends mentioned that he's been staying here regularly. I guess you've seen them—they've visited him a few times now."

The old man looked thoughtful, pausing to suck contemplatively at his yellowed teeth. "Just the one fellow."

"Which one?"

"The fellow with the funny curly hair." At my inquiring look he added, "Curls up from the front here"—he indicated the center of his own bald pate—"like one of those ribbons on a birthday package, the kind you run the scissors over and it comes out all twisty."

Gerry Cushman would probably not have been flattered by the description. "Oh, that's Gerry," I said. "I haven't seen him in ages. When was he by?"

"Two weeks ago? I can't recall for sure, but that sounds right.

He said he'd spotted your friend Wilkonson leaving, but hadn't been able to catch him. I told him about the standing reservation, so I guess they got in touch. Hard to tell who's visiting who in this place, but that's like it should be. The guests have a right to their privacy."

Bet they don't get to exercise that right much with you on the desk, I thought. I fished a scrap of paper from my bag and wrote my home number on it. "Will you call me if Frank comes in? Without telling him I've been here? I want to surprise him."

The old man's eyes grew shrewd. He'd probably spent his adult lifetime on motel row; he wasn't all that easy to fool. He said, "It was worth twenty dollars to your friend Gerry to surprise him."

I reached in my bag for my wallet. "It's worth twenty to me, too."

The old man smiled. "I like surprises as well as the next man."

When I arrived at the Murphy Windmill, the green Ranchero still stood under the cypress tree. Two parking tickets fluttered against the windshield. I pulled the MG onto the verge behind it and studied the mill.

It was close to eleven; the day had turned sunny and warm. Joggers pounded by; bicyclists pedaled lazily along; riders on horses rented from the park stables paused to look at the decaying windmill. By now the people who called the mill home might either be inside or out taking advantage of the good weather. It didn't matter which because there was no way I could investigate further until the park users cleared out and darkness fell.

I made a U-turn and headed for home.

Watney was not pleased with me. He grudgingly accepted the food I placed in his empty dish, ate ravenously, and then stomped off into the blackberry vines. Probably the Curleys had assumed I'd be home long before this; poor old Wat had had to depend on his own rusty hunting skills. It didn't particularly bother me; the creature was too damned fat for his own good. But his greeting set the tone for the rest of the day.

First I dragged the cordless out onto the sunny deck and tried to call Jack Stuart. Hank answered the phone at All Souls and told me Jack wasn't expected back until around noon the next day. I asked him if he knew anything about the beneficiaries under Rudy Goldring's will, and he said no, Gilbert Thayer had drawn it up. Since none of us had bothered to ask Gilbert where he was going when he'd quit the co-op, I had no idea how to reach him—nor did I particularly want to talk with him.

Next I tried to call Ben Gallagher for an update on the Goldring investigation. Ben was on duty but out of the office, and they didn't know when he'd be back. I left a message.

Then I sat for a while, thinking about the Lasser-Cushman connection. Maybe my initial assumption had been wrong; maybe Irene's connection was with Gerry, not Vicky. She could be one of the women he played around with. He could have loaned her his wife's car. Perhaps that was what had provoked the fight Gerry and Vicky had had last night. If so, I doubted I'd get any more out of Gerry than I had his wife. I especially doubted he'd tell me why he'd been at the motel asking after Frank Wilkonson. The thing to do was find Lasser.

I went inside and burrowed through the closet where I keep my collection of Bay Area phone directories, checking them for Irene Lasser, I. Lasser, I. Johnstone, I. L. Johnstone, and other variants thereof. None of the combinations was listed. I also checked for Susan Lasser, on the off chance the daughter was old enough to have her own phone. The results were just as negative.

On my way back outside, I stuck my head through the door of the half-completed bedroom in what had once been my back porch. I'd been remodeling the house—a cottage built to shelter victims of the 1906 quake and fire—piecemeal since I'd bought it; I was likely to still be remodeling it in 2006. The space looked more like a demolition site than a construction zone, and it made me feel as frustrated as my lack of progress on untangling the relationships between Goldring, Wilkonson, *et al.*

I shut the door on the mess and went back to the deck. The sunshine quickly perked up my flagging spirits, and I grabbed the cordless and called the Kingsway Motel. Wilkonson still hadn't checked in. Next I punched out Rae's number; no one answered. Undaunted, I decided to call Anne-Marie. Hank was at All Souls, so it was a perfect time for us to get together for a heart-to-heart. Both of us were reticent where our private lives were concerned, but she'd helped me a lot at the time of my breakup with Don, and perhaps I could return the favor.

All I got was the machine, and the damned thing cut me off before it even beeped.

I put the phone down and leaned back in my lounge chair. Thought of my youngest sister, Patsy, who, together with her new husband Evans, had recently opened a restaurant in Ukiah. I couldn't call them—Sunday dinner would be going on. There were other friends here in the city I could call—Paula, Carolyn, Liz, Alison—but on nice Sundays San Franciscans tend to take to the out of doors, and they probably wouldn't be home. I should call my mother, but I didn't want to. Since my breakup with Don, Ma had been harping at me because she was afraid I'd never get married. I even considered phoning my old friend Wolf, a fellow PI with whom I'd shared a case, but I knew on Sunday he'd be with his lady friend, Kerry Wade.

Why is it, I thought, that when you're in the mood to talk, no one calls? When you *want* peace and quiet, the phone never quits ringing.

I stayed there on the lounge chair for a long time, until the sun patch had moved away from the deck, across the scraggly backyard, and into the shadows of the pines at the rear of the lot. At about five-thirty I got up and went into the house for a glass of wine. I'd recently started drinking the good stuff—the varieties with corks—rather than the jug brands that had been a staple of my youth. The cork in the bottle of white zinfandel that I tried to open was dry—so much for the good stuff—and when I finally wrenched it free, the corkscrew skewed sideways and made a jagged slice in my thumb.

Sunday, I thought. Sunday evening coming down.

SEVENTEEN

Wilkonson never did check into his motel, and I decided it would be unproductive, if not foolhardy, to return to the windmill. So at six the next morning, after a good night's sleep, I waited halfway down the Cushmans' cul-de-sac in my MG. I suspected that sooner or later one of them would make contact with Irene Lasser; I'd follow whoever left first today, and if that didn't produce results, concentrate on the other tomorrow.

As I waited, staring at the row of golden-leaved poplars, I felt a twinge of guilt over neglecting my duties at All Souls. But I pushed it aside, reminding myself that my desk was relatively clear. Also, it was time Rae began shouldering her share of the work. I'd tried to reach her up until ten the previous night; there had been no answer. So I'd decided to proceed on the assumption she'd arrive at the office on time and deal with any urgent business.

The Cushmans obviously didn't believe in tackling the world too early on a Monday. It was close to eight when the automobile gate opened and Vicky's BMW emerged. I slouched down in my seat as the car went past me, then sat up and turned the key in the ignition.

The BMW proceeded with the flow of rush-hour traffic down Oak Street, the east-bound arterial bordering the Panhandle of Golden Gate Park. I stayed a couple of car lengths behind it, straining to get a glimpse of its occupants. Vicky appeared to be wearing a dark scarf over her wilted curls; a couple of blond heads bobbed in the back seat. She must be taking her girls, Betsy and Lindy, to school.

The BMW turned on Divisadero and drove to Pacific Heights. When we reached a block on Broadway where buses and cars disgorging children jammed the street, I realized the Cushman daughters attended the Abbott School, a bastion of upper-middle-class respectability that for generations had shielded the offspring of the city's affluent families from the ugly realities and poor instructional quality of our public institutions. The girls delivered—properly uniformed and waving happily—Vicky headed back to the Haight.

Instead of turning toward the cul-de-sac, however, she climbed the hill on one of the roads that skirt Buena Vista Park. The land above the park is steeply terraced, and the small streets twist and turn. I followed slowly, downshifting all the way to first gear on the switchbacks. Rounding a curve, I found myself a few yards from the BMW's rear bumper. As I backed off, it pulled to the curb in front of a vacant lot surrounded by a double line of young grapevines. Beyond them was a rough board shed and regularly laid-out rows of plants. Some of them I recognized: brussels sprouts, artichokes, lettuce.

It was one of the community gardens that seem to be springing up on vacant lots all over the city. Given her background in horticulture, Irene Lasser might very well be involved in organizing this one, and Vicky might have come here to see her. I eased the MG to the curb in front of a small apartment house, hoping she hadn't noticed me.

But the woman who got out of the BMW wasn't Vicky. What I had taken for a dark scarf over blond curls was a rich fall of chestnut hair fastened at the nape of her neck.

It was Irene Lasser who had driven the Cushman girls to school.

I gripped the steering wheel with tense fingers as she went to the rear door, opened it, and leaned in. When she backed out and straightened, she had a small child in her arms. She set the child down, took it by the hand, and they walked toward the garden.

Even though I couldn't actually tell the gender of the child, I assumed it must be Susan Lasser—the daughter whom no one in the Hollister area seemed to know existed. She looked to be about two, meaning she would have had to have been born a number of months after Lasser had fled the Burning Oak Ranch.

Whose child, then? Harlan Johnstone's? Frank Wilkonson's? Or had Susan been fathered by someone her mother had met after she ran away?

I remained in my car while the Lassers went inside the shed and emerged with gardening tools—a hoe and spade for Irene, a plastic bucket and shovel for Susan. They carried the tools to the back of the lot where there was an area that apparently had been cleared of the summer crops. Irene proceeded to cultivate the earth, while Susan squatted nearby, filling and emptying and refilling her bucket. Irene moved in a steady, strong motion, breaking up the clods and leveling the fine soil. Every now and then she would pause to say something to the child, or wipe sweat from her face and refasten her heavy hair. The rhythm of her movements and the way she serenely squinted up into the clear sky while resting exuded an air of contentment. Susan played quietly, her round face now and then breaking into a delighted smile; when she spoke to her mother, she seemed to laugh, and Irene replied in kind.

I watched for a while, knowing that soon I would have to shatter their shared tranquillity. As I did, I tried to figure out an approach that would not panic Irene. She would recognize me, of course. I was sure Vicky had told her of my visits—probably with a good deal of melodramatic embellishment and speculation as to my motives. It made approaching Lasser a tricky proposition.

Vicky and Irene—now that was interesting. What *was* the relationship between them? Irene used Vicky's car, drove Vicky's children to school. Did she also live at The Castles? From the relatively early hour that she'd left with the kids, I guessed she must.

I have to admit that my sometimes evil mind immediately suggested *ménage à trois*. But no—while such an arrangement might fit what I knew of Gerry, it was nothing Vicky would go along with. Gerry had wanted an open marriage many years before, at least that was what Vicky had told me. She'd also said, *I can't . . . I won't. . . .*

So what *was* the relationship between the two women? Were they just friends? Related . . . ?

And then I thought of Vicky, frazzled and overworked by her numerous causes. Too overworked to properly care for her daughters. And I remembered her comment about the woman who worked for her, who had said she should take up a hobby, "something peaceful that will give me a chance to be alone with my thoughts." A peaceful hobby such as Irene was indulging in right now.

I also remembered Betsy coming into the living room and asking her mother if it was all right if Rina and Lindy and she made popcorn in the adjacent kitchen. Rina—a nickname for Irene.

No wonder Vicky's negative response had been so vehement and out of proportion to the request. She'd just gotten done insisting she hadn't loaned her car to the woman with the long chestnut hair, didn't even know anyone of that description— and there was her daughter, about to parade that very woman through the room. Vicky had reacted in a similar way yesterday morning, when I'd suggested we go to the kitchen and I cook something for her—probably because it was about the time when Irene would be there, preparing breakfast for the kids.

Irene was the Cushmans' nanny, nursemaid, governess, or whatever such people called them. She must live on the grounds of The Castles, possibly in the structure originally built for servants. She and her little girl had been there all along.

But why the secrecy? Because Irene was hiding from her former husband? Because Frank Wilkonson was looking for her? Because Susan was the daughter of one of the men, and Irene didn't want him to have contact with her? In any event, lying to the police in a felony case seemed extreme.

But then, I reminded myself, people like the Cushmans often feel they're above the law. They're the first to howl about inadequate police protection, the first to arm themselves with handguns. But they're also the last to volunteer information that might help the cops make a collar.

The thought made me angry. To hell with the gentle approach, I decided. I didn't care anymore if I scared Irene Lasser. I just wanted some truthful answers.

As I started to get out of the car, however, two men in jeans and plaid shirts who had been ambling down the sidewalk veered off into the garden. Irene waved to them, and they waved back and went to the shed for tools. Soon they had hung their shirts on grapestakes and were working beside her, pausing occasionally to roughhouse with Susan. Within half an hour two older women had shown up; they dragged out long hoses and began watering. A young man appeared with two kids about Susan's age; the kids joined her and they set to building an elaborate dirt castle. The young man hung around Irene, talking to her and generally getting in her way. After a while she spoke sharply to him, put her tools away, and called to Susan. They left the garden, waving good-bye to the other laborers, got in the BMW, and drove off.

I debated following them but decided against it. It was after eleven; chances were they were going back to The Castles for lunch. If Vicky was there, I wouldn't be able to set foot inside the wall. Instead, I got out of my car and wandered into the garden.

The first person I came to was one of the women with the hoses. When I spoke to her, she turned abruptly, and the stream of water ran over my boot. "Sorry about that," she said. "But you shouldn't be wearing such good dress boots in here anyway. The heels'll sink into the mud and it'll ruin the leather."

"They're old and the leather's already shot," I said. "Can you tell me—was that Irene Lasser and her daughter, Susan, I just saw leaving?"

"The woman with the little girl? I don't know her name. I'm in town from Fresno, visiting my sister Beth, and she dragged me along. Beth'd know, though. That's her over by the shed."

I thanked her and moved toward the shed. The other woman—tall and muscular, with salt-and-pepper hair cut sleek and close to her head—was leaning against its wall, deep in conversation with the young man who had seemed to be trying to hit on Irene. As I approached, I heard her say, ". . . can't do things like that. She's not interested. Besides, that's not what the garden's all about."

"I was only—" He broke off when he saw me.

"Hi," I said to the woman. "Are you Beth?"

The young man said, "We'll talk more later," and moved to where the kids were still building their mud castle.

Beth stood shading her eyes against the sun. "What can I do for you?"

"Your sister told me you might know the woman and the little girl who just left in the BMW. I think they might be old friends of mine, Irene and Susan Lasser."

Beth had stiffened slightly, but there was a quick relaxation when I said the name "Lasser." It must be something from the old days when she had been surnamed Johnstone that Irene was afraid of. "Old friends from where?" she asked.

"Not Hollister, if that's what you're thinking. I know all about that business, and I don't blame any of Irene's friends for being wary."

"Where, then?" Beth's expression was pleasant enough, but she hadn't completely let down her guard.

I remembered that Irene's divorce papers had come from a Los Angeles lawyer. "L.A.," I said.

"Ah. You must have been one of the people who helped her before Susan was born."

"Yes."

"I'm sorry to have acted so suspicious of you, but we have to be careful."

"Of what? Has Harlan Johnstone—"

"Oh no, not him. He hasn't been a problem for quite some time. No, it's Susan's father. Irene's terribly afraid of him."

"Who *is* Susan's father?"

"Irene didn't tell you?"

"She never wanted to talk about him."

"She doesn't want to talk to us about him, either." From the slightly wistful way she spoke, I sensed she was telling the truth.

Before she could ask more about my alleged friendship with Irene, I said, "Did Irene plan this garden? She has such a talent that way."

Beth nodded. "Yes, it was her idea. Vicky Cushman—that's Irene's employer—got a friend to donate the land. Irene is really on the cutting edge of the urban gardening movement."

"Oh, really? I'm seeing more gardens all the time, but I didn't know there was an actual movement."

"Well, it's pretty loosely organized, but the San Francisco League of Urban Gardeners—they go by the acronym SLUG, if you can believe that—took a census a while back and found there are at least sixty community vegetable gardens in about twenty different neighborhoods. Most of them aren't as progressive as ours, of course, because they don't have Irene's ideas behind them."

"Such as?"

"Irene views the urban garden in terms of helping develop the world food supply. She says it's possible for us to set an example as to how cities can become more productive in the agrarian sense. Urban planners don't tend to think in agrarian terms, but there's a lot of space just crying out to be used— rooftops, parks, planter boxes, those grassy areas between the sidewalks and the streets, even freeway median strips. Think of what that kind of planning in places like Bombay or Nairobi would do for the Third World food supply! And there are secondary benefits: a single tree is capable of filtering pollution equal to what twenty cars put out—"

"So this garden is a sort of ecological experiment—"

"Not 'sort of'! It *is*. Do you see any waste space here? Any land lying fallow?" Beth flung her arm out at the rows of vegetables and freshly tilled earth.

"None."

"That's right. Irene is planning to establish others just like it all over the city, with Vicky Cushman's help. She's carving out a career for herself while working to aid world hunger. She consults to organizations like SLUG and Urban Resources Systems, and to UC–Davis." A shadow touched Beth's animated face. "At least, she'd be carving out a career if she didn't have to hide and worry about this damned man."

"What exactly is she afraid of, do you know?"

"No. I've gone on the assumption that he's violent or perverted or crazy—you know, that sort of thing."

I knew that sort of thing. "And you say Irene works for Vicky and Gerry Cushman?"

"She lives at The Castles and takes care of their daughters. Do you know the Cushmans?"

"Quite well," I said. *Too* well. "How do you suppose Irene got to know them?"

"I gather they're old friends."

"Tell me, has Irene ever mentioned another old friend named Rudy Goldring?"

The name didn't seem to mean anything to her, but now Beth's eyes were growing wary. My questions were too numerous, my way of asking them too practiced. ". . . No."

"Well," I said, "thanks for talking with me. I think I'll run down to The Castles now and see if Irene and Susan are at home. If not, it'll give me a chance to catch up on things with Vicky."

"You said you and Vicky are good friends?"

"We have few secrets." And I was very close to finding out those that she'd kept from me.

EIGHTEEN

When I arrived at All Souls half an hour later, Ted handed me a stack of message slips. I leafed through them, saw they were all routine. "How come you didn't refer these people to Rae?"

"She hasn't come in." Ted—so long as the news isn't too awful—actually likes to be the bearer of bad tidings. Now he leaned across his desk toward me, savoring what he was about to impart. "Doug's in the hospital, went in yesterday. Food poisoning, Rae said. What *I* think is that it was a suicide attempt."

"Dammit!"

My vehement response made him draw back. "Well," he said, "I'm sure he'd have thought twice about it, had he known how put out you'd be."

"It's not that, and you know it. I'm upset for Rae; Doug's problems are already more than she can handle. What is it that makes you think he tried to kill himself?"

"He was taken to SF General early yesterday morning, but when she called at eight *this* morning, she was as upset as if it had just happened. More upset than you would be over a simple case of food poisoning. Besides, she said something about them having to keep him under observation for seventy-two hours."

"Ah." Seventy-two hours is the length of time hospitals are required to psychologically evaluate would-be suicides. "I suppose I should try to reach her—"

"She said she'd call you at home tonight."

I nodded and took the message slips upstairs, wondering how this turn of events would affect her performance and future at All Souls. Then I pushed the thought to one side and began working my way through the stack of messages.

It was the noon hour; most of the people I tried to call were out at lunch. I dragged the phone book out of the bottom drawer of my filing cabinet and looked up the area code for Hollister, then got numbers from Information for both the Burning Oak Ranch offices and Frank Wilkonson's home. As I'd expected, Wilkonson hadn't come into the office that morning; the secretary's businesslike tone was underscored with uneasiness. When I called his home number, it rang eight times before Jane Wilkonson answered.

"Mrs. Wilkonson, it's Alissa Hernandez."

"Who?"

"Alissa Hernandez. From Allstate. We talked on Friday—"

"Oh, of course I remember." She sounded sluggish, as if I had awakened her, and it made her Texas twang more pronounced.

"I've been trying to reach your husband, but they tell me he didn't report for work this morning. Is he at home? If he's available, I need to speak with him."

"He's . . . no, he's not here."

"I see. Do you have a number where I can reach him?"

". . . No."

"You don't know where he is, then?"

"No, I don't."

"Did he make his weekly trip on Saturday evening?"

Long pause. "Yes. He left at quarter to ten, same as always."

"But he didn't come back this morning."

"No."

"And you have no idea where he intended to go, what he intended to do?"

"I told you he never says anything about that." The sluggishness was gone now, the pitch of her voice sharpened by nervousness, or perhaps fear.

"Did he act differently before he left? Differently than the other times?"

"I don't know what you mean by that."

"Was he excited? In a hurry? Nervous?"

"No. Everything was normal."

Except it was hardly a normal situation to begin with. "Have you contacted the sheriff, Mrs. Wilkonson? The hospitals?"

". . . I can't."

"Why not?"

"I can't, that's all." She paused, then added, "Look, Ms. Hernandez, I shouldn't have told you all the things I did on Friday. It's private business, between Frank and me. Will you just forget what I said?"

"It will remain private, yes." I wasn't sure that would be possible in the long run, but there was no point in further alarming her now.

"Thanks. I better get off the phone now. Frank might be trying to call me."

"All right. Why don't I check back with you later this afternoon?"

"What for?"

"I'm concerned for you. I'd just like to know everything's all right."

Jane Wilkonson's reply was tinged with surprise. "Thank you," she said. "It's nice to know *somebody* cares."

Even if that somebody was practically a stranger.

As soon as we were done talking, I dialed the SFPD, so I wouldn't be forced to dwell on the unhappy implications of Jane Wilkonson's last statement. Gallagher was in the squad room.

"Any progress on the Goldring investigation?" I asked.

"What, are you making sure you're getting your taxpayer's dollar's worth?" There was an edge to Ben's words—and I knew all too well why. San Francisco has a very low solution rate for homicides—at last report, the second-worst in urban California. Four out of every ten murders in the last decade have gone unsolved. When you're one of the investigators accountable for such a figure, you naturally become defensive.

I said, "I'm just interested, that's all. The guy was my client."

"Sorry—it's Monday. You know Mondays."

"I sure do. Are you still concentrating on Bob Choteau?"

"Yeah. The son of a bitch has vanished into the park."

"What about other leads? Did you ever find out who Goldring's ten o'clock appointment was with?"

". . . No."

"I suppose you checked his list of customers. You *do* have a list of men who bought their shirts from him?"

"Of course we do."

"Any chance of me getting a look at it?"

"No."

"Ben—"

"Sharon, you forget how long I've known you and how you operate. Maybe you can get away with sticking your nose where it doesn't belong when it's one of the lieutenant's cases, but not when it's mine. No list." And then he hung up on me.

I took the receiver from my ear and raised my eyebrows at it. The years certainly *had* changed Gallagher. In fact, he sounded remarkably like Lieutenant Greg Marcus—with one exception. Greg had respected my instincts almost from the first; had I called *him* asking about the list of Goldring's customers, he'd have wondered what I was on to, and insisted on hearing it all.

Still, I could understand Gallagher's one-track approach to the investigation. Random killings—those where there is no discoverable connection between the victim and the murderer—account for roughly three-quarters of San Francisco's homicides. When an investigator turns up a lead that indicates a link between the victim and his killer, he pursues it relentlessly. Besides, by now Gallagher had more immediate cases to attend to; the Goldring murder had happened a week ago, was old stuff. Most homicide investigations—unless the victim is exceptionally prominent or controversial—are backburnered after seventy-two hours, simply because the odds of cracking a case have been proven to drop dramatically after three days have elapsed. I knew that from my frequent visits to Greg Marcus's office; I'd seen the boxed case files stacked against the walls of the squad room. The department is too overworked and understaffed to pursue them, unless by some miracle a fresh lead turns up.

It was these problems that were making Gallagher behave as he had with me. And it was the same set of problems that made me reluctant to call him back and tell him why the list of Goldring's customers was important to me, and even less inclined to tell him where Bob Choteau was hiding. The facts I possessed about Frank Wilkonson and Irene Lasser were too nebulous to constitute the fresh lead he needed, and if he made the collar on Choteau, he'd close out the file and turn it over to the district attorney. Once closed, the investigation would be

extremely difficult to reopen. Once Choteau was charged, I
might never be able to interest Gallagher in an alternate
suspect. And worse yet, an innocent man might be convicted.

I tapped my fingers on the desk and stared out the window
at the line of fog that hovered to the south, somewhere over
Daly City. Would the offices of Goldring Clothiers still be open?
I wondered. If so, Mrs. Halvorsen, the woman who seemed to
run things there, would be able to help me.

Mrs. Halvorsen was, she explained on the phone, staying on
until the company could be sold. "The sale was stipulated in
Mr. Goldring's will," she added, "since there are no heirs to
carry on the business."

"What about Irene and Susan Lasser?"

"Them? Oh, they're not relatives, and those were just small
bequests. I know because I witnessed the will."

"You know Irene Lasser, then?"

"Of course. She's a delightful woman, came to visit often.
She gave Mr. Goldring all the plants that we have here in the
offices, you know."

"I don't quite understand the relationship. If Irene's not
family . . . "

"Well, she practically is. Irene's father and Mr. Goldring
were roommates at college, and even after Mr. and Mrs. Lasser
died, she kept in touch. Then, after her divorce, when she
needed a job, Mr. Goldring arranged for her to work for one of
his customers."

"Gerry Cushman."

"Yes. It was an ideal situation; the Cushmans needed someone to look after their little girls, as a live-in; they have plenty
of room, and no objection to a woman with a little girl of her
own. Also, I've the impression there was some need for
security for Irene—a jealous ex-husband, perhaps—and The
Castles is about as well protected as anyplace in the city. But
here I've been babbling on. What can I help you with?"

I wished I'd thought to talk to Mrs. Halvorsen earlier; it
would have saved me a great deal of trouble. "You've already
answered my question," I said. "Thank you so much."

It was after one, time to try to return my calls again. But
before I started in, I looked up the Abbott School and dialed its
number. Classes let out, the switchboard told me, at three-
thirty.

*   *   *

At three-twenty I leaned against a plane tree in front of the school. The Cushman BMW, with Irene Lasser at the wheel, had just joined the line of cars idling in the street. Soon a school bus drove up and blocked my view of it—which was fine, because it also blocked Irene's view of me.

In truth, I felt a bit like a pervert lurking around the schoolyard; when the Cushman kids appeared it probably would be all I could do to keep myself from asking if they wanted to see my Walnetto. I found myself grinning, then glanced guiltily around to see if anyone was staring at me. Why, at tense times such as this, did I often lapse into mental silliness—such as recalling the old gag from the long-dead TV show *Laugh-In?*

At three-thirty kids began to emerge from the school. I don't know why I expected them to be sedate; kids of affluent families don't hold any more of an option on good behavior than the working-class McCones had. But the exuberance with which these leapt and bounded out the doors and raced toward the buses and expensive automobiles caught me off guard. In the confusion I almost missed Betsy Cushman coming along the sidewalk in the company of a slightly older girl who resembled her so closely that she had to be her sister Lindy.

Betsy's green uniform skirt was badly wrinkled, and her white blouse hung untucked on one side. Her lackadaisical walk emphasized her chunkiness. Lindy was taller and more slender, but she hunched her shoulders; her long blond hair looked greasy and snarled. Both of them seemed as downcast as if they'd just received bad report cards.

I shook my head, feeling for them. Mom was too busy to notice their appearance. But what about Irene—Rina, to them? Wasn't it her job to see that these kids were properly groomed and clothed? The entire Cushman household seemed to be on a downslide, with Lindy and Betsy its innocent victims.

Quickly I moved away from the tree and went to greet Betsy. "Hi," I said. "Remember me—your mom's friend Sharon?"

The girl's face brightened and she turned to her sister. "Lindy, remember I told you, the other day . . ."

Lindy, however, was her mother's daughter. She stopped and looked me up and down critically. "You came to see Mom on Thursday. She yelled at Betsy because we wanted to make popcorn, and later that night she threw a fit."

"I guess you're pretty tired of that, huh?"

"You bet we are. So is Dad. She's driving him crazy, and us crazy, and we're afraid if it keeps up Rina will quit—" She broke off, scanning the street. "Where *is* Rina?"

"Over there, behind the bus." I started shepherding them that way. "What do you think is wrong with your mom?"

Lindy shrugged. "She's going nuts. It happens. My friend Judy's mother went bananas and cut her wrists and there was blood all over the bathroom before they could break down the door. Gross."

I thought of my own childhood; at the time it had seemed I had innumerable crosses to bear. My father had been a Chief Petty Officer in the Navy, and at sea a good deal of the time; Ma had had to hold the family together pretty much on her own. We'd never had enough money for the things each of us thought he or she needed. The house had seemed far too small for all seven of us, and I'd spent my teens praying for peace and quiet. But nobody had ever cut her wrists in the bathroom; nobody had gone bananas.

I said gently, "Well, I'm sure it won't come to that with your mom."

"You don't know that," Betsy said. We were at the curb now. I was surprised to feel her hand slip into mine preparatory to crossing the street. "Mom's getting worse all the time," she added. "She threw a real bad fit Saturday night."

"Who told you that?"

"Nobody's got to tell us." Lindy's voice was bitter and years older than the eleven or twelve I judged her to be. "We can *hear* when they leave a window open."

"What exactly did you hear?" I slowed my pace, giving her time to talk before we got to the car.

"The usual stuff. Mom was screaming at Dad about him having an affair." At my swift glance, she added, "Yeah, we know all about affairs. He said he wasn't. She screamed some more and said he was behaving like a fool, that he was going to ruin everything. She said he wouldn't have done what he did for *her*. Then she threatened to tell where . . . then there was glass breaking. When she really gets going she throws stuff."

It fit with what Vicky had told me—that the argument had been merely another episode in the soap opera of their marriage—and yet in a way it didn't. This affair must be more important than most of Gerry's, for Vicky to claim he was going to "ruin everything." Important, or perhaps too close to home. . . .

"Lindy," I said, "exactly what did she threaten?"

The girls exchanged conspiratorial glances. *We promised each other not to tell.*

"Was she going to tell somebody where Rina is?" I asked.

Lindy nodded.

"Who?"

"I don't know. She just said she would tell."

"Is Rina the one your mother thinks your dad is having an affair with?"

Lindy abruptly looked away. Betsy nodded, her eyes suddenly brimming. "Rina *wouldn't*," she said.

Not Daddy wouldn't—Rina. These kids were growing up fast.

We were only a couple of yards from the car now. I said, "Of course she wouldn't. Your mom's just—"

"Nuts," Lindy said flatly.

I had no answer for that. As we approached the BMW, I saw there was a child's seat in the rear, a small head sticking up from it. "You guys jump in the back with Susan, okay?" I said. "I want to sit with Rina."

They both nodded and ran ahead to the car. As Lindy climbed in the back door, I slipped into the front passenger's seat.

Irene had been turning to greet the girls, but she jerked her head toward me. Her face went very pale.

"Hi, Rina," I said. "The girls are kind of down today. Maybe we could take a drive and get them some ice cream."

Irene bit her lower lip and glanced over her shoulder. Betsy was chattering and cooing at Susan, but Lindy sat very still, watching us. "Sure," she said after a moment. "That's a good idea."

Slowly she put her hand on the key and turned it. She then placed both hands on the wheel, checked the side-view mirror before pulling away from the curb. Her motions were like those of a person who is just learning to drive and has to consult a mental checklist before each step.

I said in a low voice, "Sorry—I don't mean any harm to you, but we have to talk. Let's just act normal, for the kids' sake."

She looked quickly at me, then back at the street. I sensed a small degree of relaxation within her. "How was your day, girls?" she asked. Her voice trembled only slightly.

"Awful," Betsy said. "The lace of my gym shoe broke, and I got called on twice in math when I hadn't done the problem, and the lunch sucked—"

"Betsy."

"Lunch was Tuna Surprise, and that *sucks*."

Irene's mouth twitched and she looked over at me. I smiled too. That seemed to reassure her, because when she spoke again, her voice was level. "No more of that, Betsy."

"Mom says it all the time. 'UC Med Center sucks. Those fucking chain-store capitalists suck.'"

"Betsy! Do you want to be dropped off at home before we go for ice cream?"

"No ma'am!"

"Then no more of those words."

Betsy lapsed into silence. I looked back at Lindy and saw she was determinedly staring out the window.

I said, "So where should we go?"

Irene concentrated on her driving. "You choose."

"How about the park?"

"Fine—but where?"

"The Murphy Windmill?" I waited to see how she would react to the mention of the place Bob Choteau was hiding.

She merely looked puzzled. "Is that the one they've restored? The gardens are nice, but I don't think we can get ice cream there." The response seemed genuine—and that puzzled *me*.

"What about Stowe Lake?" I said. "We could get ice cream cones at the snack bar and rent the girls a paddle-wheel boat. It would keep them occupied while we talk."

She smiled faintly. "You seem to know how to handle kids."

"I ought to. My older brother has two, and between them my younger sisters have nine."

Irene looked over her shoulder at the toddler in the car seat. "Well, I only have the one, and she means everything to me. I'd kill before I'd let anyone harm her." Her suddenly grim face matched her words; they were intended to be a warning to me.

NINETEEN

Close to an hour later Irene, Susan, and I arrived at the Chinese Pavilion on Stowe Lake. We'd rented the girls a paddleboat and told them to go around the lake until we could see them from the pavilion; then we'd start back to meet them at the landing.

The pavilion is a small pagoda-style building that sits on the large island in the middle of the lake. It is accessible only by a couple of pedestrian bridges and pine needle–carpeted footpaths that wind around on the shore below the steep incline to Strawberry Hill Reservoir. Its bright red pillars and gilt and green roof festooned with mythical beasts present a sharp contrast to the wild underbrush, palms, and cypress that surround it. Beyond it stretch the mirror-smooth waters of the lake; seagulls and other aquatic fowl glide there, and snapping turtles take the sun on half-submerged logs.

Irene led the way across the bridge and along the path to a multitiered waterfall that channels the reservoir's overflow into the lake. There I took hold of the front bumper of Susan's stroller and helped carry it across the rugged stones at the falls' base. Around the curve was the pavilion. Again we lifted the stroller—up the white concrete steps—and seated ourselves on mushroom-shaped stools at the round green marble table directly under the pagoda's peak.

It was chilly here, the hill blocking the late afternoon sun. Irene pulled her sweater tighter, shivering. When she first spoke, the roar of the nearby falls distorted her words. I leaned closer.

"I suppose you want to talk about Rudy," she repeated.

"Rudy, and Bob Choteau. You and Susan and the Cushmans." I paused. "Frank Wilkonson and Harlan Johnstone."

Her face went pale, as it had when I'd gotten into the car. "You *do* know quite a bit," she said after a moment. "Vicky warned me that you have a reputation as a rather . . . determined investigator. That was why we thought it best that you have contact only with Rudy." A sheen of tears appeared in her huge blue eyes. "And look what happened to him," she added softly.

"You think he was killed because he knew your whereabouts?"

"Yes."

"By whom? Frank Wilkonson?"

She shrugged and looked down at Susan.

"Why don't you tell me all of it," I said. "From the beginning."

She compressed her lips and placed her hands on the table. It had a brass plaque inlaid: a commemoration in both Chinese characters and English of the gift of the pavilion to San Francisco from her sister city of Taipei. Irene's forefinger moved to it and she rubbed it over the signature of the mayor of Taipei before speaking. "All right. I guess I can't hide any of it anymore. You know I was married to Harlan Johnstone?"

"Yes. I got that part of the story from Walt Griscom, the tavern owner down in Tres Pinos."

"Well. You certainly do get around. Walt is a nice man. I'm sure he didn't say anything . . . unfair. But I guess he told you Harlan and I weren't very happy after the first couple of years. Harlan is . . . a very domineering man, a jealous man. When I began to make friends in the area and participate in community activities, he became insecure and eventually demanded I give everything up and stay close to the ranch. In order to have something to do, I worked in the office. That was where I got to know Frank."

"You had an affair with him."

". . . Yes."

"Is Susan his daughter?"

She was silent, her eyes fixed on the plaque. Finally she avoided the topic entirely, saying, "After I became pregnant, I couldn't stay on the ranch. Harlan would have known the child couldn't be his—he'd had a vasectomy years before, because his wife was in poor health and couldn't risk any more children. I couldn't bear to have an abortion; I'd always wanted a child, and this might have been my last chance. After all, I was thirty-five—the old biological clock, you know. Even under the circumstances, the pregnancy seemed like a reprieve from a lifetime of disappointment."

"What about Frank? Did you tell him you were pregnant?"

"No." She was breathing faster now, and shallowly, still not looking at me. "He'd been unhappy in his marriage for years; he would have wanted to divorce Jane and marry me. But there were their six kids to consider." Finally she glanced up; I must have looked skeptical because she added, "I know. I should have thought about those kids before I started with Frank. I genuinely cared for them; I cared a great deal for Jane. But in these things, we're not always rational."

"I know. Go on."

"Even if it hadn't been for his family, I wouldn't have wanted to marry Frank. He's the controlling type, just like Harlan, and he has a violent temper. It's ironic that I would have become involved with the same sort of man as my husband—but that's what we women tend to do, isn't it?"

"Sometimes."

"Well it's what I've always done. At any rate, I was deter-mined to break out of that pattern, and pregnant or not, I would have had to get off that ranch eventually. I couldn't breathe or grow there. I just wanted to be myself. So I left without telling anyone I was going, went to a women's shelter in Tustin, Orange County. And I had my baby."

"Do you think Frank's looking for you just because he wants you back, or does he know about Susan?"

"Oh, he knows. You see, Jane realized I was pregnant. I'd been exhibiting signs, and she's had too many children of her own not to recognize them. She thought the baby was Harlan's—she didn't suspect about Frank's and my affair—and she innocently mentioned it to Frank. That was the day before I left there. He came to the ranchhouse demanding to see me. I claimed to be sick and had Hal, my husband's son, send him away. But from the things he said to Hal, I knew what he had in mind. That's why I left in such a hurry."

"How long did you stay in Orange County?"

"Close to a year."

"Frank looked for you down there, did you know that?"

"No. How did you find that out?"

"It's too complicated to go into now. I suppose he realized where you were because the divorce papers came from there."

She was clearly agitated now. I looked away to give her time to compose herself. There was a heap of debris over against the pagoda's curving wall—beer cans and a wine bottle—and it made me think of Bob Choteau. We'd get to that in a few minutes, I told myself.

Irene said, "That would have been because of the divorce papers, yes. But him finding out I was living up here—that was entirely my fault. Once I read an article on how a person can disappear successfully. The main point it stressed was that you had to completely cut your ties with your past life—friends, associates, everything. But I violated that rule by sending Jane Wilkonson a birthday card about six weeks ago. I didn't put a return address on it, but I guess the postmark gave away the general area."

"For God's sake, why did you do that?"

"It was stupid; I realize that now. But I cared about Jane, and I knew she would have been worried about me. I put a note in the card—just said I was okay, that I'd had a baby girl named Susan. I told her I had a good job and was keeping my hand in at my old profession, horticulture. It never occurred to me that she'd show the card to Frank, or that he'd come looking for me."

I studied her, not believing that for an instant. But her expression was guileless; possibly she believed it herself. Irene struck me as one of those odd—although not uncommon—types of person who possess a strong mercenary streak, coupled with an incongruous capacity for compassion and affection. In order to reconcile the two, they often lay claim to far nobler motives than a given situation would indicate. My suspicion was that she had sent the card because she wanted Frank to know about their daughter—perhaps even wanted him to come after them. Another possibility—which was nasty enough that I didn't care to dwell on it—was that she had wanted to needle him about the fact he had a child he'd never get to see.

I said, "You violated that rule another time, too—by contacting Rudy Goldring."

"I know. I was unhappy down south; I'm a northern Californian by birth, and everything seemed so fast paced and . . . *alien*. So I thought of Rudy and got in touch. He got me the job with the Cushmans."

"How did you find out Frank was making a habit of coming to the city on weekends?"

"From a friend who works at a little nursery in the Inner Sunset. Frank stopped in there one Sunday and asked about me. His manner made her nervous, so she put him off, said she thought one of the other clerks might know me and asked where she could reach him. He gave her a local phone number. She passed it along to me. And that's how I found out about the motel on Lombard Street."

"So you asked Gerry Cushman to find out more."

"Yes, Gerry talked with the desk clerk and found out about Frank's patterns during those stays. I had to know what he was doing, how close he was getting. I was afraid of that temper of his, and I wanted someone to assess his mood, so I asked Rudy to hire an investigator. I couldn't have Gerry or Vicky do it— it would have been too direct a link to where I was living."

It amazed me, how people fell in line to do Irene's bidding. Annoyed me, too, how she got by not on her own initiative and abilities but by using others.

She must have sensed my reaction because she looked down at her hands again. I realized she was crying when a tear fell onto her whitened knuckles. "I'll never forgive myself for involving Rudy," she said. "He told me to come over late on Monday afternoon. He said he'd have your report by then, and we could decide where to go from there. But when I got to his flat . . ."

I suppose I should have felt sorry for her, but I remembered Rudy Goldring's discomfort at the lies he'd been forced to tell when he hired me. And the picture of the old man lying on his kitchen floor in his own blood was too clear. I said, "Do you want my report now?"

She looked up again, her cheeks wet, expression hurt and reproachful.

I didn't wait for an answer. "Frank had asked about you at more than that one nursery. He'd misinterpreted your note to Jane and assumed you meant that the job was in the field of horticulture." I gave her a capsule summary of what I'd observed that Sunday.

When I finished, she shook her head. "How on earth did he ever imagine he'd find me that way? I've never gone to that plant sale or to the flower mart. Half of those nurseries I've never even heard of. And the conservatory—it used to be a place I visited every time I came up to the city, but I haven't been there since I moved in with the Cushmans."

"Perhaps he just assumed he'd work at it until he got a lead. That's the nature of detective work, you know: a lot of boring legwork for very small results."

"I guess that's why he finally tried to force the information out of Rudy."

"You think he killed Rudy?"

"Yes."

That assumption interested me. "How could he have connected the two of you?"

"I've been thinking about that, and the only thing I've come up with is my letters. I left the Burning Oak in such a hurry that I couldn't take my mementos with me or destroy them. There were letters, birthday and Christmas cards from Rudy in a trunk in the attic of the ranchhouse."

"How could Frank have gotten his hands on them?"

"If he wanted to, he'd have found a way. He must have gone to Rudy's flat on that Monday and tried to make him tell where I was. Frank has such a violent temper—"

"Irene, Frank didn't kill Rudy."

"What?"

"He was at work on the ranch at the time Rudy died."

"Then who . . . ?"

"I don't know."

"Oh God, this makes it even worse—"

A childish voice shouted our names. I looked toward the lake and saw Lindy and Betsy waving from their red and white paddleboat.

"We'd better start back," Irene said.

I remained seated, wanting to talk more, to ask her about Gerry Cushman and the affair Vicky thought they were having. But she suddenly seemed eager to be out of my company, and I didn't want to destroy what fragile rapport we had. Irene could be useful to me—but only if she thought I was on her side.

I stood and helped her carry the stroller down the steps of

the pavilion. As we started along the path toward the waterfall, I said, "Maybe Bob Choteau *did* kill Rudy."

"I don't think so."

"Me either. Irene, do you know where Bob is hiding?"

"No. The paper said he might be in the park, but that was days ago."

"Well, he *is* here, and someone's been taking him food— someone from your household, I think."

She stopped at the edge of the stone blocks below the waterfall and faced me. "Why do you think that?"

I explained about the shopping bag full of provisions, omitting where I'd seen it. When I finished, Irene put her right sleeve to her forehead and swiped at it; whether the moisture there had blown from the falls or was nervous perspiration, I couldn't tell.

I said, "I need you to help me find out who took the bag of food to Bob—"

"I can barely help myself."

"You'll *be* helping yourself—and Susan."

She looked down at the stroller. The little girl had gone to sleep, her head lolling over onto one shoulder. "All right," she said.

"I'm pretty sure it was Vicky," I told her, "but I need to know for certain."

Irene shivered and glanced upward, where a bridge crossed the lower tier of the falls. For a moment the fear in her eyes made me think someone was there; I looked in that direction myself but saw no one. What she was experiencing, I supposed, was that free-floating, indefinable dread that comes over people when they feel menace but can't identify it.

"Will you do it?" I asked.

"Yes. I have to. Otherwise I won't be able to sleep another night inside those walls."

TWENTY

I spent the evening at home, waiting to hear from either Irene or Rae. Neither called.

Jack Stuart phoned around eight. I filled him in on what I'd been doing, and he said I should give the information to the police. I explained about Gallagher's tunnel vision, but he still thought I was making a mistake. I told him I'd assume responsibility for it. I wanted to give myself twenty-four hours more; by then I was sure I'd have something solid enough to force even as a single-minded a cop as Gallagher into changing his tack.

At nine-thirty I phoned Jane Wilkonson. No, she said, Frank hadn't returned or contacted her. She sounded badly on edge, even angry, and clearly in no shape to carry on a conversation. In the background I could hear a child screaming. I told her I'd be in touch the next day. Then I took a long hot shower and went to bed.

I was in the office at eight-thirty the next morning, hoping Irene might have gotten mixed up and left a message for me there rather than calling my home number. There was nothing from her, but a slip that someone had placed in the middle of my desk said Rae had called at eight and would be home until ten. I dialed her number quickly. Her "Hello" sounded strained.

"How's Doug?" I asked.

"Not so good. I guess you suspect what really happened. Ted does, and he's such a blabbermouth."

"I have a pretty good idea. Why did he do it?"

"Who knows? He claims it was an accident, that he couldn't sleep because he was worrying over whether to take the terminal M.A., and just took too many sleeping pills. But you don't take that many pills by mistake."

"How are you doing?"

"Not so good either. You know the worst thing?" She lowered her voice, in spite of Doug still being in the hospital where he couldn't hear her. "I can't feel sorry for him. All I can feel is mad, that he'd do such a thing to himself and to me. Isn't that awful?"

"No. It's perfectly natural."

There was a long silence. Then Rae said, "Look, Sharon, I don't think that I can go on working for you."

"Why not?"

"I think my job is part of Doug's problem. If I give it my all, I can't pay him enough attention. Look what he did as soon as I started taking on more responsibility."

For Rae's sake I didn't voice my opinion of Doug's tactics.

She added, "What if next time he succeeds?"

I took my time before I spoke, choosing my words carefully. "A lot of suicide attempts are simply cries for attention. You know that from your psychology courses. I'm not saying you should take what Doug did lightly—any self-destructive act, no matter what the reason behind it, has to be viewed seriously. But I do think you shouldn't be making any decisions about the job until you know more about his mental state. Have they finished evaluating him yet?"

"I'm supposed to talk with the shrinks this afternoon."

"Well, wait and see what they say. They'll probably recommend some sort of therapy program, maybe even one you can participate in. That could make a great deal of difference in what you decide."

"But in the meantime I'm letting you down—"

"Don't worry about me. I handled all the investigative work here for years before you came along. I'll survive for a while longer." As I said it, I nervously eyed the stack of folders on my desk, knowing there were more, plus a dozen or so documents to be filed, downstairs in Rae's IN box.

"Thanks."

"No problem. Just don't make any snap decisions."

The morning progressed slowly as I worked on reports and correspondence. I kept glancing at my watch, wondering why Irene hadn't called. Every time the button on my phone flashed, I hoped it would be her. But all the calls were routine, most of them easily disposed of. When Hank buzzed me shortly after eleven, I advised him of Rae's situation and asked if he could get one of the junior partners to help out with delivering or filing documents. He said he would or, if necessary, take care of it himself. Then he said wistfully, "I suppose because of this you're too busy to have lunch with me."

I hesitated, looking at my remaining paperwork.

"Seems we never get to talk anymore," he added.

I pushed back my chair and swiveled around so I couldn't see the desk. "I'm not too busy. But let's get out of here—I've been spending too much time in this damned place lately."

My reckless decision had left me in a holiday mood, and Hank seemed to share it. We decided to make an occasion of lunch by driving out into the Avenues to one of our favorite Italian restaurants, the Gold Mirror. Once there, we ordered the eggplant parmigiana and a carafe of red wine. After discussing Rae's dilemma for a while but coming to no helpful conclusions, Hank segued into a description of a divorce case he'd just handled. It involved a provision for cat support; a dispute over a hundred-dollar picnic basket listed as a major asset; and a harrowing battle over which party would take— rather than get—custody of the couple's teenaged son, who was into what he called "heavy-metal science fiction" and claimed to be building a "nuclear death device" in the garage.

The story would have been howlingly funny in the old days, but the way Hank told it was tinged with melancholy. He became more animated as he talked, but he drank more than he ate, and I managed to snag a good portion of his eggplant. When they cleared our plates, he suggested we have more wine, rather than coffee. I said okay, sensing that he might be getting ready to discuss what was really bothering him. We adjourned to the bar, where he told two more divorce stories, which weren't nearly as funny. I realized he was skating around the issue, getting closer, but unwilling to address it.

I was sure that part of his reluctance stemmed from my own close friendship with Anne-Marie. Another part came from the fact he'd always viewed me as a sort of substitute little sister, to be chided and guided but never leaned upon. What I said now could tip the balance of our future relationship.

So, craven coward that I am, I said nothing. After two more glasses of wine, we drove back to All Souls in my MG, Hank clutching the edge of the seat and looking around warily, the way he always does when I'm the one at the wheel.

When we stepped into the front hall, Ted said, "Oh, wait a minute—she just came in," and held out the receiver of his phone to me.

Hank said, "Tough luck," and wandered down the hall toward his office. I'd been complaining all the way back about how I really should have gone to the bathroom at the restaurant; I didn't need this delay.

I took the receiver from Ted and said, "Sharon McCone."

"Sharon, Walt Griscom. From the tavern—"

"Of course, Walt. How are you?"

"I've just heard some news over the police band. It made me think of you, so I dug out your card. Frank Wilkonson's dead."

That sobered me up fast—and made me forget my bathroom problems too. I sat down on the edge of Ted's desk. "How? Where?"

"Couple of hikers came across his body this morning, near the San Luis Reservoir. He'd been shot in the head. Looks like a dump job."

"Where is the reservoir?"

"State recreation area forty-some miles northeast of here."

"Any idea how long he's been dead?"

"No, that's all I've got now. Apparently he'd been missing a couple of days."

"What about the weapon?"

"You mean was there one at the scene? No. But from what I heard over the radio, I'd say it was a small caliber, probably a .22."

The homeowner's gun of choice. Also favored for plinking and varmint shooting on ranches. "And that's all you've heard?"

"So far. You planning to come down here?"

"It doesn't seem worth the trip. I've got no official status. You, on the other hand . . ."

"Ms. McCone, I'm retired."

◢

"Mr. Griscom, I bet you have plenty of friends in the sheriff's department. And it's obvious that you like to keep your hand in at your former profession."

"Yeah. I'll see what I can find out. Will you be at this number?"

I thought of where I'd last seen Frank Wilkonson. "No. Will you be at the tavern?"

"Up until closing."

"Then I'll call you there."

The western perimeter of Golden Gate Park was relatively unpopulated at four o'clock that afternoon, in spite of the continuing clear weather. A few wayward tourists stopped to gaze at the Murphy Windmill, but they didn't venture too close. They wouldn't have noticed me anyway, tucked into the hidey hole I'd occupied a couple of days before, during those hours that are neither properly Saturday night nor Sunday morning.

I was suitably attired now, in dark clothing that blended in with the discarded lumber and rusty corrugated iron. I'd brought sandwiches and fruit and a thermos of strong coffee. After a while I began to regret the wine Hank and I had drunk at midday; I was dehydrated and had a mild hangover.

Disgraceful behavior, McCone, I scolded myself. This is the age of sensibility and moderation. What's wrong with you?

Sensibility and moderation are boring, my rebellious inner voice replied. I'll take wine and eggplant parmigiana over Calistoga water and health food any day.

Time passed slowly. The shadows in the surrounding thicket deepened; the checkerboard pattern of missing shingles on the windmill changed with the shifting light. The whine of traffic on the Great Highway stepped up as rush hour got underway. At about half past five a skinny man with shaggy reddish hair and tattered clothing came along the path from the west. He paused to look around, then skirted the mill on the far side, out of my line of sight. A few seconds later I heard the windmill's door grate open and closed.

I poured coffee into the thermos's plastic cup and sipped it as I waited. I wasn't sure exactly what I was waiting for, but I felt a growing expectancy, a sense that something was about to happen.

Darkness was falling quickly now. Birds began homing to the

open windows of the mill. The temperature dropped, grew chill; the air seemed more moist and smelled strongly of the sea.

The grate of the windmill's door alerted me. I set my coffee down and leaned forward, peering through the dusk. A shaft of flickering light briefly extended over the concrete entryway; before it was blocked by the closing door, I saw two figures emerge. They came up the declivity toward my hiding place. I drew back as they passed the debris pile.

It was the man I'd seen earlier and an older, heavier man with white hair. They carried burlap sacks, like the scavengers who picked through the trash bins behind my former apartment building. I waited until I was sure they were gone, then poked my head out of the hiding place and studied the mill.

When I'd inspected it the other day there had been evidence of three people living there. The flickering light I'd seen indicated one was still inside—very possibly the one I wanted to see. At any rate, it was a number I could handle.

I reached into my bag for my .38. Then I crawled through the opening in the debris and slid down the slope to the windmill's entryway.

TWENTY-ONE

The windowless interior of the mill was illuminated only by the candle in the red glass globe. Its light reflected bloodily off the eight angled walls; a gust of wind swirled through the door behind me and set the rays to shivering over the rough stone surface.

I left the door open—an avenue for quick escape—and stood with my back to it, gun ready. Another chill blast flung the door against the wall and spiraled upward through the hole where the stairway had once been. The sound of the door hitting the wall was shattering; as the echoes died, I heard the cries of birds that had been nesting on the upper floors, and their wings flapping as they flew out the windows.

At first I thought no one else was in the mill. Then a startled interrogative grunt came from the rear of the room, beyond where the candle sat on the floor.

I peered over there, narrowing my eyes. The halo of light showed the recumbent figure of a man on one of the nests of blankets. He struggled to a sitting position. It was Bob Choteau.

"Unh?" he said again. It was both a question and a protest.

I took a couple of steps forward, my gun extended in front of me in both hands. Choteau's beard and hair were wildly unkempt; his eyes had a vague, glassy look—the eyes of a man who was either very drunk or stoned.

It took him several seconds to focus on me, several more to react.

"Unh!" This time it was a growl. He flailed about and got up in a crouch.

I raised the gun higher. "Take it easy, Bob," I said. "I'm not here to arrest you."

He remained as he was for a moment, then dropped back to the floor.

"Do you remember me, Bob?" I asked. "I came to Rudy Goldring's a couple of weeks ago. You let me in the door."

He shook his head as if to clear it and put a hand to his eyes.

"Are you all right?"

After a moment he said, "Just drunk. Red had some gin left over from . . . he had some gin. Thought I didn't know about it, but I got into it while he was out. Not used to gin." He took his hand away from his eyes. They were still glazed, but worried now. His brows drew together. "Red's gonna *kill* me, he finds out I drank it all."

"Red's the fellow who just left with the white-haired man?"

"Were they here? Guess so. Red's my friend, knew him back when I was . . . long time ago. Helped me hide from the cops, let me move in here. And I stole his gin. How low can you get?"

Choteau drew his knees up against his chest, wrapped his arms around them, and began to rock back and forth. I couldn't tell if he was frightened of Red or ashamed of his own treacherousness or just wallowing in self-pity. I said, "Tell you what—I'll give you some money to replace Red's gin."

"Why'd you want to do that?"

"You have some information I need. I'll give you ten dollars to answer my questions."

"About what?"

"Let's start with this: A man came here late Saturday night, around one o'clock on Sunday morning, actually. What happened to him?"

Choteau motioned for me to come closer. I moved into the circle of light made by the candle, but stopped well out of his reach, the gun still trained on him. He looked me over for a moment, his eyes clearer now, and recognition began to seep into them.

"You're the private dick," he said. "Captain hired you to follow Rina's boyfriend."

"How do you know about that?"

"Wasn't a lot went on there I *didn't* know. Made it my

business to listen in on things. Man's got to protect his interests."

"Did Mr. Goldring know you were aware of what went on?"

"Hell no. The captain was a good man, but people like me weren't real to him. I mean, he cared I got enough to eat, he was free with the beer. Let me sleep in the shed off the garage when I wanted to. But he didn't see me as a person. You know what I mean?"

I thought he was wrong about that; Rudy Goldring had thought him enough of a person to leave him five thousand dollars. But I merely nodded.

"Still," Choteau went on, "a damned good man. Sure as hell knocked me for a loop when I saw him lying there dead."

I lowered the gun and sat down on a wooden crate so I could talk with him on eye level. I wasn't particularly worried about him trying to overpower me now. Besides being drunk and off his guard, Bob was looking forward to getting his ten dollars. "Tell me about that day. Why'd you go up to the flat?"

"Door was open. I'd been off the stoop for a while, so I thought the captain might've gone up for just a few minutes. When he didn't come back down, I rang the bell. No answer. So I went up . . . see if he was okay."

Or to see what you could steal, I thought. "Go on."

"He was there in his own blood. I got out fast. Sort of thing the cops love to pin on people like me. Afterwards I realized I'd dropped my pouch. Guess that's why they're looking for me."

"What time was this?"

"One o'clock? Don't recall exactly. I'd been back of the restaurant around the corner, see if they'd thrown out anything good. So it might've been later—they don't quit serving till two."

"Were you there all morning?"

"Only till about ten. Captain came out of the offices and started upstairs. I complained I was out of beer, he gave me some money, told me to go to the liquor store."

As Choteau had said, Rudy Goldring had been free with the beer. Rudy had told me it was harmless enough, and I suspected that in the back of his mind he also thought it wiser to keep Bob happy and somewhat sedated. But to hand him money and send him off to the liquor store as soon as he complained . . . "Did you get the feeling he was trying to get rid of you?"

Choteau hesitated. "Well, he came up with the dough pretty quick, even for him."

"When did you get back?"

"Not till later, after I checked out the restaurant."

"Okay, let's go back to that afternoon. Where did you go after you saw Mr. Goldring was dead and left the flat?"

"Over to the Haight. Knew I had to get out of that neighborhood, and I'd heard Red was living here in the park. Hung around down on Stanyan and connected with him after a couple of hours. He brought me here."

"And you've been here ever since?"

His eyes shifted away from mine. "Sure."

"What about early Sunday morning when the man came?"

"What man?"

"A tall fellow. Slim. Limp brown hair. Wears western-style clothes."

"Never saw anybody like that around here. Wasn't nobody here but Red and the old man and me."

"The three of you weren't here, either—at least not after the man arrived. Did you take him someplace else?"

"Look, lady, I don't know about no man. At one in the morning I was probably asleep."

"You weren't that morning. I came inside, and the windmill was empty."

"You came . . . that was you went through our stuff!"

"Yes. Where were you?"

"A lot of nerve, going through our stuff that way."

"Don't change the subject. What happened to the man?" .

"I said I don't know no man!"

I decided to let it go for now. "You get out of here a lot?"

"Not much. Like I said, where would I go?"

"Out foraging, maybe. Over to the Haight—"

"Lady, cops are looking for me. I been thinking I ought to get clear out of town, maybe catch a freight up to Oroville, maybe Portland. But winter's coming on. What I'd like to do is put a little money together—"

"Is that what you were hoping to do when you tried to get in touch with Irene Lasser?"

"How'd you— No, why would I do that?"

"When I went through this place, I found the sack of food she brought you."

"*He* brought it."

"Who?"

Silence.

"*Who?*"

"Man she works for. I never even saw Rina."

"Why did he bring it?"

"How the hell should I know? Probably Rina asked him to."

"Start at the beginning. You went up to The Castles . . ."

"That what they call that place? Well, yeah, I went there couple of days after the captain bought it. Knew where Rina lived, guess I thought she might help me."

"Only you saw Gerry Cushman instead."

"Yeah, him. I was trying to sneak in there. Didn't want to see anybody but Rina. Set off the alarm going over the wall. Son of a bitch came at me with a gun. Honest to Christ, I thought he was gonna shoot me. But then his wife—what's her name?"

"Vicky."

"Yeah, Vicky comes running outside and yells for him to stop. She knows me, see. She'd been to the captain's with Rina."

"What happened then?"

"They took me inside and we talked. They said I couldn't see Rina, she was still too upset. But he gave me some money, told me he'd bring food later."

"He brought it here?"

"No, I was afraid it was a trick to turn me over to the cops. I mean, why bring food when he could just've given me cash? So I met him over near the Beach Chalet on the Great Highway."

"And then?"

Again his eyes moved away from mine. "That's it."

"You didn't go back and try to see Rina? Try to get money from her, too?"

"No! Why the hell would I? He promised me plenty—"

I waited.

Choteau tugged at one earlobe and shifted position, squirming around on the filthy nest.

I said, "Promised you plenty of money to do what?"

"You got it wrong. He promised me plenty of food. Said Rina didn't want me to go hungry—"

"You just said you only *thought* Rina wanted him to bring you the food."

"No, I *know* she did. Getting me confused. And you haven't given me my ten bucks yet."

"I'll give you twenty if you'll tell me the rest of it—and what happened to the man who came here."

"There isn't any more! There wasn't any man!"

"Twenty dollars, Bob."

He stopped, raised his head and listened.

"What is it?"

"I think Red and the old man are coming back. They might get violent, they find you here."

I didn't hear anything, and I wasn't sure whether to believe him. But his cohorts might indeed become violent—or he might incite them to it. In any case, I doubted I'd get anything out of him, given his present resistance. I got to my feet and moved toward the door.

"Hey, what about my ten bucks?"

"You'll get it when you tell me the rest of it."

"You said twenty—"

"Twenty. Twenty or nothing." I fumbled in my bag, pulled out one of my cards, and dropped it on the floor. "Call me at that number when you're ready to talk."

Choteau gave a wounded howl. I went out the door.

TWENTY-TWO

I drove slowly through the darkened byways of the park, thinking about Bob Choteau and Gerry Cushman. Some of what Choteau had told me had been lies and evasions, but one thing rang absolutely true: It was strange that Gerry had brought him the bag of food when he could simply have paid him to go away and leave the residents of The Castles alone.

It meant Gerry thought he had a use for the derelict—which was further confirmed by Bob's slip about Gerry promising him "plenty" of money.

For what, though? Something to do with Irene? If so, I was reasonably sure she had no complicity in it; her innocent reaction to my mention of the windmill had been genuine. Gerry had not told Irene where Choteau was hiding, if he knew himself—might not even have revealed that Bob had tried to see her.

One explanation for Gerry's actions might lie in what the Cushman girls had inadvertently—or maybe not so inadvertently—told me: Vicky thought Gerry was having an affair with Irene. The girls had said Rina wouldn't do such a thing, but children, even prematurely worldly children like Betsy and Lindy, don't like to believe anything negative about the people they love. And it was clear they did love Rina, possibly more than the mother who was swiftly becoming a candidate for the psychiatric hospital.

I thought back to Lindy's description of the quarrel her

parents had had Saturday night. Vicky had told Gerry he was going to "ruin everything," had said he wouldn't have done what he had for *her*. Ruin what? Their marriage? Their lives and those of the children? And what was it he'd done? Taken the bag of food to Bob Choteau, rather than turn him over to the police? That seemed minor in the scheme of things. Besides, Gerry had done that earlier in the week, probably Wednesday or Thursday. Vicky wouldn't have waited until Saturday to air her displeasure. What else had Gerry done? . . .

Saturday night was when Frank Wilkonson had gone to the windmill and disappeared. I was certain Choteau knew something about that; his evasion of my questions had been too obvious. And now Wilkonson had been found shot to death.

I gripped the steering wheel harder as I turned right out of the park onto Stanyan, where the Panhandle begins. It was nearly dark now and the perimeter of the park bordering the Haight was deserted. The streets were well populated, however, but not with the scruffy types I remembered from ten or even fifteen years ago. These people were relatively well dressed, many of them in business attire, and the warmly lighted establishments they homed in on were chic restaurants and shops. When I looked at my watch, I was surprised to find it was not quite seven.

I parked on Stanyan and dodged traffic as I ran across the street to a print shop owned by my friends Daphne and Charlie. I have a long-standing arrangement with them that I can drop in and use their phone in exchange for steering All Souls' clients' business their way. The shop was noisy and busy even at this hour; a collator clattered, copiers whirred and clunked, phones rang, and somebody—Charlie? Yes, Charlie— was swearing mightily behind a broken-down offset press. I hurried past the commotion to the rear, where Daphne was clearing her desk in her usual serene manner. She waved in greeting and moved calmly through the storm to the door— going home to their Clayton Street flat, where she would probably whip up something fantastic in the kitchen to soothe Charlie when he returned later, all ink stained, sweaty, and irate.

I sat down at the other desk, looked up the Cushmans' number, and dialed. A childish voice answered. I said, "Lindy?"

"Yes."

"Hi, it's Sharon. Is Rina there?"

There was a long pause. "Oh, that's great, Megan. Listen, can I call you back? From my own phone?"

"Sure."

". . . Oh, you're not at home? Okay, give me the number."

I repeated the number of the print shop and hung up, mystified. It was a full five minutes before the phone rang. I snatched the receiver up.

"Sharon?" Lindy said. "I'm sorry it took so long. I had to make an excuse to Dad and get over here to my room. I just hope he doesn't pick up the extension."

"Are you okay?"

"Sort of."

"What's going on?"

"Oh . . ." Her voice broke. "Oh, everything's terrible, and . . . I don't know. Something awful must have happened this afternoon, because Rina didn't pick us up at school, and she never forgets. Finally we caught the Muni home, and Mom was hysterical and Dad was furious, and Rina . . . she's gone. *Gone*."

The hollowness and misery in her voice made me ache for her. "Do you mean gone for good? Did she take Susan with her?"

"She took Susan. I don't know if it's for good or what. Dad won't talk about it, and Mom's in their bedroom screaming again. Dad fixed us dinner and now he's watching TV with Betsy and acting like nothing's wrong. Daddy scares me, Sharon. He really makes me afraid."

I noted that she'd slipped into a little-girl vernacular—not at all the sophisticated, semicynical talk of the kid I'd met outside of the Abbott School. She added, "He's different tonight. It's like . . . he just watches the TV and smiles this funny little smile. It's all so . . . oh . . ."

"Lindy—"

She began to cry. "Will you come and get us out of here? Please take Betsy and me away from here?"

"Lindy! Stop crying!"

Her sobs cut off abruptly. Then she snuffled.

The poor kid, I thought. She's seen so much in her short life, and she's probably had to fend for both herself and her little sister. It's made her capable of turning off her emotions like tap water.

I said more gently, "Lindy, I'm not angry at you for crying. I just want you to calm down, because something needs to be done. I want to talk with your dad."

"No! If he finds out I lied about Megan calling—"

"It'll be all right. Please do this for me. Go back to the other castle and ask him to pick up the extension."

There was a long silence. "Can you help us?"

I didn't know, but for her sake I lied. "Yes, I can help. I promise."

"Don't hang up." There was a scuffling noise, and then dead air for about two minutes.

While I waited, I thought some more about Gerry: his acting as if nothing was wrong while his wife screamed in her bedroom; his refusal to explain about Irene and Susan's absence; his "funny little smile." Something was drastically wrong at The Castles, but I didn't think Gerry would hurt his children. If anything, he'd go to great lengths to spare them whatever further horrors awaited. On the other hand, if I went there, he might do something to hurt me. By the time his voice came on the line, I'd decided what course of action to follow.

He said, "Hello. Is this Sharon McCone?"

"Yes."

"Lindy didn't know your last name."

"Well, we weren't formally introduced. Gerry, I need to talk with you."

"Come on up. We'll have a drink."

"No, I don't think that's a good idea." I wanted to meet him on neutral—and safer—ground. I told him I was at the print shop on Stanyan Street and gave him the address. "Can you meet me here?"

"I can't leave the girls. Our nanny is away, and Vicky's—"

"I know." Out of the corner of my eye I saw Charlie emerge from behind the offset press—ink stained and sweaty and irate, as I had expected. "Bring the girls with you. My friend here is about to go home, and he'll take charge of them for a while." Charlie and Daphne always have room for one or two more at their flat—be it adult or child. Betsy and Lindy would be safe there until this matter was resolved.

"I don't know if I should leave Vicky alone."

"Gerry, take a good look at your daughters. Those kids *need* to get out of there. I need to talk with you. And as near as I can tell, you're not doing Vicky any good by staying at home."

In the silence that followed, I was afraid I'd angered him. But the appeal on the basis of the girls' well-being seemed to have worked. He said, "I'll be there. Give us fifteen or twenty minutes."

After I'd explained to Charlie about the Cushman girls— saying that their mother was in bad emotional shape, but omitting the fact that their father might be involved in two murders—I went back to the phone and called Walt Griscom at his tavern in Tres Pinos. Against a background of revelry, Walt told me what he'd been able to find out from his contacts at the San Benito County Sheriff's Department.

"Like I suspected, the gun was a twenty-two. That doesn't do much to narrow the range of suspects. Every ranch in the area and half of the households have at least one on hand."

And, I thought, so would a great many of the households in San Francisco, where Wilkonson had disappeared. "How long had he been dead?"

"Nothing official on that yet—they don't get autopsies performed any faster down here than in San Jose or San Francisco. But the man I talked to is a long-time veteran of the department. He says at least forty-eight hours before the body was discovered, maybe more."

That would make the probable time of death Sunday morning—or even Saturday night. "I take it he wasn't killed where he was found?"

"Nope. Lividity indicates he'd lain on his right side for quite some time. He was found lying on his face."

"That area around the reservoir is pretty much deserted?"

"This time of year it is."

"So he could have been dumped either at night or during the day?"

"Yeah."

"But it's not a place that only area residents would know about?"

"Hell, no. Anybody with a map or a Triple-A guide could find it easily enough."

Like the caliber of the gun, the place where Wilkonson's body had been dumped didn't help to narrow the range of suspects. "How's Jane Wilkonson taking it?"

"She's bearing up. Woman's got guts, she'll weather this

one. Let's just hope Frank was well insured. Six kids is a lot of mouths to feed."

"I'm sure Harlan Johnstone will see they're provided for."

"Don't count on it. Old Harlan was pretty bitter about Irene running off like that."

"Well, it's not Jane or the kids' fault that she and Frank— Wait a minute, you didn't tell me Harlan had heard the rumors about his wife and Wilkonson. In fact, you said they weren't true."

"That's because I didn't believe they were."

"But now you do."

"I don't know. Wilkonson's been murdered, though; maybe there is something to them."

"How did Harlan hear the rumors? Surely no one would have talked to him—"

"Young Hal told him, after the divorce papers came through. Told him he ought to forget about Irene and why. Harlan went after Frank. They had a pretty violent confrontation. Hal managed to keep them from killing each other, and that's when Harlan started to drink so heavy and Hal took over the hands-on management of the ranch."

"I wish you'd told me this earlier."

"So do I. But I didn't think it was relevant, and I didn't want to make the Johnstones—Harlan, Hal, or Irene—look bad."

I thought back to the chronology of the story he'd told me, readjusting for this new information. "Stupid of Hal to have brought it all into the open at that late date, wasn't it?"

"Not so stupid—the boy's running the ranch now, isn't he?"

"Yes, he is." I'd have to think a bit more about Hal Johnstone.

Walt didn't have anything more to tell me, so I hung up and called All Souls. To my surprise, Anne-Marie answered. After business hours phone duty falls to whoever is standing closest to one of the red push-button instruments that are—for some long-forgotten reason that probably was terribly significant at the time of their installation—an All Souls tradition. Usually Ted, who lives in a rather rococo cubbyhole on the second floor, beats the others to the phone from force of habit. Anne-Marie had been there so seldom in the evenings since she and Hank married that hearing her voice disoriented me.

I said, "I tried to call you on Sunday, but your machine hung up on me."

"It has that habit." She sounded dull and lifeless. "Was it anything important?"

In the old days she wouldn't have asked such a question. "I just wanted to chat. You sound tired. What're you doing there so late?"

"Trying to round up my wandering husband. We're supposed to go to a cocktail party, a fund-raiser for"—she named a liberal state senator—"and I was supposed to pick Hank up here. But he seems to have flown the co-op."

I laughed, glad that not everything had changed. "Flown the co-op" was a pun Anne-Marie and I had invented, part of that special shared vocabulary that exists between good friends. But this fund-raiser! . . .

Hank, in spite of a growing fondness for designer suits and first editions of obscure "cult" writers, has managed to survive this decade with his leftist ideals relatively intact. (Although he likes to think of them as slightly to that side of Mao Zedong, while everyone else claims they're more compatible with the philosophy of FDR.) The candidate Anne-Marie had just mentioned was one Hank considered a cop-out artist—and not a very good one at that.

I suggested, "Try the Remedy."

"That's what Ted said." She sounded particularly dispirited now. "He's been spending a lot of time there lately, hasn't he?"

"A fair amount."

"He never used to drink this much."

"No." I had half a mind to tell her about our drunken lunch, but now wasn't the time. She needed to extricate Hank from the clutches of the Remedy, and I needed to check for any messages. "Look," I said, "let's talk soon."

"Why, has Hank said something to you about me?"

"No. You're my friend, and I'm worried about you."

When she spoke, she sounded slightly chastened. "We'll talk soon. I promise."

"Good." In order not to further delay her, I asked for Ted.

Ted is the world's perfect secretary—so long as you can put up with his eccentricities. He is thoroughly immersed in his job, willing to work long hours for very little pay. He is blessed with a set of hyperactive ears and a nose that can smell gossip at seven leagues. If sworn to secrecy, however, Ted will defend the pact to the death. I, for one, have often found his talents highly useful.

Tonight he read me my message slips without complaint— even though I'd interrupted his dinner. There were five: from three clients, Rae, and my mother. (I knew I should have called Ma on Sunday; when she starts phoning the office, she's worried and I'm in deep trouble.) Bob Choteau hadn't called.

Talking with Bob—if and when he decided he wanted his twenty dollars—could be vital. I said to Ted, "Are you going to be there all evening?"

"As far as I know." Which meant until something interesting turned up.

"As long as you are, would you make sure to answer the phone?"

"Are you expecting an important call?"

"Yes. I really need to get the message if this Bob Choteau calls. And look, if he does, and you decide to go out before you hear from me, would you leave the message at this number?" I gave him Daphne and Charlie's.

It upset me that Bob hadn't called by now. Possibly he had gotten more drunk or stoned and had forgotten all about my visit to the mill. But when I set the receiver back in the cradle and looked toward the front of the print shop, I saw a far better lead walk in with his daughters.

TWENTY-THREE

After Charlie had left with the girls, Gerry and I walked over to a coffee shop on Haight called The Beanery. Three days of uninterrupted good weather had finally brought the fog in. It gusted out of the park and down the street, making pedestrians pull their outerwear closer around them and head for home.

Gerry had on the same baggy houndstooth jacket he'd worn Sunday. He hunched inside it, hands deep in its pockets, head thrust forward as if he were hunting for change on the sidewalk. I had the idea that tonight the oversized jacket was less a fashion statement than a shell within which he could hide from the emotional storms around him. There was no way of telling what he was feeling or thinking inside there; his defeated posture was sharply at variance with the little smile that continually played on his lips.

The air inside The Beanery was warm and steamy, its aroma an odd mixture of various types of coffee, in which no single one dominated. I studied the chalkboard that listed the day's offerings. To me, coffee is coffee—sometimes good, often bad, usually indifferent. This array of roasts and blends and what I supposed could be called nationalities confused me. It was a moment before I settled on Kenya Peaberry—simply because I liked the name. Gerry ordered a New Orleans blend that the clerk warned was exceptionally heavy in chicory. That seemed to please him; possibly he found the choice of something bitter as apt as I did.

We took our mugs to a table in the window bay that overlooked the sidewalk. I removed my old suede jacket and hung it over the back of the chair, but Gerry kept his jacket on, not even bothering to unbutton it. He sipped his coffee and made a face. I tasted mine: it was odd, slightly acidic, yet smooth and winey. I wasn't sure whether I liked it or not.

"How's Vicky doing?" I asked.

The folds of the jacket rippled in what I interpreted as a shrug. "By the time we left, she'd barricaded herself in the bathroom. There's a phone in there, so it probably means she was getting ready to call her shrink."

"She's in therapy, then?"

"If you can call it that. She's been seeing this woman for eight years. There's been no visible progress. I think she lies to her. I know she doesn't tell her the whole truth."

"How do you know that?"

"Vicky tells me about the sessions—in every excruciating detail. Here's one example: Originally she started seeing the shrink because our relationship wasn't all she wanted it to be, but she didn't want to divorce me, either. She sat in the woman's office for two solid years talking about everything else under the sun before she got around to admitting what the real problem was."

"Is that so unusual?" I asked, thinking of Hank talking around and around his own problem.

"I don't know. Maybe not. I don't believe in therapy, myself."

I didn't either—at least not for myself. The idea of baring my soul to a total stranger was both distasteful and unnerving. "I'd probably lie, too," I said. "Therapists seem so . . . well wrapped that I'd be afraid mine was sitting in judgment of me. I'd want to make myself look better than I really am."

"Yeah, I guess that's Vicky's problem. It's ironic, though; she wants to look good for someone she's paying to listen to her problems, but she can't be bothered to put up a good front for her own kids. They're going to have great memories of their mother when they grow up: stoned or drunk, screaming or throwing things. I'm not saying I haven't contributed to Vicky's problems. God knows I've got problems of my own. But I've tried not to inflict them on the kids."

"A lot of people have worse memories of their childhoods

than Lindy or Betsy will. They're good kids, they'll survive, and probably be all the stronger for it."

"Yeah, well, they won't have to live with it much longer." The incongruous little smile flickered across his lips. "I'm filing for divorce and asking for custody. My lawyer says I have a damned good chance, given Vicky's mental state."

It didn't surprise me. "Is this what precipitated her fit tonight?"

"That and other things."

"Such as Irene Lasser leaving?"

He sighed. "I was wondering when you'd put aside your phony concern for Vicky and get down to business. Irene told me you'd tracked her down and forced her to talk to you."

My anger flared. I took a deliberate sip of coffee to allow myself time to get my emotions under control. "In the first place, Gerry, my concern for Vicky isn't 'phony.' I don't like to see anyone in the state she's in. And while I realize it would take a psychiatrist to help her in any significant way, I'm available if she needs to talk or just to have someone hold her hand. Secondly, I didn't exactly 'force' Irene to talk to me. By the time we finished, she seemed damned glad we'd talked."

"That isn't what she told me."

"I suspect she was just saying what she did to stay on your good side. She was quite nervous because someone in your household had taken food to Bob Choteau. Did you admit you were the one who'd done it?"

"Yes. And Irene understands I did it to protect her."

"To protect her from Choteau?"

"Of course."

"If you really wanted to do that, why didn't you just pay him to go away?"

Gerry looked down into his cooling coffee. Beads of sweat were breaking out on his forehead—whether from wearing the heavy jacket in such a warm place or from stress, I couldn't tell.

"Gerry," I said, "are you having an affair with Irene?"

No answer.

"Vicky thinks so. The girls suspect it, though they won't even admit it to themselves."

He looked up, the strange smile flickering. In stark contrast to it, his eyes were black and mirthless, their pupils dilated so much that I thought of the black holes in the universe that astronomers talk about.

"I'm going to marry Irene," he said. "As soon as my divorce from Vicky is final, I'll take my girls and go away with Irene and Susan."

He didn't look like a man who was contemplating future happiness. Unease stirred in me. I said, "Did you tell Vicky that?"

"Yes. This afternoon."

"Is that why Irene left?"

"No."

"Why, then? Did it have to do with Frank Wilkonson's murder?"

He didn't appear surprised I knew about it. "In a way. She received a phone call from her former stepson around noon. I don't know how he knew where she was, but he did. He told her Wilkonson was dead."

Now Gerry began speaking quickly in a peculiar singsong rhythm. My unease blossomed into full anxiety, and I gripped my coffee mug with suddenly cold fingers.

"She came to my studio," he went on. "I was working at home, as I always do in the initial stages of a project. I thought she was there to remind me to eat lunch. I often forget to eat when I'm working well. She told me about the call and said she was afraid. First Rudy and then Frank—murdered. She said she knew who must have done it, and that she couldn't stay at the house anymore. I told her I would take her away. We'd pick up the girls at school and go someplace safe. She wouldn't let me do that, and she wouldn't tell me where she planned to go. She just packed up and called a cab and went. I don't know where she is now. But I'll find her. And we'll be married. Just like I planned."

"Was this before or after you told Vicky you were filing for divorce?"

"Before. About an hour after Irene left, Vicky came back from one of her damned meetings. I told her she'd have to pick up the girls herself, and she started ranting. She went on and on about how busy she was with all her *important* causes. About how tired she was because she was trying to *set things right*. About how *good* she'd been to Irene. About how *much* she'd done for her and Susan. About how *rotten* it was of Irene to leave without giving any notice. Then she started in about Irene and me. She was really laying into Irene. I couldn't listen to that kind of talk. So . . . I told her." His voice cracked and he looked down again.

I felt slightly breathless, as if my emotions had been running to keep pace with his. To give us both time to pull ourselves together, I said, "Do you want some more coffee?"

He cleared his throat. "Yeah. Get me some decaf French roast or something, would you? I can't drink this shit."

When I came back with two fresh mugs, Gerry was staring out the window at the fog. I set them down. He didn't look at me, just picked up the coffee, drank, and watched the drifting grayness.

I said, "Gerry, what kind of cab did Irene leave in?"

"What? Oh, Checker. She always used them when Vicky's car wasn't available. The number's posted on the bulletin board next to the phone in our kitchen. Why?"

"I may be able to trace her. What time did she call?"

He glanced hopefully at me. "It was about quarter to one. I know because I looked at my watch, to see how long it would be before Vicky was due to come home. Vicky hates Irene, but she likes having someone to deal with the girls, and I thought she might be able to persuade her to stay."

The idea of Gerry using his wife to persuade his mistress to stay didn't set well with me. I said, "You know, Gerry, this isn't the first time Irene's had an affair with a married man."

Anger flickered deep in his eyes. "You mean Frank Wilkonson."

"Yes. Did you ever think it might be a pattern with her—"

"Now you sound just like Vicky. That's the first thing she brought up when she accused me of being involved with Irene. I know all about Wilkonson. That was different. Different from what we have. So was my marriage. I love Irene in a way I never loved Vicky, never loved any woman. I'd do anything for her."

That brought me to the real reason I'd wanted to talk with him. "Such as?"

"I don't follow you."

"Vicky says you did something for Irene that you would never have done for her. Something that could ruin everything. What was that?"

He put his hands to his forehead and swiped at the beads of sweat. "When did she say that?"

It was possible he didn't remember; he probably tuned out a

great deal of his wife's ranting. "Saturday night—to you."
When he didn't react, I played a wild card. "Sometime after
Frank Wilkonson disappeared near the Murphy Windmill."

His pupils dilated even more. I thought of the black holes
again, and how their gravitational pull supposedly is so great
that nothing escapes them. Then I realized I'd moved back
from the table, away from the pull of Gerry's stare.

He licked his lips and seemed to fumble for words. When he
spoke, the dryness of his mouth made his voice thin and reedy.
"Wilkonson never came to the windmill," he said.

"Yes, he did. He left his car on the drive and walked toward
the mill. That's the last I saw of him."

"*You* saw him?"

"Yes, Gerry, I was there. I followed him all the way from the
ranch to San Francisco. He disappeared in the park. As far as I
know, no one ever saw him again—except his killer."

Gerry shook his head. He raised his mug, but his hand was
trembling so much that the coffee spilled down onto the sleeve
of his jacket. He had to use both hands to lower the mug to the
table.

"Jesus," he said. "Jesus, am I in trouble."

There was only one reason for him to feel he was in trouble.
I said, "Did you call him and ask him to come to the windmill?"

"No! I . . . no, I didn't."

"You had Bob Choteau call him, then. That's why Bob
expects you to give him more money. That was why you didn't
just buy Bob off in the first place. You planned to use him."

No response. Gerry merely stared at me.

"I suppose Choteau told Wilkonson he had information
about Irene's whereabouts. That would be certain to lure him to
the mill. Did you hire Bob to kill him, too?"

"No! It wasn't like that!" Gerry realized he was shouting now
and looked around before leaning across the table and speaking
softly, rapidly. "Look, Choteau *did* call Wilkonson. Promised to
take him to Irene if he'd come to the mill. Instead, I went to
meet him."

"Why the windmill? And why didn't you just call Wilkonson
yourself, rather than have Choteau do it?"

"I suppose it was stupid to have him make the call, but it was
in the back of my mind that if I heard Wilkonson's voice,
confronted the reality of the man, I might not go through with
it. As for the mill, it would be dark and deserted—I'd bribed

Choteau and his pals to stay away by buying them booze. Wilkonson wouldn't be able to see me all that well, and there would be no clues as to Irene's whereabouts."

"Did you plan to kill him?"

"Christ! What do you think I am? I was going to give him some information that would make him leave us alone, that's all. And if that didn't work, I was prepared to pay him. I just wanted him to *go away*, so we could be happy."

His voice had slipped into the singsong cadence again, underscored by raw emotion. "You can understand that, can't you? All we wanted was to be happy. Is it so goddamned bad to want to be happy?"

It is, I thought, if you destroy other people's lives in order to achieve happiness. I said, "Tell me what happened with Wilkonson."

"Nothing."

"Come on, Gerry. You went to the trouble of luring him there—"

"He never showed. I waited inside the mill for two hours, but he never came."

"That can't be. I saw him walk across the road from his car. It wasn't more than ten minutes, fifteen at the outside, before I went inside the mill. He wasn't there—and neither were you."

"I tell you, I waited two hours! I waited until ten, and then I gave up and went home."

"Ten? He arrived there after one in the morning."

"Why would he have done that? The appointment was for eight. What happened was, Choteau reached him around four. Wilkonson said he had to go back to the ranch offices for a while, but he'd leave early, in time to get there by eight. I wouldn't have thought he'd have wanted to be late; he thought he was going to be taken to Irene."

"He was late, though. I don't know what delayed him, but I guess he got there as soon as he could. Whoever killed him must have known about your meeting—and I doubt it was Bob Choteau."

Gerry became very still. He didn't even seem to breathe. "Who else knew you were meeting Wilkonson, Gerry?"

"Vicky," he said quickly. Too quickly.

"Who else?"

He shook his head, horror seeping into his eyes.

"Who else?"

". . . Irene. But she didn't know where, only that I was going to talk with him."

"She could have followed you."

He was silent.

It was coming together, I thought. All of it.

"Well," I said, "that solved her problem of Wilkonson trying to claim his daughter, didn't it?"

Gerry shook his head in denial. Then his mouth twisted bitterly. "If he'd been on time, if I'd been able to talk with him, there would have been no more problem."

"Oh yes—what was the information you intended to pass on?"

"The key fact that would have put a stop to it all: Wilkonson wasn't Susan's father."

TWENTY-FOUR

For a moment I didn't believe him. "Who is her father, then?"

"I can't tell you. But it wasn't Wilkonson. He *thought* he was the one who had gotten Irene pregnant, and until he started hunting for her and Susan, it seemed better just to let him believe it."

"Better than what?"

"The truth."

"And that is . . . ?"

"Not mine to tell. I've already said that."

"Look, Gerry, this is no time to keep confidences. We're dealing with two murders here, and as you also said before, you're in a lot of trouble."

He pushed back his chair and headed for the door.

"Come back here!" I stood up and started after him. The sleeve of my sweater somehow got hooked on one of the uprights of the ladderback chair at the next table. I wrenched at it, and the chair tipped over, blocking my path. By the time I'd shoved it out of the way and gotten to the door, Gerry had vanished.

"Great," I said aloud. "Just great." I went back to the table, snatched up my bag and jacket, and stood there thinking.

Given what I'd just found out, it was probably time to turn this over to Ben Gallagher. Acting in cooperation with the San Benito County authorities, he could pick up Gerry for questioning and put out an APB on Irene Lasser. But I felt so damned close to the solution that I resented not being in at the finish. Besides, what had Gallagher done in the Goldring investigation except routinely search the park for Bob Choteau? He'd been so absorbed in his pat theory that he hadn't even *noticed* I was on to something. There was no guarantee he would listen to me any more now than he had before.

No, I decided, I'd see this one through, at least until tomorrow morning. And if I did turn over the information about where Frank Wilkonson had gone shortly before his death, it would be to the San Benito County Sheriff's Department.

I left The Beanery and hurried back to Stanyan Street. The print shop stayed open until nine; I could use its phone again. Once seated at Daphne's desk, I dug out the M–Z volume of the Yellow Pages and turned to taxicabs. I was about to dial Checker when I reconsidered and looked up its address; it was on Eighth Street, not too far from the Hall of Justice. I'd get better results, I reasoned, if I made my inquiry in person.

Next I called Daphne and Charlie's flat. She answered and said the girls were still there, amusing themselves on the home computer. I told her she might be stuck with them for quite a while; Gerry hadn't bothered to ask their address, and anyway, he hadn't looked as if he were thinking about resuming the responsibilities of fatherhood when he'd stormed out of the coffee shop. Daphne said that was fine, the girls could always sleep on the couch, and if Gerry did show up, she'd handle him gently.

I pressed the disconnect button and redialed. Ted answered the phone at All Souls. No, he said, there was no message from Bob Choteau. The only one was from Rae. She'd said it was urgent—

"I can't deal with that now. If she calls again, tell her you haven't heard from me."

"She sounded upset—"

"Ted, I'm working a case. Rae's problem will have to wait."

"Okay, if that's the way you want it, I'll say you haven't checked in." He sounded disapproving.

I handled it the same way I've been handling my mother's plaints about my unmarried state all these years—by ignoring it, but not without guilt. Then I set off for the Checker Cab Company.

* * *

The dispatcher in the office inside the cavernous, echoing garage was busy. It took her forty-five minutes to search the trip logs for the cab that had picked up Irene Lasser, and its destination. The only reason she did it at all was that she was one of those people who are fascinated by private investigators. She kept mumbling about some TV crime show with the word *hire* in its title. Since I don't watch much TV—except for the news and old movies—I didn't know what she was talking about. But I nodded and commented vaguely and smiled and worked at concealing my impatience. At close to ten she finally located the correct notation in one of the afternoon logs.

The cab had picked up two fares at The Castles and traveled to Rudy Goldring's building on the block-long alley called Stillman Street.

It surprised me, but I didn't think it strange that Irene would go there again. She and Rudy had been good friends; it was likely that she had a key to his flat. And the flat would make an ideal place to hide: it was in a commercial area where few people would see her coming and going, and no one save for Mrs. Halvorsen—the skeleton staff of Goldring Clothiers—would even suspect she was there.

One thing bothered me, though. Had I been in Irene's circumstances, I was not sure I would have taken my small daughter to stay in the place where a close friend had been murdered. I especially would not have wanted to spend a night there after I'd had the traumatic experience of discovering his body.

Irene had more nerve than I'd previously suspected. Or maybe she hadn't really been such a good friend to Rudy.

Either way, in a short time I'd find out what was going on. Stillman Street was close by.

The short street was deserted now. Most of the vehicles that crowded its curbs by day were gone. The old warehouses and factories were monolithic, their blank facades broken only by high many-paned windows that glinted blackly in the light from the street lamps. The fog hung thick and motionless; it seemed to mute the sounds from the surrounding streets and the hum of traffic on the elevated freeway.

I stopped the MG across from Goldring's Victorian and stared at the upper windows. The bay of the front room was heavily draped, but a telltale strip of light outlined it.

Stupid of Irene, I thought. If she doesn't want anyone to know the flat is occupied, why doesn't she stay in back, in the bedroom or kitchen?

Then I remembered the kitchen, and Rudy's body sprawled in front of the stove. Of course she would keep as far from that room as possible.

I remained in the car, considering my options. Ringing the bell would produce no results, except to panic Irene. She wouldn't answer the door, and she might flee again—this time to Lord knew where. I couldn't loid the lock; it looked to be a dead bolt. The offices downstairs would be similarly secure. Break a window? Too much noise.

Then I remembered Bob Choteau saying that "the captain" had let him sleep in the shed off the garage. That meant the shed had been left unlocked for him. Would anyone have thought to lock it up after Rudy died? If not, there might be some way to enter the building from there.

I studied the house some more. The garage was under the two-story window bay; a narrow cement path ran alongside it. It was dark back there, so I reached behind my seat for the good-sized flashlight I keep there. Of course it had rolled forward and was wedged tight; finally I had to get out of the car and move the seat to get at it.

Flashlight in hand, I hurried across the alley to the pathway.

The shed was about six feet back from the sidewalk—a small structure with a sharply pitched roof that leaned against the main building. There was a padlock on its door, but when I touched it I realized it was merely positioned to look closed. It broke apart easily; I removed it and tugged at the hasp. The door opened, scraping on the concrete.

Quickly I turned the flash on and stepped inside, closing the door behind me.

It was a cozier space than the one Bob Choteau currently occupied: about four by six, cleanly swept, empty except for some wood planks stacked against the wall that adjoined the house. There were a few shelves holding the usual array of dribbly-sided paint cans, rusted tools, glass jars full of screws and nails, and ends of rolls of wallpaper. There was no door leading into the garage. Or was there? . . .

The lumber looked carefully stacked. Too carefully, consid-ering the disorder of the shelves. I went over and shined the flash around it. There was a door, all right; the lumber had been arranged to conceal it.

I set the flash on the end of a shelf and went to work moving the lumber, all the while reflecting that it was the simple contrivance of a man who had been more trusting and naive than he ought to have been. The type of lock on the door confirmed my impression; it took me only a minute to force it.

Inside the door was the garage. A handsome old Buick—the kind with portholes—stood there. Beyond it were an ancient washer and dryer, and then stairs leading to the first floor. The door at their top opened into the gray-carpeted hallway of the offices. I paused outside the door, listening for sounds of occupancy. The place held that humming silence that tells you no one is there.

I had an idea that there might be another stairway at the rear, where service porches have been added on to many Victorians, so I moved along the hall to the area where Rudy had said he did his fittings. When I pushed open the door at the very end, there was a sudden flare of light and motion.

Adrenaline pumped through me. I flattened myself against the wall and took out my gun.

Nothing further happened.

After a moment I pushed the door further open and shone the flash inside.

Its beam glared off the silvered glass panes of a mirrored room. The motion I'd seen had been my own, reflected back at me. I stepped inside and swung the light around. There were mirrors on three walls, so the customer could view his body from all angles. The fourth wall contained a wet bar flanked by comfortable chairs. As I crossed to a door next to the bar, I caught sight of my own rueful smile.

Beyond the door was an enclosed service porch crammed with cardboard cartons; the stenciling on them said they contained mailing boxes. There was a stairway to the second story, but the cartons blocked access to it. I shoved at one of the stacks and found it too heavy to move. Finally I set the gun and flash down and began moving them one at a time.

Before I started up the stairs I turned off the flashlight and jammed it into my bag. The gun I continued to carry. I groped slowly upward, splinters from the wooden railing pricking at my fingers. The stairway stopped at a landing and then switched back on itself; when I rounded the turn, I could see a rectangle of light spilling over the upper porch.

I crept to the top of the stairs and looked around. The light came from the kitchen window, which overlooked the porch. I remained where I was, listening. At first I didn't hear anything, but then there were voices, growing louder, as if people were coming along the hall to the kitchen.

One voice sounded like Irene's. The other was a man's and seemed familiar, but I couldn't place it. Nor could I yet make out what they were saying.

The porch was crowded with stacks of bundled newspapers, pop bottles and wine jugs, bags and boxes full of aluminum cans. Obviously Rudy had been a recycler. I crouched lower and moved among the clutter toward the window, avoiding the patch of light.

The voices were clearer now—not the words, but their tones. Irene's was high-pitched, seesawing up and down. The man's was deep, made ragged by anger. I crept directly under the window and leaned up against the wall.

The man's words became distinguishable first—but his voice was muffled enough so that I couldn't quite place it. ". . . none of this would have happened if you hadn't sent that card to Jane. Wilkonson wouldn't have gotten all stirred up about the kid he'd never seen—"

She interrupted him, but the words were muted.

"Don't give me that! You knew she'd show it to him. It's almost as if you *wanted* all this to happen. And now if you're right about who killed Wilkonson—"

More garbled syllables.

"No, we're not going back to the living room. I want you to face up to what your selfishness has caused. Take a look, Irene—that's where your friend Goldring died. Take a good look at the chalk marks and the bloodstains."

She must have turned toward the window then, because her voice came louder. "I told you I couldn't stand to come back here!"

"Poor sensitive Irene can't stand to come into the room where Rudy died. Couldn't bear to bring her precious baby girl to the place where a murder was committed, so she foisted her off on friends."

That surprised me. Gerry Cushman might have lied about Irene taking Susan with her, but I didn't think so. He had no reason to, and besides, the cab company's log showed that two fares had been picked up at The Castles and dropped at this address, with no intermediate stops. If the second fare hadn't been the child, who was it? And where was Susan?

The man added, "You're always such a victim. And you'll never take responsibility for anything, will you?"

"*Me* take responsibility? If it wasn't for you—"

Irene's words broke off in a scream of pain.

My hand tensed on the gun.

Silence. Then I heard her sob.

"Go ahead, cry."

I wished I could place that voice!

"I don't see the point of this," her tear-clogged voice said. "We should be doing something."

"What?"

No reply.

He said, "It's all coming unraveled now. If you just hadn't sent that card. If Wilkonson hadn't started running around like a crazy man. Even then you could have defused it, or I could have—if only Goldring would have told me how to contact you."

Irene said, "You tried to get Rudy to tell you where I was? How did you even know about him?"

The man didn't reply; he must have realized the slip he'd made. I did. Perhaps Irene did, too.

She said, "Never mind—I think I can guess. You had no right. . . . *When* did you go to him?"

"A long time ago." Now his reply was too quick.

"I don't believe that. You were the one who came to see him last week. How else would you have known where he died?"

"*You* were the one who said you couldn't stand to come into the kitchen. Besides, there are the chalk marks—"

"No, I said I couldn't stand to go into the *back rooms* of the flat. I didn't say anything about the kitchen."

Another silence. Then, "Well, whatever happened, it's all your fault. Everything, damn you."

She screamed again. I'd once heard a dog scream like that—when it was hit by a truck. But this deliberate torture of a human being was even more terrible.

I looked at the door to the kitchen; it was secured by a dead bolt. The window was closed, probably locked.

There was a thump, and Irene began to cry hysterically.

I stood up and thumbed the safety off the .38. Snatched one of the heavy wine jugs with my left hand. Backed off a step and swung at the window. The lower pane shattered. I dropped the jug and aimed the gun two-handed through the opening.

"Freeze!" I yelled.

I couldn't see Irene. The man had his back to me but was pivoting.

"Freeze!" I yelled again.

He completed his turn, then dodged to one side. In the millisecond before I fired, I recognized him.

Hal Johnstone.

TWENTY-FIVE

My shot missed Johnstone. He lunged for the window. I stepped back, fired again. The bullet tore into the frame. Johnstone leaned across the sill, karate-chopped at my hands.

Pain shot through my wrists. I dropped the gun. As he jumped down onto the porch, I scrambled away.

The gun wasn't in sight. I darted behind a stack of newspapers. Shoved it at him.

It hit him across the thighs; he stumbled. He was panting, and blood trickled down from a cut on his right cheek. I backed toward the stairway, tipping over a bag of cans and sending them rolling. I still couldn't see my gun.

Johnstone righted himself and shoved the newspapers aside. I whirled. My shoulder bag caught on the newel post; I wrenched its strap off my arm and kept going.

Johnstone was close behind me. His hands slammed into my back. I pitched down the stairway.

I raised my hands to break my fall; they met with nothing but air. My knees hit the bottom step, and I fell forward and my head smashed into the wall of the landing.

The stairs shook under Johnstone's weight. He hurtled over me. There was more pounding and shaking, a crash from below.

Then I was aware of nothing but the twin waves of pain—one from my legs, the other from my skull. My vision blurred and I doubled up, trying to clutch at my head and my knees at

184

the same time. The waves met at my midsection; bile rose to my throat. I cradled myself about my middle, forcing the nausea down.

Other footsteps—tentative ones—came down the stairs.

I said, "Unnh?"

Irene bent over me, her hair straggling down from its coiled braid. She said, "Are you okay?"

I let go of my midsection. The pain was diminishing—but not nearly fast enough. I tried to sit up, fell back against the floor.

Irene grabbed my arm and got me into a slump against the wall. There was a searing in my back.

When I could speak, I said, "Where's Johnstone?"

She squatted down next to me. "By the time I got to the top of the stairs, he was gone. Then I heard the front door to the offices slam, and a few seconds later his car started."

I hadn't noticed it in the street. "Are you sure it was his?"

"Yes, I know the sound of that Porsche."

I let out a sigh that hurt my ribs. "Neither of my shots hit him."

"No."

For a moment I wondered why the shots hadn't attracted any attention; then I realized that at night this neighborhood was given over to the derelicts—and they would have a vested interest in not noticing.

I said, "Did you see what happened?"

"Part of it. He'd pushed me to the floor before you smashed the window."

Then I remembered her screaming. "What did he do to hurt you?"

"Applied pressure on a nerve." Her voice was bitter. "He's skilled at little things like that. He's got a degree in physiology, as well as veterinary science. I've always been amazed at the kind of knowledge he picked up in school."

I recalled my initial negative reaction to Hal Johnstone. My judgment hadn't been so far off after all. "Had he hurt you before like that?"

She dipped her head slightly, looking ashamed. Possibly she believed him when he told her everything was her fault.

"Can you help me upstairs?" I asked.

Slowly Irene got me to my feet. Fingers of pain played over my backbone; my head and knees throbbed; but nothing seemed to be broken. I leaned on her all the way up the stairs and across the porch to the kitchen.

Somewhere inside the flat a child was sobbing. Irene said, "My God, I forgot about Susan!" She left me leaning against the counter by the door and hurried out of the room.

So the child was here after all. Why had she told Hal she'd left her with friends? Was she afraid he'd also hurt Susan?

After a moment I went back out onto the service porch. My purse was still hooked on the newel post at the top of the stairs. The gun turned up under a stepstool to one side. I put the safety on, slipped it into the bag, and went back to the kitchen. On my way over to the table I stepped on Rudy Goldring's chalkmarks. It gave me a chill, as if I were walking on his grave. Then I thought, *Doesn't matter now.*

As I sat down at the table, Irene came back into the kitchen. "Susan's asleep again," she said. "Do you want a drink—some brandy?"

"Please." I watched her as she went to a cupboard and removed a bottle and two glasses. "I thought you told Hal that Susan was with friends."

"With the Cushmans, yes. For obvious reasons, I didn't want him anywhere near her. I gave her a mild sedative and put her to bed in the room next to this one; then I told him I was afraid to come to the rear of the flat because of Rudy dying here. I should have known that would make him want to drag me back here."

As she set the glasses on the table and sat down across from me, I studied her. Although her hands trembled, she seemed remarkably in control now, considering what she'd just been through. I said, "You weren't afraid to come here, after what happened to Rudy?"

"No. After the initial shock of finding him, it hasn't seemed quite real. I've been through something . . . traumatic like this before, and for a long time I kept on as if nothing had happened." Her eyes strayed toward the floor in front of the stove. "Of course, reality eventually sets in."

"Hal as much as admitted killing Rudy, you know."

She nodded. "Apparently he went through the trunk of letters that I left in the attic at the ranch and found I had a close friend here in the city. He must be the one who came here that day. He knew which room Rudy died in. He seemed to know where this place was without me giving him directions. Stillman's really only an alley; it's not someplace you'd know about unless you'd been here before."

"Without *you* giving him directions? Did you ask him to meet you here?"

"Yes."

"Why?"

"When he called to tell me Frank was dead, he said there were things we needed to discuss."

"What things?"

She shook her head, looking down into her glass.

The man was a sadist who had hurt her before. She'd been so afraid to have him near her child that she'd concealed Susan's presence. It made no sense that she would agree to meet him alone, in such a deserted place. Unless what they needed to discuss concerned something—or someone—she feared more than him.

I backed up a little, asking a question that had been bothering me. "Irene, how did Hal know to call you at the Cushmans' this afternoon?"

"I assumed Vicky had told him. She'd threatened to call both Harlan and Frank, you know. But Harlan's . . . ill, and if she called the ranchhouse, she would most likely have reached Hal."

"I see. What he needed to discuss with you must have been pretty urgent, for him to drive all the way up here rather than go into it on the phone."

Silence.

"Dammit, Irene! The man's a murderer! You've no right to protect him."

"It's not Hal I'm protecting."

"Who, then? The person who killed Frank?"

No reply.

I was tired of her games, angry with her silences. I said, "Irene, I spoke with Gerry tonight. He told me Susan wasn't Wilkonson's child."

Slowly she raised her head. "He wouldn't tell you that."

"But he did, and he was planning to tell Frank, too—if Frank had shown up for their meeting at the windmill last Saturday."

"No! He wouldn't have— "

"Mama, I'm scared!"

We both turned toward the doorway. Susan stood there, wearing yellow terry-cloth sleepers, her pale blond hair tousled. She was blinking against the light; when Irene didn't reply immediately, she thrust her thumb into her mouth.

I transposed Irene's facial features on the little girl's. Then transposed Hal Johnstone's. Looked back at Irene.

I said, "That's what all this is really about, isn't it? Hal is Susan's father."

Irene paled and sat very still. Susan's face puckered; she was being ignored. Then she took her thumb out of her mouth and began to cry. The sound brought Irene out of her chair and across the room, where she knelt cuddling the child, as if to shield her from me with her own body. After a moment Susan quieted. Irene lifted her and said, "I'll put her back to bed."

Once again, while she tended to her daughter, I waited, sipping brandy and thinking of all the questions I would need to ask.

When Irene returned—a good ten minutes later—she had freshened her makeup and repinned her unruly braid. There was a stiffness to her carriage; her eyes glittered as if they were covered by a thin skin of ice. She sat, folded her hands on the table, and looked steadily at me.

Apparently in her absence she'd reordered her emotions as well as groomed her person. I sensed now that the truth was out, there would be no more outbursts or evasions. It would make it easier for both of us, but I couldn't help wondering what would happen when she finally gave full vent to her feelings.

I said, "I was right, wasn't I? Hal *is* Susan's father."

"Yes."

"Who knows?"

"Only he and I. And now, Gerry."

"Is he trying to reclaim his daughter?"

"God no! Hal hates children. Hates me, too—he's detested me since he first set eyes on me, at Harlan's and my wedding."

"If he hates you, why did he have an affair with you?"

She was silent.

I tried another tack. "Why did he hate you at first sight?"

"It has very little to do with me, personally. Hal wants the Burning Oak. But under community property, it would have come to me. Initially he gave up on the ranch, stayed back east, tried to make a life for himself there. But I guess he changed his mind, because from the day he moved back here, he did everything he could to drive me away. Then, when I admitted I was pregnant and that the child was his, he made me leave there and promise never to let Harlan know."

"I still don't understand why the two of you would sleep together—"

She interrupted me, going on with her story as if it were a speech she'd memorized. "Since Frank started looking for me, most of Hal's energy has been directed toward worrying that somehow it would all come out. If Harlan suspected Hal had fathered my child, he'd write him out of his will."

"Why would he suspect? He must know how the two of you feel about one another."

She shrugged. "I didn't say Hal's fears were rational."

I thought of how Hal had told his father about Irene's affair with Frank Wilkonson. A bit of self-serving misdirection there. "What about Rudy?" I asked. "Did he think Susan was Frank's?"

"Yes."

"And Vicky?"

"Her, too."

I hesitated, still wondering why she had slept with Hal, then asked something else that was bothering me. "Are you sure Susan is Hal's daughter? She resembles him, but you *were* having an affair with Frank at the time she was conceived."

"I'm sure. I wasn't seeing Frank anymore then. Or anyone else. I broke off with Frank a few months after Hal returned to the ranch. Hal suspected what was going on, and I knew as soon as he had proof, he'd go to Harlan with it. Besides, Jane had had her baby by then and was suffering a bad case of postpartum depression; she needed Frank more than I did."

I was still skeptical of her motivations toward Jane Wilkonson, but that wasn't the central issue now. "Go on."

"Then I got pregnant by Hal."

This further refusal to elaborate on what seemed to be highly inconsistent behavior made me snap at her. "Could you be more specific? You've already said he hated you. Obviously there was no love lost on your side, either."

She was silent, her fingers so tightly interlocked that the tips of their nails were white.

"Irene?"

"Yes. I'm just trying to think of a way to say it."

"It's best just to get it out quickly."

"Yes, all right." She took a deep breath, expelled it. "Hal raped me," she said.

The tone in which she delivered the words was so flat that at first I thought I had heard wrong. Then I saw her eyes: the ice had melted, tears welled to the surface.

I touched her hands. She unclasped them and pulled away. Beneath the tears, I saw a flicker of fear.

She's afraid I don't believe her, I thought.

It's common for rape victims to be disbelieved; in fact, it's the only crime I know of where the burden of proof is placed squarely on the victim's shoulders. Irene didn't have to prove a thing to me, though. Unless they're severely disturbed, women stand to gain nothing and lose everything by falsely accusing men of rape—no matter what the she's-framing-him or she-asked-for-it schools of thought claim. Certainly making the agonizing admission to me had cost Irene dearly.

I said, "Tell me what happened."

Some of the fear left her eyes and she wiped the tears from their corners. Then she resumed speaking—calmly and matter-of-factly, as if we were discussing the weather.

"As I said, Hal suspected about Frank and me. Even after I broke it off, he would make remarks—off-color, but subtle enough that no one else would get their meaning. Then he started trying to hit on me, thinking, I suppose, that that might be the thing to drive me away. When I'd resist, he'd hurt me."

"I can see why you couldn't go to your husband about it, but why didn't you tell Frank?"

"Frank had problems of his own, and besides, I was afraid of his temper, what he might do to Hal. I decided to handle the situation myself."

"But obviously you couldn't."

"No. One night Harlan had to come up here to San Francisco on business. I begged him to take me along, but he refused. I thought of leaving the ranch myself, but I knew if Harlan found out, there would be trouble—he was that jealous. And I had nowhere to go, no friends to cover for me, since Harlan had made me quit all my outside activities. So I stayed."

"And that's when it happened."

"Yes. I can't go into the details."

"No need."

"I have accepted what happened, believe me. I was in therapy for a long time after I went to the women's shelter in

Tustin. It helped a lot and affirmed my decision to keep the baby. And I came to realize that it wasn't my fault—no matter what Hal said. It was something twisted and violent in him that was to blame."

"I heard him tonight, telling you you were to blame for everything."

"He's that way, evades responsibility entirely. To Hal, what went wrong in his childhood was his mother's fault. It's easier for him to blame her than Harlan, since she's dead and can't defend herself. When he got older, the blame fell to teachers, professors, girlfriends, employers. And then there was me."

I toyed with my glass for a moment, disturbed by her calm. I'd seen this same type of reaction in other victims—of muggings, robbery, attempted murder. They tended to dissociate themselves from the event, speaking of it in a detached manner that made it sound as if it had happened to someone else. It made me wonder if Irene's therapy had helped as much as she claimed.

I said, "After the rape, how could you go on living in the same house with him?"

"I didn't. You see, Hal had left. He'd never intended for things to go that far. He was afraid I'd go to his father or Frank, so he invented a request from a fellow veterinarian for emergency assistance in his practice and took off the next day. And I was in no shape to go anywhere, anyway. I didn't sleep much, and when I did, I had nightmares. I cried a lot, flew into rages for no reason. Had trouble concentrating, remembering things. A lot of the time it was as if I was on one side of a pane of glass, looking out at reality but never touching it."

"I know what you mean." I myself had experienced that pane-of-glass phenomenon earlier in the year, during a period of burnout when the cumulative weight of the misery and tragedy and horrors I'd seen professionally had threatened to incapacitate me. "How did you react when you realized you were pregnant?"

"At first I just plain denied it. It couldn't be happening to me. I felt terribly ambivalent—I'd always wanted a child, but I didn't want Hal's. I knew I should do something, either get an abortion or make plans for myself and the baby, but I didn't feel equal to the effort. It took Hal coming back to the ranch—after three months, when there had been no repercussions—to snap me out of it. I left two days later."

"But in the meantime, he found out you were pregnant."

"Yes, from Frank—when he came to the house thinking the baby was his and wanting to see me. From the timing, Hal figured out he must be the father. He confronted me, and I admitted it. He told me I'd have to leave the ranch. I'd already made up my mind to go. I suppose my meekly complying is one of the reasons Hal claims I'm a victim. Well, I was once. But never again."

Now she seemed drained. She slid her hands along the tabletop toward me, then leaned forward, her head against her forearms.

I put my hands over hers. This time she didn't pull away.

"Irene," I said, "both you and Hal seem to think you know who killed Frank. I heard you discussing it when I was out on the service porch. Who is it?"

"Harlan."

"Why?"

"Frank tried to see him a couple of times, to ask about friends or relatives I might have in the Bay Area. Hal was able to intercept him both times, but Frank was so determined that they fought, and Hal suspects he may have gotten to his father another time. Harlan's been drinking more heavily than ever in the past few weeks, and the reservoir where Frank's body was found is a place he knows well, one where he would have supposed a body wouldn't be found until spring. It all fits."

It did—and yet it didn't. I said, "Where do you think Hal's gone? I've got to have an APB put out on him."

She slipped her hands out from under mine and sat up. "Back to the ranch, I suppose. No, wait—Hal thinks Susan is at The Castles. He might go there—to try to get hold of her, so he could force me to keep silent about Rudy, as well as about Harlan. He might harm the girls. Or Gerry."

I noticed she didn't mention Vicky, and decided that she probably didn't care what happened to her. Then I reminded myself that I shouldn't be so quick to judge a situation about which I really knew very little. Besides, I thought—somewhat uncharitably—Vicky was so crazy that she was more than a match for Hal.

I said, "The security system at The Castles is very good. And Gerry and the girls may not even be there." I explained briefly about my earlier meeting with him, and how he'd stormed out·

and neglected to reclaim his daughters. "The best way to deal with this," I concluded, "is to call there."

There was a phone on the wall behind me. I got up and dialed the now-familiar number for The Castles. Vicky answered, sounding normal for a change. I identified myself and asked for Gerry.

"Sorry," she said, "he's not here. He went off a few hours ago with the girls. He even forgot to take his keys to the compound. I suppose they'll be late and I'll have to wait up and let them in."

"I think the girls are going to be spending the night with a friend of mine."

"Oh? Who's that?" She sounded oddly unconcerned.

I explained about Daphne and Charlie.

"I know them. They own the print shop I use. I suppose I could go round and collect the kids."

"They're probably asleep by now."

"You're right, it's better they just stay there. Besides, it's Gerry's fault they're there at all; let him take responsibility."

Something about the way she spoke made me uneasy. "How are you doing, Vicky?"

"What's that supposed to mean?" Now the undertone I'd heard surfaced: that out-of-kilter, losing-control tremor that presaged what her daughters called "one of her fits."

"Vicky—"

"Where the hell is Gerry, anyway?"

"I don't know."

"You do too. He's finally run off with that bitch, hasn't he?"

"Of course not."

"He has too. Answer me, you!"

I hung up on her. If I'd thought she would have listened to me, I'd have advised her to call her therapist.

I glanced at Irene. Vicky had been screaming loud enough that she'd heard a good part of it. Before she could speak, I said, "Don't blame yourself for her condition. You may have contributed, but this has been coming on for a long time."

"I know."

I turned back to the phone and called the SFPD. Gallagher was off duty, but I told another inspector in his unit that I'd overheard what seemed to be the next best thing to a confession in the Goldring case. The inspector took down the particulars and said he'd try to get in touch with Gallagher. I should stay right where I was, he told me, until Gallagher called back.

Finally I called Daphne and Charlie's. She answered, sounding exhausted. The kids were still there, bedded down on the couch. There had been no word from Gerry. There was a message from All Souls for me, however.

She went away from the phone. When she returned, I could hear her yawning. "Ted called," she told me. "He said Bob called. At eleven forty-five. That's an hour ago."

I looked at my watch, feeling surprise at how late it was and guilt at disrupting my friends' lives this way.

"Bob says he'll talk to you," Daphne went on. "For fifty dollars. Not twenty—fifty. If that's okay, you're to meet Red— Are you following this?"

"Uh-huh."

"Meet Red at the McDonald's on Haight at one o'clock. That's fifteen minutes from now."

"Thanks. I owe you guys a big one."

"Don't worry," she said dryly. "We'll be sure to collect."

I hung up the receiver. Irene was watching me. "You'd best take Susan to a hotel," I told her. "It's not all that safe to stay here."

"All right. Are you going to wait for that cop to call?"

I thought of Gallagher; there was no telling how long it would take to reach him. Then I thought of the meeting with Red; he wouldn't be likely to wait. "No, I've got to go. When you're settled in somewhere, leave a message on my answering machine so I can reach you."

"Wait—where are you going?"

"There's somebody I have to meet."

I didn't know if I could get across town to Mac's Steak House—as Hank calls it—on time, but I'd try. There was one thing Gerry had told me earlier that I needed to confirm with Choteau. If I was now interpreting it correctly, it could present a whole new solution to the case.

TWENTY-SIX

Even the hard white neon of the McDonald's restaurant across from the park was softened by the fog. I left my car in the mostly deserted parking lot and hurried inside. It was one twenty-five.

Three customers hunched in widely separated booths in the dining area. They were all shabbily dressed men, but none was Red.

I turned toward the serving counter, where a plump young woman stood staring vacantly at a spill on the fake terra-cotta floor. The trays under the warming lights were almost empty; from the area behind them came the sound of desultory conversation. The soft drink machines hummed, and hidden mechanisms clicked and whirred.

When I asked for a cup of coffee, the woman barely shook off her lethargy. She fetched it at a plodding pace; when she rang up the price on the computerized keyboard, I noticed dark smudges under her eyes. I paid her and asked, "Have you seen a skinny man with longish red hair hanging around in the last half hour?"

A silent shake of her head was all the reply she could muster.

I took the coffee to a window booth from where I could see the corner of Haight and Stanyan. Traffic was light, foot traffic even lighter. Beyond the intersection, the park lay in impenetrable fog-filtered darkness. I thought about Red and Bob, and the secret lives they lived there. I tried to picture how the park—so familiar by day—looked when rendered alien by nightfall.

When I next checked my watch it was one forty-seven. No one had come into the restaurant after I had; those there before me had scarcely moved. I felt as if I were caught in some frozen bubble in time—one that was harshly lit, exposing me for the rest of a hostile world to view.

One fifty-three. I finished my coffee. Briefly I considered another cup, decided against it.

Come on, Red, I thought. *Now!*

As if in response to my summons, a figure emerged from the park and started across the intersection. It was a man with longish red hair held off his forehead by a blue bandanna. He wore a light-colored down jacket that fluffed out around him as he walked. He looked to be the same man I'd glimpsed twice near the windmill.

The man came to the street side door of the restaurant and looked around furtively before entering. When he stepped inside, the woman at the counter became more alert. He scanned the room, saw me, and started toward my booth.

The counter clerk opened her mouth to call after him, but I held up a staying hand. Red glanced at her, then grinned nastily, showing crooked yellow teeth. "Fuckin' people," he said. "Aways tryin' to run you off if you look like you don't have the price of a fuckin' hamburger." He sat, eyes narrowing slyly. "Buy me a burger, lady? And some fries?"

"Quarter Pounder or Big Mac?"

"Quarter, with cheese. Coke. Large fries."

I went up to the counter and placed the order, throwing in a hot apple pie for good measure. The woman looked curiously at me but boxed it up silently. The food had probably been standing in the warming trays for some time, but I didn't suppose Red would mind.

When I got back to the booth, he was licking sugar out of a packet some previous customer had left on the table. He nodded brusque thanks and started eating rapidly, as if he were afraid the meal might be taken away from him.

I said, "Where's Bob?"

He gulped Coke. "I'll take you there—after you hand over the cash."

I shook my head. "You'll bring Bob to me—after you get *half* the money."

"He don't want to leave the park."

And I didn't want to go there—not with Red, at night. "I won't make him go far. You know the lane that runs alongside Kezar Stadium?"

He nodded.

"It's dark there and not patrolled much. Neighborhood people cut through there and use it to park their cars; if anyone notices us, that's what they'll think we're doing. I'll be there in fifteen minutes, in a red MG parked next to the chain-link fence."

Red hesitated, chewing thoughtfully. "Okay. Here's how it is: I want twenty-five for me, fifty for Bob."

"What I heard was a straight fifty."

"Lady, I'm taking a risk bringing him there. He's wanted; they could get me as an accessory."

I sighed. These days, everybody's a lawyer. "All right. I don't have time to haggle. I'll give you thirty-five now, the rest after he and I have talked. Are you ready?"

He balled up the wrappings from the fast food, stuck the apple pie in his jacket pocket, and held out his hand.

I counted out thirty-five dollars and passed it over to him. "Remember—fifteen minutes. Don't be late."

The lane next to the old and largely unused stadium was deserted. I pulled up next to the fence and killed the MG's engine. It was silent there, save for the regular bellow of the fog horns out at the Golden Gate and the occasional swish of tires on the streets to either end. A security light shone down through the branches of the overhanging cypress trees, casting a web of shadows on the hood of my car.

I was edgy and keyed up, sure my investigation was approaching its climax. My nervousness may have been heightened somewhat by the place I'd chosen for the meeting: years before, one of the principals in another case had been murdered only yards from here. Now the scene returned vividly to my consciousness. I shook off the memory, took the .38 from my bag, and set it on my lap.

Ahead of me was the intersection where King Drive winds off into the park, between the heavily vegetated area known as Whiskey Hill and the children's carousel and playground. There was a traffic light there, but it was set to cycle only when cars approached from the park, or at a pedestrian signal. I watched the occasional car pass through it. A police cruiser went by. A few minutes later I saw another. The patrols seemed unusually heavy for this hour; I began to wonder if the search for Bob had been stepped up. If so, I might have unwittingly led him into danger.

Fourteen minutes went by. Sixteen.

I thought of Gallagher. By now the inspector who had caught my call would have contacted him. Gallagher would have called Rudy Goldring's flat and gotten no answer. He'd be furious with me, justifiably so. I'd better have something to deliver.

Nineteen minutes. Twenty.

And then I spotted Red's down jacket, fluffing out peculiarly as he walked. Bob was next to him; they were approaching the traffic signal, looking around cautiously, waiting for a van to go by. They started across—

A siren whooped. Red and blue flashes stained the pavement. The men froze in the headlights of a black-and-white that had suddenly appeared. It skidded to a stop across the mouth of King Drive and its doors flew open.

Red started running back toward the park. Bob just stood there. One of the cops was on the cruiser's microphone now, yelling for them to freeze.

Red dove into the shrubbery at the periphery of Whiskey Hill. A warning shot boomed out. Bob raised his hands above his head.

"Goddammit," I said as I watched the cops approach him. "There goes my thirty-five bucks."

It was gross self-interest, but I felt far worse about the loss of the money and my inability to question Bob than I did about him being arrested. At the jail he would be fed, clothed, given a warm place to sleep and medical attention, should he need it. By the time they apprehended Hal Johnstone and released Bob, he would be in much better shape for a winter on the streets. And given that Rudy Goldring had left him five thousand dollars, he might not have to spend another night out in the cold for a long time—if ever. I'd make sure to seek him out and convince him I hadn't deliberately led him into a police trap. Perhaps I could find him some sort of job similar to his post as "doorman" that would supplement his small inheritance and provide beer money.

I didn't want to attract attention to myself, so I huddled in the MG, waiting for the police to leave and figuring out how to proceed. I would have liked to have been able to confirm with Bob that I was putting the correct interpretation on what Gerry had told me, but in lieu of that, I'd just have to act on the assumption I was right. Besides, I didn't think there was any immediate danger to anyone involved in the case. . . .

Or was there? I thought back to my conversations with Irene and Gerry, then further back to my talk with Lindy and Betsy. And I saw the imminent potential for violence.

The police had gone. Quickly I replaced the gun in my bag and turned the key in the ignition.

In the flatlands the fog had been stationary and heavy; on Ashbury Heights the wind gusted strongly and erratically, swirling the mist. My little car shuddered in the up- and downdrafts. When I put on the windshield wipers, they made a smear, and I had to slow until it cleared.

I turned into the Cushmans' cul-de-sac and parked near the corner. I'd approach The Castles on foot and, if everything seemed all right there, return to the car and keep watch. Possibly nothing would happen here tonight, but I needed to make sure. I felt a somewhat irrational culpability in Frank Wilkonson's death, and I wanted to see that no harm came to anyone else.

As soon as I stepped out of the car, the wind chilled me. Fog—more like tiny droplets of rain—clung to my face and eyelashes. I turned up the collar of my jacket and started down the cul-de-sac.

It was very dark there. Few lights showed in the houses on either side, and those that did were faint, obscured by the trees' swaying branches. Ahead I could see the turrets of The Castles, illuminated by pinkish security spots. The leaves of the row of poplars shivered and snapped like tiny flags; some flew loose, and one clung wetly to my sleeve. I caught the acidic smell of eucalyptus, heightened by the damp.

A few cars were parked on either side of the pavement: a sleek sports car, two sedans, and next to the wall of The Castles, a shabby Japanese-make station wagon. I started over to inspect it, paused when I heard a buzzing noise.

The noise stopped. I waited, listening. It came again: the entry signal on The Castles' front gate. I peered over there but couldn't make out who was being admitted. All I could see was the steeply canted slate roofs of the turrets, bathed in the pinkish glow. The automobile gate was closed.

I moved over by the ivy-shrouded wall, the heels of my boots sinking into the damp earth. The eucalyptus smell was strong now and vaguely unpleasant; all around me trees soughed and creaked. My hair trailed limp against my back; my hands were cold and clammy. I flexed my fingers as I walked toward the gate.

Halfway there I heard a banging sound. I tensed, then relaxed some when I realized it was only the gate, being thrown back on its hinges by the wind. I crept over to it and peered inside the compound.

The mist swirl was so thick that I could barely see the curve of the path. Dead leaves scudded along the ground. There was no one in sight.

I stepped inside the gate, my hand in my bag, closing around the butt of my gun. The slate path was slippery. I skidded on it, regained my balance, and stepped off onto the packed earth.

Visibility here in the compound was better than in the street, but the eddying of the fog played tricks on my eyes. For a moment I thought someone was standing on the path a few yards away from me; then I saw that the path curved the other way, and what I was looking at was a shrub. I mistook a wind-blown tangle of vegetation for a cat, thought I heard footsteps but couldn't identify their source. Then I got turned around and blundered into the eucalyptus grove, losing sight of the turrets. I stumbled over exposed roots, whacked my head on a low-hanging branch. Finally light appeared ahead of me.

It was the main castle—fully lit, but with the blinds pulled across the windows. All the other buildings were in darkness. A figure stood between me and the front door: tall and dressed in a loose-fitting jacket that billowed out in the wind.

Gerry had returned. He'd probably spent the evening wandering or drinking in a bar, then returned and found he'd forgotten his keys. Vicky had buzzed him in; she'd complained on the phone that she'd have to wait up for him.

But now that Gerry was home, he seemed to have doubts about staying. He stood only yards from his front door, facing the oddly proportioned building as if he were studying it.

Perhaps he was, I thought. Perhaps he was wondering why he'd come back here. Was wondering if returning to this place he'd planned to flee, to Vicky and her insurmountable problems, was really worth it.

I opened my mouth to call to him, but a sound came from the trees behind me. I looked back, saw a great curl of bark peel loose from a nearby eucalyptus and rattle to the ground. When I looked at Gerry again, he was walking slowly toward the castle door.

And then the shots came.

There were three, close together. Firecracker reports from a small-caliber handgun. From someplace between the main castle and the one that housed the bedroom.

Gerry crumpled to the ground.

Another shot.

I went to the ground, too.

I yanked the .38 from my bag and inched forward. There was a metallic taste in my mouth and my whole body tingled. My eyes probed the swirling mist for the sniper.

No one.

I came out of the trees, crawled toward the path, stones cutting into my knees. My fingers were icy, welded to the butt of the gun. Near the door at the end of the path, Gerry lay unmoving.

I kept crawling forward. Flattened as another figure came running from my left—a figure in white that emerged from the mist like a strange ectoplasmic being and went lightly, soundlessly, to where Gerry lay.

I jumped up, grasped the gun in both hands, and said, "Stop right there, Vicky!"

She froze, then whirled toward me. Something flew from her right hand and landed on the lawn with a faint thud. Her long loose nightgown shivered around her. White nightgown, except for the spatter of red stains that were probably from the wine she'd thrown at the fireplace Saturday night—stains that now looked like blood.

Behind her, Gerry hadn't moved.

"Sharon," she said, "I heard shots." Her eyes moved to the gun in my hands. "You were shooting—"

"No," I said. "No, Vicky, *you* were."

She spread her hands wide. The nightgown caught in a gust of wind and flared out, making her look like a demented angel. "How could I?" she said. "I don't have a gun."

But I'd seen her throw it away. I motioned at her. "Move over by the door."

She stayed where she was. I stepped closer. Now I could see her expression, the little furrow between her brows that made her look like she was trying ever so hard to understand.

Again I motioned with the gun. She looked at it for a moment, then shrugged and went over by the door. She had to walk around Gerry to get there, but she didn't so much as glance at him.

I went over and located the gun on the lawn where she'd thrown it. It was the .22 she'd mentioned she and Gerry kept in their bedroom. I picked it up by the tip of the barrel so I wouldn't destroy her fingerprints and placed it in the outer compartment of my bag. Then I went to Gerry and knelt, still training the .38 on Vicky.

At some time during that evening, I thought, he must have exchanged his fashionable sport coat for a heavy nylon jacket. The dark stain near one shoulder was spreading. I heard a low moan. Grabbed his other shoulder, moved him slightly to see if he could speak.

And realized with a start that I had been right after all.

Vicky moved then. I jerked the gun up, but she was merely reaching inside the door of the castle and flicking a switch. Light spilled down from a flood set high on the wall. It bathed the grass, the path—and the pain-contorted features of Jane Wilkonson.

Vicky tiptoed forward. Looked down. And started to scream.

"I thought it was Gerry," she kept saying. "I thought I was killing Gerry!"

TWENTY-SEVEN

In the confusion that followed I almost didn't find out all the things I needed to know.

After realizing she'd shot a total stranger instead of her husband, Vicky went inside the main castle and threw a fit of crippling hysterics. I checked to see how badly Jane Wilkonson had been hurt; the wound was high on her shoulder and she was in no immediate danger. I covered her with a couple of heavy coats I found in a closet off the entryway, then went inside looking for a phone.

Vicky huddled on the floor between the couch and the coffee table, knees drawn up against her breasts, arms clasping them, rocking back and forth and crying. I looked at her long enough to confirm my original impression that the stains on her gown were old wine, not blood. Then I bypassed the living room phone and went into the kitchen.

The room resembled a war zone, domestic variety: Dirty dishes were stacked everywhere, interspersed with empty wine bottles. A paper sack of garbage overflowed onto the floor; next to it another one had fallen over and broken, leaking damp coffee grounds. There was some sort of green substance that had run down into the sink; on the wall above it was a smear of similar-looking stuff. When I saw a colander with the remains of spinach clinging to it, it didn't take much imagination to figure out that its contents had been flung at the wall.

The phone was next to the bulletin board Gerry had mentioned earlier. As I called 911, I stared at the reminders of typical family life posted there. But they were not all commonplace or reassuring: Betsy had drawn Halloween pictures for Daddy, Mom, and Rina, signed with love; the one for Rina had been ripped in half, and part of it lay on the floor at my feet.

After I'd called 911, I also dialed Gallagher's extension at the Hall. He was there—and furious with me.

"Where the hell are you?" he demanded. "We picked up Choteau near the park about forty minutes ago, while I'm sitting here looking at some vague message from you about a confession in the Goldring murder. And the number you left doesn't answer."

"I'm sorry, Ben. But I've got even more for you now." I filled him in on what had happened in the last few hours. When I finished, he seemed somewhat mollified and said he'd see me in about fifteen minutes.

I went back outside to see how Jane was doing. She lay unconscious under the heavy coats, but her pulse was steady.

Gerry arrived at the same time as the police and the ambulance. He'd obviously spent the evening drinking and had forgotten all about leaving his girls in the care of total strangers. When he heard what had happened, he sobered up quickly and went to see if he could do anything for Vicky. I watched him walk toward the door, stooped and faltering as an old man, but before he went inside he pulled himself erect, squaring his slender shoulders. Gerry was a better man than I'd thought; the woman inside had planned to kill him in cold blood, but he would try to help her anyway.

Gallagher appeared while the paramedics were checking Jane over. She'd regained consciousness and recognized me. As I hovered close by, she kept calling out for Miss Hernandez. It was a few minutes before I realized she meant me.

Ben took me aside. He looked bone-tired and most of his anger had evaporated. "She the one who killed Wilkonson?" he asked, motioning at Jane.

"Yes. His wife."

"She confessed?"

"No, but I think she will. It wasn't a cold-blooded thing."

His mouth twisted wryly. "No, none of them ever are."

I was silent. I knew the woman; he didn't.

"What was she doing here?" he asked.

I hesitated. It was my opinion that Jane had come to The

Castles to confront, maybe harm Irene Lasser. But I didn't know that for sure, and besides, she was suffering enough now—would suffer a great deal more in the future.

"I don't know," I said.

Gallagher looked skeptical. "What were *you* doing here?"

"Checking on Vicky Cushman—the woman who shot Jane Wilkonson. She's not very stable."

From inside came the sound of Vicky's voice, screaming again. "No shit," Gallagher said.

I glanced at the paramedics. They'd moved Jane onto a stretcher and gotten an I.V. started. "Look," I said, "let me ride to the hospital with her." This had been my case since Rudy Goldring had asked me to tail Jane's husband. I was not about to be cheated out of the truth at its very end.

"Why?" Gallagher said. "So you can disappear on me again?"

"Please, Ben. I can talk to her. She keeps asking for me."

"She's asking for somebody called Hernandez."

I pointed at myself.

"What did you . . . ? Oh hell. Go. I'll see you at the hospital."

He followed me over there and conferred with the paramedics. I knelt next to the stretcher. Jane was very pale and her face twitched spasmodically. I said, "How are you feeling?"

"Awful."

"I'm going to ride to the hospital with you."

"Thanks."

"There's something you should know." I told her my real name, and the reason I'd practiced the deception on her. I wasn't sure if she fully understood.

The medics adjusted the straps on the stretcher and hoisted it into the ambulance. I climbed up behind them. After they'd gotten Jane set, one motioned to a jump seat beside her. I took it as the siren started. The vehicle lurched across the lawn toward the automobile gate.

I put my hand on Jane's uninjured shoulder and squeezed it. The ambulance made an abrupt right turn; its siren was not nearly as loud when heard from inside as I'd expected it would be. I glanced at the medic, a black fellow in his twenties. He gave me a reassuring smile.

When I moved my gaze back to Jane, her eyes met mine. She moved her lips, and I leaned forward.

". . . good not to be alone," she said.

"Is somebody with your kids?" I asked.

"Lady from the PTA. Only friend I've got in the valley."

"Was she also with them Saturday night?"

She turned her face toward the side of the vehicle. After a moment she whispered, "You know."

I leaned closer, spoke low, so only she could hear. "Did you understand what I said before—about who I am and why I was following Frank?"

"Yes."

"I followed you Saturday night, from the ranch to the windmill in Golden Gate Park, where you abandoned the Ranchero. I never really saw you, so I just assumed you were Frank. How did you get back to Hollister?"

"Bus. Caught a streetcar on Judah and took it to the Greyhound station. Studied the city map beforehand so I knew how to go."

"You'd already shot Frank."

A long silence. "Yes. Thought if I left the car in the park they'd think he was killed there. Should have left him there, too, but was afraid to drive all that way with him . . . couldn't bear it. Was all I could do to take him to the reservoir, leave him there in the cold."

"When did you do that?"

"Sometime after dark. Kids were at my friend's for the night."

They'd given her something for the pain, and she was getting groggy. Hurriedly I asked her about the fact I'd planned to confirm with Bob Choteau: that he'd called Frank at home— where Jane could overhear—to set the appointment at the windmill.

She nodded. "I answered the phone," she said. "Stranger's voice. I was suspicious. Your visit—it made me think about Frank . . . going places. Remembered the times last year. Right after Irene's divorce papers came from down south. Remembered the accidents he had down there. Other little things . . ."

"So you listened in on the call, and then confronted Frank about Irene."

"Was a good time to have it out. Kids were gone. Even the baby. Friend took them so we'd have a chance to have a romantic dinner alone." Her mouth twisted. "Thought if I could keep him from going off . . ." A tear formed in the corner of each eye; she squeezed her lids shut, and the drops spilled over.

I glanced at the medic. He was watching but made no move to interfere.

After a moment Jane said, "Frank told me . . . about the baby. Said he didn't care about Irene anymore. But he wanted the baby. Wanted to bring it home so I could raise his . . . mistake. I'd been angry for a long time . . . being left alone like I was. That . . . did it."

Her eyes were still closed. She took a deep breath and went on. "Never even wanted all the kids I've got. Love them, but every time I'd wish . . . But Frank had this need . . . something to do with proving himself, I guess. Never cared that I had needs too. Something for myself. Sick of giving. Getting nothing in return. After Frank had her, he didn't want me anymore. Never came near me. So I didn't even have that. And then he wanted me to give some more . . . to his bastard."

"So you fought. And you shot him."

She opened her eyes—possibly, I thought, to avoid seeing the scene replayed against her lids. "Damn gun. Was in the cabinet, not even locked. Always told him, 'Lock it, one of the kids might . . . ,' but he said they should be better trained."

She began to cry. I squeezed her shoulder harder. The ambulance was speeding along on a level surface now, close to San Francisco General.

I said, "Did Vicky Cushman call you and tell you where Irene was living?"

"Sunday morning. Was asleep. Pretending it never happened. Maybe if she hadn't called I would have turned myself in to the police. But it made me think about Irene. How she took everything I ever cared about. Frank . . . all our good times. She and her brat were the reason I shot him. I knew what I had to do."

"What was that?"

Silence.

"Why did you go to the Cushmans' tonight?"

She still didn't speak.

I thought back to when the police had arrived, remembered her purse lying on the ground where she'd fallen. One of the cops had picked it up and gone through it; I'd watched him; it hadn't contained a gun.

I said softly, "You don't need to talk anymore. You're better off not saying anything to anybody, not even me, until you've seen your lawyer."

For a moment she studied me curiously. Finally she said, "You understand."

"Yes."

"All I wanted was something of my own. Everybody's got to have something. Is it wrong to want that?"

"No, it's not," I answered automatically. Then I thought of Irene . . . Vicky . . . Gerry. Of Anne-Marie . . . Hank . . . Rae. And of myself.

"No," I said firmly, "it's not wrong at all."

TWENTY-EIGHT

It was Sunday again—one of those clear fall afternoons that make you think winter is never going to come. I sat on my deck in the sunshine, thinking about planting the bulbs and brussels sprout plants that I'd bought on that other Sunday, which now seemed so long ago. From my kitchen came the sound of the Forty-niner game on the radio, but I wasn't really listening to it; the team was too good and won too easily this season for me to conjure up any real excitement about football. I was content just to sit there in my heavy red sweater and jeans, taking my time about getting to the gardening.

Today was the first time since the early hours of Wednesday that I'd felt reasonably perky. The events at Stillman Street and later at The Castles had left me with a low-grade depression that had taken longer than usual to shake. Hal Johnstone had been picked up near Hollister on Wednesday; he'd denied everything, hired a hotshot lawyer, and stood altogether too good a chance of going free unless Irene's and my testimony was damned convincing to a jury. And with the exception of him, I felt sorry for everyone connected with the case.

For Vicky, who was currently under treatment at the Langley Porter Psychiatric Institute—an irony in itself because the clinic was part of her archenemy, the UC Medical Center. For Gerry, who was determined to stand by his wife at least until she was well, and was playing the role of single parent to his girls at The Castles. For Irene, who had been stunned by his decision and had returned to the Orange County women's shelter, where she'd received therapy during her first crisis. For Susan and Betsy and Lindy, the innocent victims of it all.

And then there was Jane; about her I felt worst. She'd been released from SF General and turned over to the San Benito County authorities. Her arrest, on top of that of his son, had snapped Harlan Johnstone out of his drunken wallowing, and he'd arranged for a good lawyer to represent her. On Friday I'd driven down to see her at the county jail.

Jane was a very changed woman from the one I'd first seen playing drill sergeant to the young troops the week before. She sat across from me in the visitors' room, face drawn and melancholy, chain-smoking the cigarettes I'd brought her. The kids, she said, were still with her friend from the PTA. Everyone was being very kind: Harlan Johnstone was paying all her attorney's fees; Walt Griscom had taken up a collection from his customers and delivered a load of groceries to her friend to help feed the kids; some of the wives of the ranch hands had visited and offered to help in any way they could. Her lawyer thought she could get off with a light sentence or probation—some sort of diminished-capacity plea, Jane thought. The kids didn't really seem to understand what had happened yet.

"I dread the day they do," she said. "I'm afraid they'll turn against me."

"They might, at first," I said, "but eventually they'll forgive you."

"Maybe." But she didn't look heartened. After a moment she added, "You know something about the other night? Until the cops questioned me in the hospital the next day, I thought it was Irene who shot me, not Mrs. Cushman. I would have felt better if it had been; that way I could have gone on hating her. Now I don't know. Maybe if I'd been in her place, I'd have done what she did, too."

I had no reply for that. Jane didn't seem to expect one. She merely lit another cigarette and stared into space. Then she said, "I keep thinking of how it might have been different. I keep wishing we'd never left Texas and come to this sad place."

I wished they hadn't, either.

We didn't talk long after that. When I left, I said I'd come back if she wanted me to. She said she'd have her friend call and let me know when, but I doubted she ever would.

* * *

Now I shook off the gloomy thoughts and looked at the flat of brussels sprouts. The bag of bulbs sat next to it. I would have to clear a plot to plant them—the backyard was that overgrown with weeds and wild blackberry vines. I had most of the afternoon to do it, though, at least until three, so I decided to have a glass of wine first.

When I went into the kitchen the score was twenty-eight to seven, Forty-niners over the Packers at the half. I switched off the radio and went back outside. As it was, I could still hear the game from most of the TVs and radios within a four-block radius. I sat on the steps of the deck, leaning against the newel post and thinking about other people, closer to home than Jane.

Hank was still spending a lot of time at the Remedy; he and Jack had taken to staging pinball tournaments on the bar's decrepit machine. Anne-Marie still hadn't talked to me about their problem; her answering machine was still cutting people off before the beep. And then there was Rae. . . .

On Tuesday night I'd ignored her urgent message and promptly forgot about it. On Thursday morning she'd confronted me in my office, red-eyed and defiant.

"All right," she said, unwinding her dreadful blue-and-gold scarf and tossing it on the floor like a gauntlet. "All right—you wanted me to live my own dream and the hell with Doug and his, so here I am!"

I swiveled in my chair, staring at her as if she'd gone mad.

"So here I am," she repeated. "But couldn't you at least have helped?"

"I don't understand."

"Didn't Hank tell you? Or Ted?"

"Tell me what?"

She began to pace the room, picking up objects, examining them, and replacing them exactly the way she'd found them. When she looked over my gorilla mask—a gift from a client who knows I've always wanted to dress up in a gorilla suit and have lunch at Trader Vic's on Halloween—she wrinkled her nose, and I was absurdly afraid that all this had to do with my having bad taste.

Finally she said, "I called you Tuesday night. I needed to talk, but you never called back."

"Well, I guess you heard what happened. Surely you can understand—"

"I could have helped you, you know. You didn't have to go through that alone."

"It never occurred to me."

"Oh sure, it wouldn't! Do it all yourself. That's your way, isn't it?"

Her words took me aback. But it *was* my way. And there wasn't anything I could do to change that.

"Well," Rae went on, "*I* had to do things all by myself, too. So I went to Hank and made the arrangements and here I am."

It was all I could do not to tear at my hair and scream. With forced patience I said, "What do you mean—'Here I am'?"

"I'm leaving Doug and moving here to All Souls."

"What?"

"We started therapy Tuesday afternoon. Couples therapy, they call it. And do you know what that bastard admitted? He admitted that he faked the suicide attempt so I would quit my job here and go back to being a security guard and pay more attention to him. He said he knew the amount of pills he took wouldn't kill him, and all he wanted was for things to be like they used to be with us."

She began to pace again, snatched up the gorilla mask, and began tugging at its fur.

"Dammit, Sharon, he victimized me! He risked his life and did something that he knew would hurt me, and all because of his own selfishness. He wanted me to give up my dream for his, and that's totally unfair. I've got a right to a dream, too!"

Relief flooded through me. Rae wasn't going to go the way of the Jane Wilkonsons of the world.

I phrased my response carefully. "I think it's best you get out of there, then. But I wouldn't give up on the therapy. Or file for divorce yet."

"Oh, don't worry—I won't. But Doug's got to learn he can't manipulate me like that. And he's got to learn to stand on his own. If he works at the therapy, if it does him some good, then I'll consider a reconciliation. But right now I'm not counting on anything—or anyone but myself."

Then she looked down at the gorilla mask. It had a bald spot now, right in the middle of its chin. "Oh my God, I'm sorry!" she said.

"That's okay—he looks better like that. More character. When are you moving in?"

"Sunday. It's the first time I could get hold of a friend's van. Do you think you could help?"

"Sure. But what room are you moving into? They're all taken."

"My office."

"Rae, that's not much bigger than a closet!"

"Doesn't matter—I'll make do. Hank said I could store some stuff in the attic."

I thought of the spare room I'd have in my house after the new bedroom was finished. Given the prospect of rent money from Rae, I could probably justify borrowing to get the work done. . . .

Then I thought, Wait a minute, McCone. You're a loner, not a landlady. Let her sleep in her office while you think this one through.

I said, "What time should I be at your place on Sunday?"

"Three. Doug has a creative writing group that always meets then, so he'll be gone and won't freak."

Now I looked at my watch. Twenty to three. The brussels sprout plants and bulbs would have to wait. Better yet, I'd give them to the Curleys next door. They were avid gardeners, and the gift would partially make up for all the times I'd asked them to feed the cat.

Thinking of him, I tried to whistle up Watney. As usual, he didn't come. I went inside, freshened my makeup, tied my hair back, and found my car keys.

On the way out I detoured into the living room and grabbed the baboon flower. It would make a good housewarming— well, closetwarming—present.